Vertigo

by

Gwenan Haines

Vertigo

Cover Art by *Angela Anderson*

The Wild Rose Press, Inc.
PO Box 708
Adams Basin, NY 14410-0708
Visit us at www.thewildrosepress.com

Publishing History
First Crimson Rose Edition, 2013
Print ISBN 978-1-61217-811-0
Digital ISBN 978-1-61217-812-7

Published in the United States of America

"How did you get in?" Blake asked.

Declan held up a tiny black object. "Skeleton key."

Well, at least that explained how he opened the door earlier. She stepped into the living room, still holding the flashlight. Bad enough that he deliberately flouted her command to leave. Even worse that he did it when she looked about as sexy as a ratty gym towel. She knew she wasn't sizzling hot like Jenna, but she at least wanted him to regret losing her a little bit. "So I tell you I never want to see you again and you break into my house?"

He nodded. "Guilty as charged, counselor."

"I should call the sheriff on you."

"Maybe you should." He deposited the key into his shirt pocket. "Anything might happen. Only I don't recall you having a phone."

She indicated the darkened kitchen with a tilt of her head. "As of today I do. I had one installed before I left this morning," she lied, willing herself not to look away from him.

He gestured toward the entryway magnanimously. "Don't let me stop you then."

Was he calling her bluff? Or just playing with her, like a cat pawing a very angry mouse? "Of course, if I did call the sheriff he'd probably hang up on me."

"He's not a fan," Declan agreed, a smile tugging at the corner of his mouth.

Should she order him out a second time? Turn around and rush back upstairs? She knew the absolute worst thing she could do was to go on standing there looking into his dark eyes. Like staring at a cobra.

Praise for Gwenan Haines

"Ms. Haines is on my list of authors to watch for."
~Karen Doering, Parent's Little Black Book
~*~
"Gwenan Haines is a very talented writer."
~Elise Marion, The Romance Writer's Reads
~*~
"Haines is a fantastic writer."
~Diana, The Offbeat Vagabond
~*~
"Author Gwenan Haines was a new-to-me author, and oh wow, am I ever glad I found her."
~Brenda, Romance with a Bite

Dedication

To my daughter Caitlyn

I would like to thank my editor, Ally Robertson,
for her invaluable assistance.
I'm also grateful to my family and friends
for their support.

Prologue

Eagle Point Light, Maine
1922

There was no way out.

Lucy Stone gripped the railing on the lighthouse balcony, searching for a sign of her husband's boat. The fog had rolled in at sunset and settled across the horizon, making it all but impossible to see more than a few feet beyond the rocky shore below. The wind tore through her thin blouse and cotton skirt, chilling her to the bone. Her chattering teeth told her what she already knew—if she stayed out on the catwalk much longer she would freeze. But somehow freezing was preferable to what awaited her.

As she peered into the impenetrable blackness she could hardly breathe, as if someone had thrown a wet, wool blanket over her face. Despite its dangers Lucy had always loved the fog, the way it enshrouded reality in mist and made anything seem possible. It held the promise of magical things, a life of enchantment and adventure. Or it had seemed to.

Until she met Billy.

No light shone from the tower—her husband had seen to that—and the darkened shore seemed devoid of life. Had the weather caused a delay? Or had Billy accomplished what he needed to and headed home? To hope his task would take longer than usual seemed almost as horrific as the crime he was about to commit. But every minute he was delayed meant she had one more minute until he arrived back at the lighthouse. A little more time to come up with a plan to save herself and Hazel.

At the thought of her one-year-old, her heart knocked against her chest. Leaning over the railing, she strained to hear her daughter's cry but the sound of the sea crashing against the rocks below was deafening. Would Billy keep her locked up there all night? Or would he let himself into the tower and drag her back to the keeper's house to receive the worst beating of her life? Even more important, would he hurt the baby?

She had no idea. The only thing she was certain of was her husband's wrath. To think Billy might have a change of heart and forgive her was as fantastical as the dreams the fog had carried to her as a girl.

Billy Stone had no heart.

Over the course of three years Lucy had learned that lesson well. The handsome nineteen-year-old sailor who had charmed her with stories of adventure on the high seas was the opposite of what he'd seemed. Beneath his devil-may-care demeanor was a man who knew nothing of love or tenderness. Sometimes, in one of the intervals when Billy's cruelty waned, she told herself it was the monotony of life on shore that drove her husband to violence.

Of course, it was hard to believe for very long. When they were first married she had done everything in her power to please her new husband. But somehow she never did please him. The biscuits were hard as rocks—or they were soggy in the middle. The blueberry pie was runny, the fish undercooked, the kitchen a filthy, stinking mess.

By the end of the first year she knew that it mattered not that the biscuits were hard or the fish undercooked. Nor did it matter that the keeper's house was neat as a pin or that she had learned never to raise her voice to him or look him in the eye.

What mattered was survival. The handsome boy Lucy had fallen in love with had been replaced by a grim stranger and if she wanted to live she had better endure it. Or at least that's what she had thought until Hazel came along.

By that time she had already spent two years doing what she could to avoid her husband. She went to bed early and woke before sunrise. If Billy was too drunk to man the lighthouse, she volunteered. She spent hours polishing the lens and the lighthouse glass, hours writing in the logbook and inventorying supplies in the service room. The longer it took her, the happier she felt.

It wasn't until after Hazel's first birthday that she started to think about escape. Though Billy had never hit their daughter, Lucy didn't trust him with her. She would carry Hazel up to the tower and let her watch as she manned the light, a task she had been doing more and more in recent months. If she hadn't been so frightened it would have struck her as funny—the fact that Hazel was safer 100 feet above the treacherous, unforgiving sea than in her own home. At night, after Hazel was asleep in her crib and Billy drifted off into a drunken sleep, she formed a plan that would free them both and put a stop to Billy's nocturnal activities.

She had come so close.

She was putting up the last of the dinner plates when his arm clamped around her neck. Before she knew what was happening Billy hauled her across the yard and threw her into the lighthouse. The door swung shut, and the key turned. The tower base was pitch black but she'd inched her way forward until she reached the spiral staircase that led to the lantern room. She was locked in, away from Hazel, but at least she could light the lantern as a warning to nearby ships.

Or so she thought.

When she climbed nearly to the top her foot missed a rung in the darkness. She slid downward, catching herself just before she fell to the cement floor below. Slowly, she regained her grip and climbed on until she wondered if she would ever reach the top. At last her hands brushed against the trap door and she pushed it upward with all her strength. To her surprise, its ancient hinges creaked and the door lifted. Had Billy forgotten to secure the padlock? Surely he wouldn't have wanted her to gain access to the light. Carefully hoisting herself into the cold room, Lucy stood half bent for several minutes with her arm braced against the glass. It had been a long climb and she couldn't catch her breath.

The door to the catwalk was a few feet away. Normally she didn't like to go out onto the balcony. Though it didn't bother her to spend time in the lantern room, the catwalk truly scared her. She had a fear of heights and it was more than a hundred feet to the rocks below.

So easy to lose one's balance.

But she couldn't breathe. She waited several minutes and her gasps didn't lessen. If anything, the wheezing was getting worse. Finally she crossed to the door and stepped outside. The wind swept back her skirts as she leaned forward, taking big gulps of air. She felt better.

The door slammed shut behind her. Frantically, she rushed over to it and grasped the iron handle with both hands, pulling on it with every ounce of strength she possessed. The door, locked from the inside, didn't budge.

No way to escape and save herself. No way to light the lens and save anyone else.

Far below, at the base of the tower, a dark form emerged out of the blackness then disappeared so quickly she could almost convince herself she had imagined it. But the part of her that had grown adept at dodging blows knew better. After three years of violence it was as if she'd developed an extra sense. Her intuition had been honed to an infinite thinness, a kind of internal blade that snapped open when danger was near. Within her, the blade sang with fear.

He was coming.

The scream rose from the deepest part of her. Though she couldn't hear his footsteps mounting the stairs, she knew he was on his way. The screams kept coming, reaching a mad crescendo that was lost in the breaking storm.

The sky opened and sheets of rain pelted her face as Billy lifted the trap door to the lantern room and hoisted himself up inside. A slow smile lit his face when he looked up and saw her watching him from the other side of the glass. Despite the stumble in his walk, there was nothing uncertain about the heavy-lidded look he gave her. It was the drowsy, hypnotic stare of a cat that's finally got its mouse.

Chapter 1

Did every woman go a little crazy when she hit thirty?

Blake Cartwright stood in what passed for a driveway, staring at the ramshackle two-story cape she now owned. What had looked quaint yet spacious on the internet was dingy and run-down up close. The sunny blue skies of the photos were nowhere to be seen, even though it was the middle of July. Dark spruces surrounded the place, their pointy spires disappearing in a ghostly mist that hung over everything. The rocky coastline that had seemed stunning a month ago looked threatening and unfriendly now. As for the lighthouse, she didn't even want to contemplate the amount of money it was going to take to make it presentable.

What the hell had she been thinking?

She hadn't been thinking. That was the problem. For twenty-nine years she had done things by the book and her life had been one long, picture-perfect Kodachrome moment. Up until six weeks ago she had the dream job, the dream apartment, the dream boyfriend. Then for the first time—after a teary night spent with her laptop and a couple of margaritas—she had trusted her emotions. For once, she allowed herself to stop planning and start imagining. She would open a thriving inn, one that would allow her to pursue her passion for cooking while freeing her from the insane hours she logged at her law firm. Even if she put some money into renovations, she could get the lighthouse for so little it would hardly dent her savings.

And this, she thought as she stood staring at the white clapboard house with its chipped paint and sagging roof, was the result.

Good call, Cartwright.

Shivering in the tank top and cut-off jeans she had thought would be appropriate for the middle of summer, Blake wondered just how cold it got in northern Maine. Did she even own a hooded sweatshirt? Overpriced Armani suits, check. Expensive Jimmy Choo pumps, check. Wool fishermen's sweaters—not a one. She pulled the old-fashioned iron key out of the envelope she'd picked up from the realtor and tried to shake off the idea that she had just made a colossal mistake.

She took a tentative step onto the first porch stair and stopped. An icy certainty that something was wrong coursed through her, making her fingertips tingle. Much as she wanted to attribute it to the lack of proper clothing, she knew the sensation too well. She always got it when she met a client who was guilty, however much they might protest their innocence. Or when she was being watched.

Feeling like a fool, she looked over her shoulder at the solitary landscape. The lighthouse stood about fifty yards away, at the end of a barren headland that jutted out into the iron-gray sea. The tower rose out of the mist, its height dwarfing the massive boulders below. She peered up at the lantern room, half-expecting to see a shadowy form or the glint of binoculars, but its windows were dull with years of disuse. The only sound was the crash of the waves against the rocks.

Clearly, no one was there.

Quit jumping at shadows. Forcing herself to cross to the door, she inserted the key into the lock and turned it. The door actually creaked as it opened and when she stepped over the threshold she found herself enmeshed in a thick layer of cobwebs. With a sound of disgust, she pulled a few sticky strands out of her hair and peered inside.

The interior was shrouded in darkness, despite the fact that it was the middle of the afternoon. A ray of weak light seeped through a crack between drawn curtains on the other side of the room, illuminating a sliver of dust motes. As her eyes adjusted to the dimness, she could make out darker, bulkier shadows looming before her. She moved a few steps further into the room, ignoring the deepening sense that she wasn't alone.

It's only furniture, she told herself. So why did she suddenly feel like the lead in a bad horror flick? Edging sideways, she ran her hand along the wall until she found a light switch. She flicked it up, then down, then up again. Nothing happened. Cursing herself for not thinking to bring a flashlight, she made a mental note to see what she had to do to get the electricity back on. In the meantime, she needed more light. After fumbling around in her purse she triumphantly extracted a forgotten lighter and ran her thumb over its jagged tip. Its flame sprang to life, bathing the interior in wavering shadows.

To her right, a staircase disappeared into blackness. To the left was what had been a living room. *Is a living room,* she amended, forcing down the queasy feeling in her stomach. She was glad the place was furnished, but its stillness was more than a little eerie. Aside from the cobwebs and the thick layer of dust that had settled over every possible surface, the room looked as if whoever had been living there had simply gotten up and walked out, leaving everything just as it had been fifty or even a hundred years earlier. The coffee table was littered with old copies of *National Geographic* and there were even a few logs piled up in the fireplace. The faded wallpaper seemed to undulate in the flickering light and the mahogany bookcases that filled an entire side of the room threatened to topple over at any moment. Even from where she stood in the entryway, she could detect the musty smell of old books and stale air.

Home Sweet Home.

Holding the lighter out in front of her like a talisman, she made her way toward the center of the room and plopped down onto an overstuffed chair that emitted a metallic protest at her presence. Things looked even worse from there.

Maybe she could phone the realtor and explain that it was all a big misunderstanding. She was a city girl, a workaholic who drank lattes and got manicures on a regular basis, not the sort of handy person who would be able to take on a project of this magnitude. Even as she imagined the phone call, she knew getting out of her predicament would be impossible.

For better or for worse, she was stuck with the place.

She felt married. But not in a good way.

She leaned back against the chair, half expecting to be attacked by a family of spiders. She still held the lighter in her right hand, keeping it steady so that its flame illuminated a small circle around her. In the shadow of one of the curtained windows an unlikely shape caught her attention.

"You have got to be kidding me," she said aloud, rising from the chair and approaching the Victrola. They didn't even make record players anymore, nevermind hand-cranked phonographs. As she ran her free hand over its square oak base, Blake tried to remember if she had ever seen one before. Certainly not outside of a museum, which may have explained why the image her mind conjured up was quite different from the machine in front of her. The wind-up phonograph was elaborately carved, with a large brass horn that hovered above its turntable. The inside of the horn had been painted a deep shade of orange and an intertwined ring of pink roses bloomed around the interior rim.

Pretty fancy. And definitely feminine. Blake lifted the needle and placed it on the edge of the record on the turntable Who it could possibly have belonged to? The realtor had said the previous owner was a reclusive old fisherman who had lived alone for forty years. Try as she might, she couldn't imagine a salty old sailor cranking up tunes on the elaborate gramophone.

Without knowing exactly why, she felt a twinge of anticipation. Before she had time to register what she was doing, she reached down and cranked the handle. When she realized she couldn't wind it any more she let it go and nearly dropped the lighter when the grainy strains of "The Charleston" filtered out across the dust-filled air. The jazzy melody seemed ghostly and out of place in the desolate, dimly lit room. She tried to imagine who might have listened to such music—so far from the energy and bustle of cities.

The tune came to an abrupt end when the needle hit the center of the record. She bent down to crank the handle again when she heard the unmistakable sound of a footstep on the hardwood floor above her head.

Then nothing. The silence stretched out for a minute, then two.

The lack of movement overhead didn't reassure her. Though she wasn't sure what had convinced her, she had the definite impression whoever was upstairs had caught on to the fact that she had heard something. Her earlier instincts had been right. Someone had been watching her.

She fought down her anger. The house might not be a palace, but it was hers, and someone had gotten inside. Pulling her cell phone out of her bag, she dialed 911 only to realize she had no reception.

Great.

She strode across the living room in the direction of the staircase, grabbing a decorative iron bookend in the shape of an anchor off the bookshelf on her way. She didn't allow herself to contemplate what might happen when she got to the second floor. Slipping out of her flip-flops, she grabbed onto the railing and inched her way up the staircase. A step creaked underneath her weight and she paused. Had the intruder heard her? Were they armed? Well, at least she had a weapon. Even if it was a bookend, it was heavy enough to give somebody a killer headache.

Smiling at her unintentional pun, Blake stepped up onto the landing and made her way down the hallway, keeping her back against the wall. A wave of doubt washed over her. Was it possible she had imagined the sounds? Old houses settled all the time, didn't they?

She reached the first closed door and her hand gripped the porcelain knob. It was cool to the touch and she stood unmoving, straining to hear what lay on the other side. All was silent. Without the feeble glow of the lighter, the upstairs hallway was nearly pitch black.

Using all her strength, she pushed open the door and shoved up against the solid bulk of something rock hard. It took her several seconds to realize she had barreled straight into a man's chest. Either that or a steel vault. Raising the anchor high over her head, she brought it down in front of her with all her might.

A voice cried out in pain. A very male voice.

Moments later a beam of light cut through the gloom, nearly blinding her as it shined into her eyes. Blake stumbled backward until she fell against a wall and found herself staring at a man holding a gun on her.

"Don't move," he said quietly. "Or you'll regret it."

Blinking in the glare of the flashlight, she saw that the intruder stood over six feet tall and had the body of a Navy SEAL. His face was shadowed, but if his voice and the gun were any indication she was pretty sure he wasn't the sort of guy she wanted to annoy.

On the other hand, she wasn't exactly thrilled herself. "Who are you?" she asked loudly, hoping she sounded a lot more confident that she felt. "And what do you think you're doing in my house?"

"So they sold the place, after all," he remarked casually, returning the gun to its holster and lowering the flashlight. "Let me guess. You bought it sight unseen."

His voice sounded amused and a bit curious—

certainly not frightened or apologetic. Even the blow hadn't done much damage. She debated whether to hit him again with the anchor or bolt down the stairs and was surprised when she did neither. The heat rushed to her face as his eyes traveled from her impeccably cut shoulder-length blonde hair to her designer handbag to her manicured nails. Even in a tank-top and cut-offs, she knew she must seem incredibly out of place. But why did she care what he thought? Straightening to her full height, she tightened her grip around the top of the anchor.

"You're not going to hit me again with that thing, are you?" he asked, rubbing his right shoulder.

She raised her chin defiantly. "I might."

"Don't take this the wrong way," he said with a grin. "But the next time you threaten an intruder you don't want to do the flip."

She tried to look as if she had no idea what he meant. "The flip?"

"The hair flip," he said. "It's not exactly intimidating."

Blake's ego ruffled at his remark. Who on earth was this arrogant person? "Well, pardon me but I haven't had a lot of experience intimidating intruders. And you still haven't answered my question about what you're doing in my house. Because if you're the neighborhood welcoming committee, I'm a little disappointed."

"Sorry, I left the flowers at home."

"And I suppose part of your repertoire is to offer tips on how to fend off potential serial killers?"

"Something like that," he said, then deftly changed the subject. "So you're a city slicker. Tired of the evils of the big, bad city."

It was a statement, not a question. And it was beyond infuriating. What made it even worse was that the man was so damned attractive. She couldn't help but react to his dark hair and brooding eyes, not to mention the Navy SEAL physique. Still, he was an intruder in her home. "I do happen to live in New York as a matter of fact," she said haughtily. "Well, I did. But before I made my offer I'd seen more than enough to convince myself I was making the right decision." Even to her, it sounded ridiculous. "And you still haven't answered my questions."

"Fair enough," he said, extending his hand to her. "Declan Hunter."

Blake refused to be mollified. "That's only one," she said, still hanging on to the anchor, pointedly ignoring his belated gesture of goodwill.

Declan stepped out into the hallway and aimed the flashlight toward the staircase. "It's not much of an explanation," he said, "but I'm a bit of an architectural buff. My specialty's renovating old houses. I was curious. When it comes to following the rules, I'm not always one for adhering to the letter of the law. The door was open so I let myself in. Then you showed up."

She tried to remember if the door had been unlocked. Come to think of it, she hadn't tried to open the door before turning the key. His story could be true. Still, that didn't give him the right to make himself at home in her home. "And you just happened to be out here sightseeing," Blake remarked skeptically, stepping out into the hallway after him, "with a gun."

He raised his hands in mock surrender, so that the beam of the flashlight danced crazily on the ceiling.

"Okay," he said. "You got me. I was out here plotting how to kill you. Happy now?"

"Believe me, that doesn't come close to what I'm feeling."

"Look, I know you have absolutely no reason to trust me, but I meant you no harm. I was indulging my passion for old buildings—I'm especially fond of lighthouses and anything connected with them. I was upstairs when you showed up and I didn't want to scare you. So I decided to wait until you took off again. I had no idea you'd bought the place."

To his credit, he really did sound astounded that she was the legitimate owner. Putting the offshoots of that thought as far from her mind as possible, she stopped at the top of the stairwell. "Glad you didn't want to scare me," she said sarcastically.

Declan turned to face her directly. "That wasn't my intention."

"But you admit you were watching me."

"Technically, yes. But I didn't mean to spy on you."

"And then you thought you'd sneak up on me and scare me to death?"

"You snuck up on me, as I recall," he said. "Am I on trial here?"

She opened her mouth, then shut it. She did sound exactly like a prosecuting attorney questioning a hostile witness. On the other hand, he was in her house. "I am—was—a lawyer. For Ross, Rand & Smith of New York City. I specialize—specialized—in white collar crime. Sometimes I fall into interrogation mode. But that doesn't negate the fact that your story is about as convincing as the latest Ponzi scheme."

He flashed her a rakish grin. "I take it that's something you hear a lot about. From your clients."

Why was it so easy for him to exasperate her? Maybe it was because his comments hit too close to home. Or maybe it was his absolute lack of concern for his situation. If anything, he seemed amused that she doubted his story. "Not that it's any of your business," she said, pursing her lips. "but that happens to be one of the reasons I'm standing here freezing my butt off. Got any ID?"

"As a matter of fact, I do, counselor."

"I'm not a counselor anymore, so you can save the titles." The man wasn't just trying to provoke her, he was trying to drive her absolutely insane. It was working, but she wasn't going to let him know that. Blake held out her hand. "Hand it over," she said as coolly as she could manage.

Declan pulled a wallet out of his back pocket and laid a laminated card onto her open palm. "My license," he said. "Do you want to see my library card too?"

She peered down at the card but there was no way she could read it in that light. Not unless she asked him for his flashlight and that was something she was not going to do. Hurrying down the stairs, Blake pulled open the front door and stepped onto the porch.

After the dark interior, even the dim afternoon light seemed blinding. She squinted at the license and read the tiny print. Declan Hunter, 128 Wiscasset Drive, Eagle Point, Maine. So he was who he said he was—or seemed to be. The issue date was fairly recent though. Still, that didn't necessarily mean he was lying.

"Satisfied?" Declan asked, emerging from the gloom. "Or do you still want to see that library card?"

She looked up from his license. Yes, the picture matched. No question that the man in front of her was the guy in the photo. God, he had a hell of a body. Now that she could actually see Declan she found it next-to-impossible not to visualize him without a shirt. Not to mention jeans. Blake reddened, though she wasn't sure if it was out of embarrassment about her interrogation or her off-color thoughts. Maybe she was being a bit too hasty. After all, couldn't her doubts spring from her city mentality, the one she hoped to lose?

"I'm planning on turning this place into an inn," she said as a kind of peace offering. She knew it must seem odd, a high-powered corporate attorney buying a run-down lighthouse in northern Maine.

If he thought so, he didn't mention it. "Eagle Point—picturesque, remote and too damn cold to leave the bedroom. The ideal spot for romantic getaways," he said. "Want some help unloading your stuff—mysterious anonymous lady—"

She couldn't help smiling. He was right. So far, there wasn't anything particularly romantic about the spot she hoped to turn into the ultimate getaway. Aside from the fact that she'd just met the best-looking man she'd seen in a year.

Even so, there were too many things about his story that didn't gel. Why the gun? And why was he in her house? The questions refused to dislodge themselves from her head. Even more troubling was the idea of Declan Hunter as a hapless architecture aficionado. She always knew a liar when she met him.

And if her intuition was right, he *was* lying. If so, she should thank him and send him on his way. That was the smart thing to do.

"Blake Cartwright," she heard herself say. "And if it's not too much trouble, I'd love your help."

But he was already on the porch, heading for her Lexus SUV. As if he'd known she would say yes. Or as if he wasn't willing to accept any other answer. She watched him lift a couple of overstuffed, lead-weight bags as if they were filled with feathers.

No, she decided, Declan Hunter wasn't just scouting architectural oddities. Her internal radar wasn't wrong. So why hadn't she gotten rid of him?

****

He watched the upstairs window from his hiding spot among the pines. The light from a kerosene lantern danced on the panes, casting a yellow glow across the misty yard. The rest of the house was dark and in the driveway her pricey designer car sat unlocked.

Already the city girl was letting down her guard.

So much the better.

Every few minutes her willowy silhouette would pass by the window, filling him with excitement so intense the only way he could control it was to press his fingernails into his palms.

His impulse was to simply kill her. A snap of the neck when she lay sleeping or a silencer held to the temple. Quick, simple, easy. Then Blake Cartwright and her ridiculous scheme would be forever thwarted.

But where was the challenge in that?

No, he'd leave her alone for the time being. At least until he figured out an alternative plan. And in the interim he had to come up with a solution to his most pressing dilemma.

There wasn't much time for him to prepare. Aside from the difficulties Blake's arrival posed, he also had to deal with the usual set of problems. The timing had to be nearly perfect, the conditions favorable. Most importantly, he needed to know he could rely on his allies on the other end of things. They had always come through before but one never knew. With so much at stake it was easy to panic. If he had learned one thing over the years it was that people always panicked.

He never panicked.

As a result, he had become an expert at manipulating people into doing what he wished. He had always been good at it, even as a child. His parents had laughed about it then, writing it off as the result of his status as the youngest of eight children. If he hadn't been able to wheedle his way into getting what he wanted he would have had to go without. Even as it was, he had gone without far more than he liked.

At the memory of his early years, he smiled grimly. His father's face, worn, exhausted, filled his mind. The old man never caught a break his whole life. Worked in the factory till the day he collapsed at his machine. And what had he gotten for all his years of toil?

Nothing. Not a damn thing but a stack of unpaid bills and a bunch of noisy, snot-nosed kids. Never had a day of peace in his whole life. He didn't believe in the afterlife but part of him wished the old man could see him now. He was never going to be poor again.

Blake's silhouette filled the window. As she stared out into the mist he could almost feel her fear. A thrill ran up his spine at the thought of her nervousness. Big-city lawyer, beautiful blonde, with her Roth IRA and her triple-digit savings. How many times in her life had she been really scared?

Not many, he guessed.

Before this was over she would know what fear really was. Something within him hated her, not simply because her presence had created immense problems. His hatred sprang from something deep within—some primal impulse that wanted to punish her for the ease women like her took for granted. She had everything and could still throw it away without so much as a second thought. Because success came so damn easily to her.

Not this time. This time she had met her final opponent.

He looked down at his hands and was surprised to see his own blood. He had been pressing his nails into his palms for so long he had punctured the skin.

He hadn't felt a thing.

Chapter 2

"That old money pit?" Angie Corelli, the owner of Cuppa Cafe, refilled Blake's oversized coffee mug. "I take it you're independently wealthy. And that you don't believe in ghosts."

Blake laughed at the statement's absurdity. "Not wealthy by a long shot," she said, emptying a package of creamer into her coffee. "But, you're right, I don't believe in ghosts."

"Well, then I hope you're a licensed electrician, plumber and handyman," Angie said. "Or engaged to one."

"No and no," she said. "But I did hire somebody last night. Declan Hunter." She stirred her coffee then took a sip, savoring the brew's rich flavor. Well, at least good coffee wasn't going to be something she would have to give up. After an hour spent wandering the streets of Eagle Point, she had been pleasantly surprised to find the hip restaurant nestled between a hardware store and a bait-and-tackle shop. Though she found the small town's brick storefronts and shingled vacation shacks oddly appealing, the cafe's rainbow of brightly painted chairs and weathered velvet couch made her feel almost at home.

"Declan Hunter?" Angie paused then shook her head, making her enormous dangly earrings dance. "Don't know him."

"He renovates old houses. The kind of tough jobs other contractors aren't interested in because they can't turn a quick profit." Blake blushed, realizing she had used the exact words Declan had used to describe himself the night before. Recalling how easily he had managed to convince her to hire him, she wondered if he'd played her and decided he had. *Most definitely.*

Angie wasn't one to miss much. "You sure you're not engaged to him?"

"I never met him until last night, actually," she said a little too fast. "I thought you might recognize the name. It's such a small town, I guess I just assume everybody knows everybody else."

"You assumed right." Angie grinned, revealing a chipped front tooth. With her short-cropped black hair, dangly earrings, and flowing madras skirt, she seemed as out of place in Eagle Point as Blake was. "I've been in this town for about fifteen years now and I can safely say I know just about everybody within a hundred-mile radius. Either your boy doesn't eat or he's new in town. Or he's a flatlander just visiting."

Blake was about to protest Angie's use of the term "your boy" to describe Declan when the cafe door swung open and a rail-thin girl wearing a Red Sox cap pulled low over her face hurried inside. She made a bee-line for the back of the café, nearly plowing into the curvaceous, twenty-something redhead who stood behind the cash register.

"Sorry I'm late," she murmured in Angie's direction, not meeting the cafe owner's eyes.

"Just get on your apron and get out front," Angie called after her. "Jenna's been waiting to get off for the past hour."

Flashing the redhead a malevolent look, the girl rushed through the swinging doors that led to the kitchen. "Sorry, Angie," she said when she reemerged, apron tied twice around the waist and her long dark hair pulled back into a pony tail. "It won't happen again. I couldn't get the baby to go down and the sitter—"

If Angie bought her excuse, the redhead behind the counter certainly didn't "That's what you said last time, Kelly," she said, cutting her off in the middle of a sentence. "Chris is taking me out on his boat. Or he was—if he hasn't left already."

Kelly's expression crumpled. Turning from the swinging doors that led out back, she regarded Jenna as if she were dirt. "He always did like a little...booty call."

For a girl who couldn't weigh more than 110 pounds soaking wet, Kelly had a surprisingly loud voice. An uncomfortable calm settled over the cafe as customers waited to see what was going to happen next. From the looks of it, Jenna—who stood at least six inches taller than Kelly and had a few years on her as well—was ready to knock her across the checkered linoleum floor.

Swearing under her breath, Angie hurried over to the two girls and said something Blake couldn't make out. From the speed with which they returned to work, she could only guess at what Angie had threatened. Turning her attention to the now silent cafe, Angie put her hands on her hips. "Now ain't everybody all worked up over a little cat fight," she said. "C'mon now. Back to your gossip."

As ordered, customers went back to their conversations and their coffee. Kelly even gave Jenna a polite transparent smile when she took over at the register. Jenna nodded curtly and disappeared out the door as Angie made the rounds with a fresh pot of coffee. The atmosphere was as buoyant and festive as it had been before Kelly's arrival—almost as if nothing had happened.

Clearly, Angie Corelli was a force to be reckoned with.

Maybe that was why Declan had stayed away? And what had she meant about Blake believing in ghosts?

****

It was nearly sunset when Blake got back. Declan was perched on a ladder, scraping paint off the chipped exterior. He waved as she drove her "slightly used" pick-up along the steep, rutted incline. She felt a twinge of guilt for the length of time she had spent in town.

Of course, she had been busy.

"You're really taking this country-life-thing seriously," he said, eyeing the weathered truck she had traded in the Lexus for at the dealership in town. "You ever driven a truck before?"

She bristled at the amusement in his voice. True, she hadn't ever driven a pick-up before her test drive earlier that morning. But he didn't need to know that. Nor did he need to know that the profit on the trade would be more than enough to pay his first month's salary. "Just because I used to live in New York doesn't mean I'm completely incapable of surviving in an area of less than a million people," she said, trying not to stumble as she stepped down out of the cab.

If her tone fazed him he wasn't going to show it. Walking around to the passenger side and grabbing a couple of grocery bags, he headed for the door as if he owned the place. "Power's on again," he said. "How about we celebrate?"

When she had turned up the road to see Declan already at work on the house, she reconciled herself to the fact that she was going to be seeing a lot more of the man than she had bargained for. That she could handle. But she wasn't about to let him insert himself into her personal life too. "I don't think so," she said, tucking a strand of hair behind her ear. "Maybe another night."

If she expected him to back down politely, she was wrong. "Come on," he insisted, "I cook a mean seafood chowder."

Blake opened her mouth to repeat her refusal but found herself temporarily incapable of speech. She had the distinct feeling things were spiraling out of control. He was too sure of himself. Too Type-A personality. Too good looking. Okay, she amended, noticing the way his muscles rippled underneath his t-shirt, scratch that last part.

Declan had apparently decided to take her lack of response for ambivalence about seafood chowder. "Okay, no chowder," he said. "How about the best damn pasta sauce you ever tasted. It's even got a secret ingredient."

Well, at least dinner would present an opportunity for a little detective work. A couple glasses of wine and he would start talking. "All right," she said sweetly. "You can stay, but only if I cook. That's half the reason I moved here."

He nodded. "Well, it had better be good. I'm a pretty tough critic—especially when it comes to food. I make Chef Ramsey look like a boy scout."

His appeal to her competitive side sealed the deal. "Is that a challenge?"

"You bet."

Grabbing the rest of the bags herself, she threw a wicked smile in his direction. "You're on, Hunter. One gourmet dinner coming up."

****

So much for plying him with liquor to make him talk. The marinara tasted even better than she'd hoped and the candles placed on the pedestal table at the center of the kitchen gave the place an intimate, casual atmosphere. Opening a bottle of Cabernet Sauvignon, she poured Declan a generous glass and waited for her chance to learn more.

"So where are you from?" she asked, only to have him veer her onto a different subject time and again. After two glasses of wine she thought he said he was originally from somewhere in the Midwest. Ohio. Or was it Missouri? Later she grilled him about what he had studied in college. History? Or was it biology? She racked her mind for one concrete thing Declan had told her and came up with absolutely nothing.

It was time to concede defeat. At least for the first round. Maybe he would be more forthcoming when it came to mysteries that didn't relate to him. "The owner of the coffee shop I went to this morning said something about it being a good thing that I don't believe in ghosts," she said, fingering her wine glass.

He didn't look all that surprised. "I guess the realtor didn't mention that."

"Don't tell me this place is haunted on top of everything else."

"Okay, then I won't tell you."

"No, I want you to," she said, unable to resist. "Don't worry, I'm not afraid of ghosts or things that go bump in the night."

Declan gazed past her through the window in the direction of the lighthouse. "About a decade ago somebody jumped from the tower into the sea. People say the spirit of one of the keeper's wives made her do it. Seems the wife—her name was Lucy, I think—committed suicide back in '20s. There have been others too. People in town say the sea would whisper to the women in Lucy's voice, sort of seducing them into going through with it."

Blake took a sip of her wine then turned to follow his gaze. It was a calm night and a full moon had risen behind the tower. Far below, waves crashed against the boulders that jutted up around the base. She had always had a fear of heights and the idea of falling from the catwalk made her stomach tighten. "Falling from the lighthouse would definitely not be my number one choice if I were going to kill myself."

He gave her a curious look. "I guess that's one reason the property was on the market so long. Nobody around here wants anything to do with the place. Or at least nobody—"

He stopped in mid-sentence, as if he had been on the verge of saying more and thought better of it.

She studied his rugged features, struggling to find a connection between the legend and Declan's presence at the lighthouse "Well, that should certainly be good for business," she said finally, raising her glass in a mock toast. "To Lucy's ghost."

He grinned and raised his glass as well, but the smile didn't reach his eyes. "To Lucy's ghost."

"Do you believe in them?" she asked abruptly, setting down her glass. "Ghosts, I mean."

"They don't seem all that logical." Polishing off the rest of his wine, he leaned back in his chair. In his plain t-shirt and faded jeans, he came off as the laid-back handyman he claimed to be. Even so, there was an air of secrecy that hung over him. "If I believe in anything, I guess I'd have to say I believe in Occam's Razor—the idea that the simplest explanation is the most likely one. Well, maybe not the simplest. But in general most of the bad things that happen can be traced back to a few basic drives—greed, jealousy, desire."

The word desire hung in the air between them. In spite of his arrogance and his refusal to reveal anything about himself, there was something about Declan that drew her to him. Was it possible he might feel the same way about her? From the intensity of his gaze, she could almost imagine he might. Then again, the man's thoughts were about as clear as mud.

"Maybe that's what Lucy's story is about," she ventured, not sure what gave her the sense that she was right. "Greed. Or maybe desire."

He shrugged. "Maybe. People say they hear the sound of crying sometimes, late at night. Some say it's Lucy, others claim it's her child crying for its mother."

The idea of Lucy having a child struck her as important. "She had a kid?"

"To be honest, I can't remember," he said, running a hand through his hair. "When I was growing up my grandmother used to tell me the story. She said at night you could occasionally see strange lights in the tower, that it was Lucy's ghost up there, pacing the catwalk."

The foggy warmth the wine and the candlelight had

generated rapidly dispersed. "I thought you said you grew up in the Midwest."

"I went to school in the Midwest," he said evenly, rising from the table and stacking her plate onto his. "I never mentioned where I grew up."

"So you were raised in Eagle Point?"

Declan gave her a pointed look. "Not exactly, counselor."

"Sorry," she apologized. "My ex hated it too."

"Ex-husband?" he asked, keeping his tone neutral.

"Ex-boyfriend," she said quickly, glancing away from him. "We weren't all that serious." With a start she realized the truth of the statement. Five years together and Henry—who was probably the most traditional person she knew—had never once spoken of marriage. Though on the other hand, they hadn't formally broken things off either. Why had she given Declan the impression they had?

Declan walked over to the counter and set down the dishes next to the sink. Leaning back against the counter, he regarded her thoughtfully. "It was probably for the best," he said. "Love can be dangerous."

Their eyes met and held. Was it her imagination of did some sort of unspoken understanding pass between them? He was warning her.

She was sure of it.

****

The baby wouldn't stop crying. She stood with her hands gripping the railing of the lighthouse catwalk, listening to her thin wails riding the wind. She knew the baby needed her, knew she had to come up with a plan before he returned to the tower. Frantically running from one side of the catwalk to the other, she looked desperately for a means of escape. The crying seemed to go on and on, endlessly summoning her. "Don't be afraid" she shouted, but her words were lost in the roar of the surf below. "I'm coming for you." Even as she said it, she knew it wasn't true. How could she leave her beautiful girl? She ran to door of the lantern room and pulled on the iron handle. Again and again, she used all her strength in an attempt to force it open. The heavy door wouldn't budge. "I won't leave you," she whispered. "I promise I won't ever leave you."

Blake sat up with a jolt in the moonlit room. Her nightgown was soaked in sweat and her pulse raced. As her eyes adjusted to the dimness, she could make out the semi-familiar shadows of the dresser, the bookcase, the bedside table. "It was only a bad dream," she said aloud, in the same soothing tone her mother had used when she was a child. Whether it was the memory of her mother or the realization that she really had been dreaming, a sense of relief washed over her.

Swinging her legs over the edge of the bed, she pressed a hand against her chest and took a few deep breaths. After a minute or so, her heartbeat quieted enough for her to tell herself she had to go back to sleep.

Or maybe not. She still couldn't shake off the dream's reality, so the idea of going back to sleep was impossible. Maybe she would just make herself a cup of tea. She tied her bathrobe around her waist and grabbed the flashlight she had left in the pocket. With the moon so bright, she hardly needed it.

When she reached the doorway, she heard a thin, rhythmic cry.

Somewhere nearby a baby was crying.

Slowly, almost against her will, she followed the sound. As she edged toward the open window next to the bed, the crying stopped abruptly—as if someone had placed a hand over the baby's mouth. She peered out into the luminous darkness but couldn't make out anything unusual. Across the yard a light breeze ruffled the sea grass, making it dance in the moonlight. The dark firs rustled quietly. If it weren't for the fact that she'd just heard a baby crying she would have described the scene as peaceful.

At the end of the point the lighthouse loomed, fixed, dark and silent. The tower windows glinted with reflected light.

She pressed her forehead against the windowpane, straining to get a closer look. What she had taken for reflections of the moon seemed, upon closer inspection, like something very different. A moment later a wide swath of light streamed from the tower. She watched in fascination as the beam cut through the darkness.

Blake closed her eyes and forced herself to count to ten. With all her being, she wanted the tower to be dark again. When she opened her eyes, it was still there, a yellow arc swinging out across the whitecaps.

She had to be dreaming. She wanted to be dreaming. Because what she was seeing couldn't be real. She knew the tower hadn't been in service for decades, not since the Coast Guard had shut down the station back in the '40s. From what the realtor had said she didn't even think the lens was still there. It was in a museum somewhere, she was sure of it.

Blake stood frozen at the window, watching the light's hypnotic path. *What on earth was happening?* Was she going mad, like the women who had imagined

Lucy's voice luring them to suicide? Or was it possible it really was Lucy's ghost? And what of the baby's cries?

Stepping back from the window, she sat down on the bed. She needed to get hold of her imagination. "Occam's Razor," she whispered, almost hearing Declan's deep voice say the words. Assuming she wasn't dreaming and that she hadn't gone mad, then the likeliest possibility was that someone was in the tower. And that there really was a baby, not too far off. A baby that needed help. Fighting the impulse to pull the down comforter over her head, she switched on the flashlight and headed downstairs.

If only she had cell phone reception. Vowing to get a landline installed the next day, she edged her way down the staircase until she was standing before the front door. With a single motion she pulled the door open and stepped outside, inhaling the crisp night air.

The lantern room, she noticed, was dark again. Crossing the yard as quietly as possible, she approached the base of the tower. The moonlight was bright enough to make a flashlight unnecessary, so she stashed hers in her pocket and crept up to the lighthouse door.

Gently, she pulled on the handle.

It didn't budge.

Shining her flashlight onto the ground around the door proved fruitless. If there were footprints she certainly couldn't see them. She edged her way around the tower, a little at a time, looking for another way. There wasn't one, at least not an obvious one, and if somebody had been in the tower they had either slipped away after she left the bedroom or they were still up there. As much as she hated to admit it, she hoped whoever it was had slipped away. Either way, there was nothing more she could do.

Which still left the problem of the baby.

She hadn't heard the cry since she had seen the lights in the tower. Had the person taken the baby into the tower with them? Had they taken the baby with them when they left? And why would someone bring a baby to this desolate place, in the middle of night?

She was halfway down the path to the house when she spotted it. A pacifier that had fallen onto the gravel, almost lost among some tangled blades of sea grass. Leaning down, she lifted it and held it before her. It was made of clear pink plastic, the kind you see in nearly every department store in America. Bringing it close to her face, she caught a whiff of the faint scent of vanilla.

Chapter 3

Sheriff Charlie Santos reached across his desk and took the pacifier from Blake almost reluctantly. "Lemme get this straight," the heavyset fiftyish man said, barely suppressing a smile. "You're telling me this pacifier means somebody left a baby on your property?"

"Yes—well, maybe," she said, ignoring the sheriff's obvious contempt for her claim. Declan stood beside her in the small office, his thick arms folded disapprovingly. Whether he disapproved of her or the sheriff, she wasn't sure. When she told him her story that morning he tried to convince her that she had been imagining the whole thing, but after she wouldn't budge about filing a report he insisted on driving her into town.

Now that they were there, she wished she hadn't agreed. The sheriff's skepticism would only bolster Declan's conviction that his story the night before had affected her impressionable mind. Suppressing the urge to scream, she pressed on. "I think somebody was using the tower last night. The lighthouse lens was on for at least five minutes. And I heard a baby crying. That's what woke me. When I went outside to try to find her, the crying stopped. On my way back I found the pacifier."

Santos placed the pacifier on the center of his

blotter and leaned back in his chair. "Listen—Miss—

"Cartwright."

"Cartwright," Santos repeated. "I know you probably think you saw, or heard, something last night—"

"I did see—and hear—something," Blake insisted, then bit her lower lip. Cutting the man off mid-sentence wasn't going to get her anywhere. But she'd be damned if she let him go on talking down to her. In the corner, she could sense another officer, probably the deputy, listening. No doubt they'd have a good laugh about it as soon as she walked out of the office.

Santos folded his hands over his ample belly and gave her an understanding smile. Obviously, he'd been through this sort of thing before. "Miss Cartwright, I know you've only been with us for a short time and that you're out there all by yourself." His glance flicked to Declan, then back to her. "No doubt you've had your head filled with a whole lot of silly ghost stories and when you went to bed it was only natural for you to dream about what you heard. The mind can play tricks on us, especially when we're out of our comfort zone. As for this pacifier, some tourist probably dropped it ten years ago and nobody noticed it till you found it."

"I know what I saw, sheriff."

"Did you find anything else?" Santos asked.

She fought the almost overpowering urge to smack him. "No," she said in a clipped voice. She cast a sidelong glance at Declan and wondered why he bothered to come with her. Here she was trying to explain what happened to a man who was openly mocking her and Declan just stood there as if his mind were a thousand miles away. Fine, she thought in annoyance. She would handle Santos myself. "Look, sheriff—

"You know she might be right," Declan said suddenly, as if he had come to a decision. "Maybe some high school kids figured out a way to get into the lighthouse. Could've been partying up there."

Santos picked up the pacifier again and studied it a minute. "I 'spose it's a possibility," he said. "Though as I remember it, there's no lens. Hasn't been for years. Did you check the door to the lighthouse, Miss Cartwright?"

"It was locked," Blake admitted. Santos seemed on the brink of believing her, but the look of benevolent skepticism settled back onto his face. "But they could have still been inside."

"Might be worth takin' a drive out there," the deputy offered, not bothering to remove his feet from his desk. "What else we got to do?"

Wrong thing to say, she thought as the sheriff's face turned a shade of deep purple.

"I'd be very grateful," she said in her sweetest utterly-helpless-female voice. "It does get real scary out there all alone." She thought she heard Declan grunt beside her and when she looked over at him, she detected an imperceptible smile tugging at the corners of his mouth. She could only hope his disdain for her acting skills wasn't as obvious to Santos as it was to her.

But Santos wasn't as much of a fool as he seemed. Raising his brows, he regarded her sagely. "If you ask me, I still say your mind was playing tricks on you. You ain't the first to see funny things out that way. I tell you what, Danny and I'll take a ride out there sometime in the next day or two," he said. "If we get the time. In the meantime, you see anything spooky, you give us a call, okay?"

****

There was even a bell. Despite her foul mood Blake smiled as she heard the familiar tinkle when she crossed the threshold into Herrick's General Store. Rows of supplies filled the store from top to bottom. Unlike her old grocery store, which had signs designating organized rows of goods, Herrick's was a mish-mash of rubber boots and canned soup, fishing rods and blow-up canoes, homemade fudge and the usual mix of tourist trinkets. Behind the counter, a grandmotherly woman sat reading a local newspaper.

With a guilty start, she realized she hadn't checked her cell phone yet that day. She hadn't contacted Henry since she'd left the city, nor had he made any attempt to reach her. The truth was she'd barely thought about him since her departure. Henry, the tax attorney who preferred vanilla ice cream to Cherry Garcia, classical music to rock, walking to running. There was nothing wrong with Henry. He didn't drink, didn't smoke, didn't do any of the things that might justify her leaving him. The man was perfect in every way. Good looking. Sophisticated. Filthy rich.

And dull as dishwater.

Grabbing a cart, she pulled her cell phone out of her purse and stared at it, then replaced it quickly without allowing herself to read the screen. She didn't want to know who tried to contact her. Or who hadn't. She only hoped Henry didn't miss her too much.

And it wasn't only Henry who was the cause of her uneasiness. No, she admitted to herself as she negotiated the cart down the narrow aisles, the person on her mind was Declan. Not that he would have called or even texted. Their parting earlier that day hadn't been exactly warm and fuzzy. She'd waited all of ten seconds after they'd left the sheriff's office to let him know exactly what she thought of his lack of support. Recalling the scene in 3D detail, she wished she had been just a little less confrontational. Or maybe a lot. After she stormed off in the direction of Herrick's she realized she hadn't even asked when—or if—he planned to drive back out to the lighthouse. Wincing at the memory of some of the swears she used, she powered up her cell phone and clicked into her message box.

Why did she always fall into the belligerent lawyer persona when she was under stress? Declan hadn't believed a word of her story, but he still offered to drive her into town and even went with her to see Santos. He had been decent and she'd been...she didn't even want to think about it.

There was no text from Declan, but Henry had sent one. Blake was a bit surprised he'd texted instead of called—or was she surprised to hear from him at all? She wasn't sure. Opening the message, she read:

Happy Birthday. City isn't the
same without you. Expect present
soon. Love, H

Automatically, she glanced at the date on her phone. *Yep, it was definitely her birthday.* How had she forgotten? Though it wasn't as if she had big plans—or anybody to celebrate with. She reread the message with a growing sense of unease. Blake was sure Henry hadn't seemed fazed by her move. His only comment after learning of her plans was an inquiry about her bank balance. But here he was sending her a present.

She hoped it was something small—but not too small. Expensive jewelry was small. Diamond rings were small. She wasn't immune to the allure of beautiful jewelry, but the last thing she wanted from Henry was a romantic gesture. Though it hurt her when he reacted so calmly to her announcement that she was moving a thousand miles away, she was relieved too. She hadn't wanted a dramatic scene where he got down on bended knee and asked for her hand in marriage. Maybe that kind of thing was all right for other women, but she wasn't the sort of girl who daydreamed about...

Who was she kidding?

All right, she conceded, there had been a time when she hoped to fall madly in love and live happily ever after. But now she was hitting thirty—hell, she *was* thirty as of today—and happily ever after wasn't anywhere in sight. But she didn't want to get married just to be married. She cared for Henry, in spite of his stodginess, but she didn't love him. So the last thing she wanted from him was the surprise romantic gesture. If he sent a ring, she prayed, let it be a key ring. She might not love him, but she didn't want to hurt him either.

The tinkle of the bell roused her from her musings. A man wearing wire-rim glasses and torn jeans ambled in and lifted a basket from the bin next to the door. He was cute in an urban sort of way, with his tangle of dark blonde hair and scruffy beard. There was something hip about him that she responded to, in part because it seemed so familiar. He looked like the kind of guy she always ended up dating: witty, ambitious...and very, very boring.

He cast a curious glance in her direction and she was surprised at her lack of reaction. It struck her as odd, considering she had spent so much time with guys like him. Probably a tourist, she guessed, as she maneuvered her cart down an aisle stocked with pup tents, flannel pajamas and—miracle of miracles!—a whole row of hooded sweatshirts. She hurried to the end of the aisle and threw three into the cart without giving a second thought to the color.

If only the women in her office could see her now. She burst into giggles.

By the time she emerged from the last aisle her small cart was nearly full. Trying not to think about the cost, she steered it toward the check-out counter and recognized Kelly, the waitress from Cuppa Cafe. As Kelly bent to retrieve her groceries from the cart, Blake couldn't help noticing again how painfully thin the girl was. There was a tiger tattoo on Kelly's shoulder and when her tank-top rode up, Blake spotted the head of a dragon on her lower back. She couldn't be more than eighteen or nineteen.

A little girl about a year-and-a-half old was seated in the front of the cart, showing off a new front tooth. Unlike Kelly, her eyes were sea-blue and platinum blonde hair curled around a cherubic face. "Mama," she said, pointing at Blake.

"No." She shook her head. "Blake."

"Mama," the girl said again.

Blake pointed at Kelly. "Mama," she corrected.

Kelly turned her attention from the baby food on the counter. "Grace calls everybody that," she said with a polite, tired smile. "She thinks every female over ten is mama."

Blake tried to ignore the sharp pang in her chest. Why did the term bother her so much? "She's cute."

The tired smile turned into a real one. "Gloria thinks I should get her into modeling."

"Looks just like the Gerber baby," said the storekeeper. "That child could make a lotta money for you."

"Takes a lotta money to get 'em started, Gloria." The bitterness in Kelly's voice was unmistakable. "Plus I'd have to buy a new car. Couldn't be driving down to Boston in that piece of junk. God knows Chris'd never lend me his precious Mustang."

"You were never one to back down from a challenge," Gloria said placidly, ringing up a jar of baby food. "You'll find a way."

Blake followed Kelly's gaze through the store window and saw a beat-up sedan parked next to the curb. There was no ring on the girl's finger and she couldn't be making much money working at a coffee shop. Her daughter was beautiful, but the idea of modeling when they were a good six hours from a major city seemed pretty far-fetched. She was still searching for something positive to say when the man with the wire-rimmed glasses appeared at the end of a nearby aisle.

"Hey stranger." Gloria's face brightened at the sight of him. "Haven't seen you in a while."

He shifted his basket from one side to another. "Just got back last night," he said. "Miss me?"

"Cataclysm's been waiting for you for six months now," Gloria said, reaching beneath the counter and retrieving a video game wrapped in cellophane. "You told me you needed it ASAP and then you up and disappear for six months." She sighed resignedly. "Where was it this time?"

"Kuala Lumpur," he said. "First International Conference on Computing in Heterogeneous and Autonomous Environments."

"Oh dear Lord," Gloria chortled, ignoring Kelly's strumming fingertips. "Where on God's earth is Koala Lumper?"

If her butchered pronunciation of the city amused him, he didn't show it. "Malaysia."

"I won't even ask where that is," the storekeeper gushed.

Kelly's back went rigid. Blake thought it odd that she hadn't even turned to acknowledge the man. Such behavior would be typical in the city but seemed out of place in Eagle Point. The strumming fingertips were blatantly rude.

"Hey Kelly." The tentative ring to his voice was hard to miss. "Sorry to hold you up."

"Not a problem." Hurriedly, Kelly pulled a wad of crumpled one dollar bills out of her bag. Her hands shook as she counted them.

As if she sensed the tension between the two, Gloria went back to ringing up baby food. Kelly lifted Grace out of the cart and settled her on her hip, reaching for the bag of groceries with her free hand. Blake and the man waited in uncomfortable silence.

"Want some help with that?" Blake asked.

"No thanks." Kelly's face closed. She wore a cynical, hardened look that aged her beyond her years. What made her so angry? Everywhere the girl went she seemed to generate tension. "I got it."

Kelly was struggling to open the door when the bag

dropped. Its contents tumbled out, rolling in all directions. Blake rushed over to help her, leaning down to scoop up a can of soup and an apple. A few inches away from the apple was a package that contained a clear pink pacifier. Picking up the package, Blake saw the phrase "New Vanilla Scent" across the top.

Kelly took the soup, the apple and the pacifier without looking at Blake. Under the gaze of Gloria and the few customers who filtered into the store, she seemed embarrassed and ill at ease. "Thanks. I appreciate it," she told Blake. Her words were rushed, as if she couldn't wait to get back out into the street.

Grace on the other hand seemed to find the entire event most entertaining. She laughed and clapped as her mother bent to retrieve the scattered groceries. "Big mess," Grace said again and again. At the sight of her daughter's gleeful face, Kelly cracked an exasperated grin. "Big mess," she repeated, to Grace's delight.

The spill was soon remedied and Kelly hurried out, the bell tinkling at her departure. Gloria had already started ringing up Blake's purchases and if the woman was curious about her arrival in town, it was overshadowed by the presence of the computer guru, whoever he was. Blake paid for her groceries and balanced an overflowing bag on each hip. Just like Kelly had with her baby.

As she emerged onto the street Blake tried to sort out the jumble of emotions within her. She felt turned inside out by the events since her arrival. Part of it was the idea that she was turning thirty in a town where she knew almost no one. Part of it was seeing Kelly with her baby.

Then there was Declan Hunter. Like it or not she

was going to have to call him. She couldn't very well walk back to the lighthouse.

She struggled to extricate her cell phone from her purse. As she dialed Declan's phone number she wondered if he would even pick up. Doing her best to ignore the weight of the shopping bags, she listened as the phone rang repeatedly. "Please pick up," she said to herself, making a vow to be especially nice to him when she saw him again.

A recording clicked on and she wondered if she should leave a message. Instead she waited in silence after the sound of the beep, feeling like a complete idiot. She hung up the phone abruptly.

On the other side of the street a pair of new mothers pushed their strollers along in sync and a man with a map was walking toward them as if he would knock them over. Further down the block, people wearing sunglasses and Crocs meandered along in twos and threes. Nobody was in a hurry. Nobody seemed particularly wary or stressed. And there wasn't a cab to be found.

Looks like I'm not in Kansas anymore, she thought wryly. *Make that New York City.*

Sitting down on a step in front of a vacant building, she found her thoughts returning to the strange events of the night before. The pacifier Kelly bought was an exact replica of the one Blake found on the path to the lighthouse. It could be just a coincidence, but she couldn't rid herself of the conviction that Grace was the baby she'd heard crying.

If so, what was Kelly doing there?

Or had someone else brought Grace—but for what possible purpose? Blake had watched Declan drive off around midnight, but it would have been easy for him to park out of sight and make his way back to the lighthouse. After all, she'd caught him sneaking around once already. It seemed more than plausible that he was the person up in the tower. But what could he have to do with Kelly's baby?

Most troubling of all were the track marks that scarred both Kelly's arms.

****

Declan shifted uncomfortably in his sleeping bag, wondering just what it was about Blake Cartwright that got under his skin. Sure, she was beautiful but he'd known beautiful women before and they hadn't made him feel the way Blake did. She was uncharacteristically silent on the drive back and several times he had been on the verge of trying to explain why he hadn't spoken up at the sheriff's office. Or why he tried to convince her she was imagining things even though he believed she'd seen something.

But he knew he couldn't do that. Confiding in her—in anyone—would put everything he'd been working toward for the past three years at risk. Yes, he felt something different with her. Even so, he couldn't take a chance.

He grinned in the darkness as he recalled the way Blake flatly turned down his tentative invitation to watch a movie that night. God, the woman could be prickly as a cactus. Maybe some of that was because she'd spent her whole life in the city. Maybe she'd been hurt somewhere along the way. Or it was possible she wasn't the kind of woman who wanted to be vulnerable? An ice princess. After all, she seemed to be doing her damnedest to isolate herself, buying a lighthouse out in the middle of nowhere.

Still, there was something alluring about her. When he remembered her laugh or her habit of tucking her hair behind her ear, he had the impulse to tell her everything.

But that, he knew, would be the biggest mistake of his life.

Outside the oil house, an out-of-use shack where he'd decided to hole up for the night, the wind picked up. It howled across the water and through the trees, its pitch high and constant. It almost did sound like someone was crying, he thought as he lay awake in the darkness. He could understand why so many people heard—or thought they'd heard—Lucy Stone's ghost. Even Blake, for all her big-city skepticism, had been taken in.

Sitting up and peering out the cracked window that was the oil house's only source of light, he was relieved to see that keeper's house was dark. Hopefully that meant Blake had finally dropped off to sleep. The lantern in her window stayed lit for hours after he'd "left for home." He wasn't sure if it were her usual habit to stay up late or if she was afraid. Either way, he'd sat in the oil house for hours watching for signs of anything unusual.

So far there hadn't been. Granted, he couldn't see much past the house. The oil house window faced the opposite direction from the lighthouse so he didn't have much of a view. More than once he considered finding a spot outdoors, but the possibility Blake might see him was enough to convince him it wasn't a good idea. Not to mention the fact that it was damn cold. He'd forgotten how cold it got up north, even in the middle of July. He'd forgotten about the fog too. It hung over the water, dense and heavy. Maybe it was romantic in movies or books, but he could do without it right about now.

His next job was going to be someplace warm. Florida, maybe the Keys. Great fishing down in the Keys, not to mention water you could actually swim in. Swimming at Eagle Point was like taking an ice bath. Yes. He would definitely put in for the Keys. But what about Blake, his conscience wanted to know. He hadn't been lying when he'd told her he renovated old houses. He'd done it for a few years before he got into law enforcement. So he could start on the projects he'd mentioned to her—finishing was a different story, though. If he got what he was looking for he'd be long gone before her inn opened.

Well, she could get somebody else to do the work. Somebody who could give her a lot more than he could offer.

The wind was screaming now, rattling the windowpanes and banging against the thin wooden door. Reflexively, his hand went to the Glock 22 strapped to his waist. He could only imagine what Blake would think if she knew he was not twenty yards from her house, watching the place with a loaded gun in his belt.

She'd be furious, no question about that. She insisted she could take care of herself. Even as she'd said it he could hear the fear in her voice, but just because she was scared didn't mean she was going to let a stranger sleep on her couch. She seemed to want to be alone, and when he mentioned something about a movie she visibly balked.

Almost as if she didn't trust him.

Well, why the hell should she?

He leaned back against a rickety wall and closed his eyes. No doubt about it, the woman had definitely gotten under his skin. If he knew what was good for him he would start distancing himself from her as soon as possible. And if her behavior toward him that day was any indication of what was to come, it shouldn't be too difficult.

He was exhausted. Despite the bone-chilling cold and the wind, the late hour was finally catching up with him. Images of Blake's face floated across his consciousness as he drifted off to sleep. He'd wrapped her in his arms and was leaning down to kiss her when he heard the screams.

He was on his feet, gun in hand, before he even realized he was awake. Kicking open the door and running in the direction of the sound, Declan made an effort to force down his emotions.

The screams were coming from the keeper's house. And the woman screaming was Blake.

Chapter 4

"There was a woman," Blake said between chattering teeth. "I saw her fall. From the tower."

When he appeared in her bedroom, she didn't ask why he was there or what he was doing with a gun. Apparently it hadn't occurred to her that she was standing before him clad only in a sheer white nightgown that showed more than it concealed.

But it definitely occurred to him.

Declan was caught between the desire to stare and the urge to hand her robe. For some crazy reason he felt protective of her. Ironically, the number one person she needed to be protected from was him. Could he protect Blake from himself? At that moment he doubted it. He doubted it very much.

Before he could stop himself he crossed the room in long strides and took her in his arms. Her skin was soft and cool to the touch. He, on the other hand, was burning up. He touched her hair with his free hand and pressed the hand with the gun against the small of her back. Though he knew it was wrong he didn't want to let go, wanted to keep her safe within his arms.

"We've got to go look for her," Blake said, taking a step away from him and making an effort to get the chattering under control. "She might be badly hurt."

She didn't say what he suspected must be true: that whoever fell from the lighthouse balcony wasn't just hurt. How could somebody fall more than a hundred feet onto the jagged rocks below and survive?

He nodded and replaced his gun in its holster. "It's pretty foggy out," he said, walking over to her window and pulling back the sheer curtain. "It would be hard to see something like that on a night like this. And the wind's so loud it does sound like a woman crying."

His words reminded him of what Sheriff Santos said. For some reason the gentleness in his voice seemed to make Blake even angrier than the sheriff's condescension.

"You didn't see anything?" she asked.

He shook his head reluctantly. "No."

Crossing her arms in front of her, she stood facing him. "I couldn't sleep. The wind kept howling and every creak sounded like footsteps to me." She stopped abruptly, as if she realized she sounded exactly like the sort of person whose perceptions couldn't be trusted. "I kept trying to tell myself maybe I imagined the whole thing the night before. Finally, I couldn't stand it anymore. I had to look outside. So I got up and walked over to the window. You're right—it was hard to see anything, at first. But after a couple of minutes, I thought I saw somebody on the catwalk. I wasn't sure—"

He peered out into the darkness. Should he tell her what he knew? Or go on acting as if he thought she were crazy? Either way, he was skeptical. It would have been difficult, perhaps impossible, to see someone from that distance. He let the curtain fall back into place and gave her his full attention. "What made you think it was a woman?"

"I don't know." Blake tried unsuccessfully to

articulate her reasons. "Nothing obvious like a flowing skirt or long hair or anything like that. Something about the way they moved—I don't know. I'd say it was intuition, but I know you'd laugh."

"Okay, let's say it was a woman," he agreed. "You say she fell?"

She nodded. "It was hard to see. At first I saw her out on the catwalk, then I couldn't see her anymore. I started telling myself it must've been something about the fog, an optical illusion or something, when I saw a body falling through the mist. That was no optical illusion."

"Did you see it hit the ground?" he asked softly.

Blake closed her eyes. "No," she said shakily, hugging herself as if she couldn't get warm. "Just the fall."

Declan hesitated, unsure what he should do. "During a storm it's pretty common for seagulls to hit the lantern room glass and fall to their deaths," he said tentatively. "Maybe that's what you saw."

If looks could kill he would be a dead man. "Sea gulls?" she asked in disbelief. "That's the best you can do."

"Looks like it, doesn't it?" he said evasively, not meeting her eyes. Blake Cartwright was one woman he would never want to take on in a court room. Or out of one.

She let her breath out in a sigh of disgust. "You're worse than Santos."

"I'm not saying I don't believe you—"

Which was true. He wasn't certain, and his instinct was to check it out. The only problem was he didn't want Blake out there with him. For the second time that night his instinct was to protect her—and for some reason the urge to do so was even stronger because she was the sort of person who resisted being protected.

"Not another word," she said disgustedly, pulling on a pair of sneakers and shrugging into her robe. "If you don't want to come, that's fine by me. But I'm not going to let somebody die if I can help it."

"All right," he said, half hoping she really hadn't seen anything. "Let's take a look."

****

Declan jogged behind her, struggling to match her rapid strides. Glancing over her shoulder, she watched him trailing after her. The man definitely had some explaining to do. Later she would ask him what he was doing out at Eagle Point hours after he bid her goodnight and drove off, supposedly to the cottage he was renting on the other side of town.

Even more troubling was the presence of the gun. She knew next to nothing about weapons, but his Glock wasn't something she wanted to be on the wrong side of. It definitely wasn't the kind of weapon she would have expected a house renovator to own. Even if she wanted to believe the story about his presence at the lighthouse on that first day, he kept turning up where he shouldn't. And he always carried a weapon. As she hurried toward the tower it occurred to her that she might have more to fear at Eagle Point than ghosts.

No time to think about it now, though.

The wind blasted her face and went straight through her robe. Wishing she'd remembered to put on a jacket, she aimed her flashlight straight ahead. Its beam cut through the fog but illuminated nothing, only more fog. Above the wail of the wind, she could hear the waves crashing against the base of the cliffs that bordered either side of the headland. If it weren't for the sound of the surf hitting the rocks, she would not have known she was near the ocean.

For a moment her thoughts turned to the ships that must have sailed those waters when the lighthouse was working. How relieved their captains must have been to see the light shining a path across the treacherous sea, guiding them to safety through stormy nights.

The lighthouse loomed above them, its darkened tower disappearing into the mist. Shining her light around the patch of sea grass that bordered its base, Blake peered into the gloom in search of a body. The roar of the wind and sea was so loud she blocked her ears.

A firm hand closed around her arm. "Be careful." Declan was shouting, but she could hardly make out his words. "Don't go near the rocks, even if you see something."

She nodded. She didn't need him to tell her what he'd left unsaid—one slip and she would be swept out to sea. Swimming on a night like this would be impossible. Carefully, she searched the perimeter of the tower, trying to keep his flashlight steady.

The fog was so thick she'd probably have to stumble over a body to find it, she thought, deliberately ignoring the chill that had settled between her shoulder blades. When Declan took her hand, she twined her fingertips through his and held on as tightly as she could. Casting him a sideways glance, she didn't know whether to be relieved or disappointed that he refused to look at her. Probably just taking precautions, she told herself, struggling not to let her heart respond to his firm grip.

After about a quarter of an hour, they had covered the entire area without finding anything. Blake wasn't sure whether she was relieved or discouraged. Despite the obvious doubt in Declan's voice, she was positive someone had fallen from the balcony. If she closed her eyes, she could still see the body tumbling through the fog.

Which meant there was a body. There must be. They just hadn't found her yet. Again, she wondered if it were possible to survive such a fall.

Lucy Stone hadn't. But then again she hadn't wanted to, something that was hard for Blake to imagine. Seeing the body fall from the tower sparked her doubts about Lucy's death. As with her belief that it was a woman she'd seen fall, she didn't have a concrete reason to doubt what she'd heard about the lighthouse keeper's wife. Yet she did. It was the idea of Lucy's child that troubled her more than anything.

She knew what it was to believe life hadn't turned out the way you hoped it would. She had experienced some of that earlier that night, when she virtually shoved Declan out the door so she could wallow in self-pity about turning thirty. Maybe that kind of sadness was the beginning of the path that led some people to take their lives. But as hard as she tried, she couldn't envision a mother committing suicide. Mothers killed themselves all the time, she knew. Still, her intuition told her otherwise.

Declan let go of her hand and moved toward the door at the base of the lighthouse. "I don't think we're going to find anything out here, not tonight," he said. "Let's see if we can get inside the tower."

To her surprise, the door opened easily when he pulled on the handle. At the sight of the darkness within, a jolt of fear shot through her. The other night it had been locked, she was sure of it. She'd even returned the next morning to try the door again, with no luck.

Someone had been inside the tower.

Or were they still there?

Declan shined his flashlight through the door and stepped inside. "Wait here," he said firmly. "I won't be long. I'll take a look around the lantern room and head back down. I shouldn't be more than ten or fifteen minutes."

Blake wavered. It was pretty clear he didn't want her to enter the lighthouse. "I'd rather go with you," she said, just as firmly. "If you don't mind." As much as she would have liked to tell herself she was doing it out of concern for the woman she'd seen, she forced herself admit the truth—she was scared to death of staying alone in the dark.

His brow furrowed. "It might be better—"

"Let's go," she said, cutting him off. If he kept asking her, she might change her mind. Stepping into the tower after him, she shined her light around the interior of the tower base. The sound of the wind was muted and their footsteps echoed strangely as they explored. There was nothing inside, only a spiral staircase at the center that disappeared into the ceiling far above. The place had a hollow feel to it, as if they were inside an empty shell.

Declan climbed the first few steps then turned and held out his hand to her. "C'mon," he said with a resigned sigh. "I hope you're not afraid of heights."

She gave him a withering stare. "We're pretty used

to that sort of thing in the city." She ignored the urge to take his hand. He was acting as if she were helpless again and she wasn't about to let him get away it, not anymore.

Declan flashed her an exasperated grin. "Glad to hear it. Because if you really want to come, you're going to have turn out your light. You'll need both hands."

It was a long way up. Despite her claims, she found herself more frightened than she was willing to admit. It was one thing to ride in an enclosed elevator, another thing altogether to look down and see the concrete floor of the lighthouse forty feet below.

As they climbed through the darkness so slowly she could hardly stand it, she tried not to think about the question that bothered her most—was someone waiting for them upstairs? When they were almost at the top, Declan stopped and shined his flashlight on the trap door that led up into the lantern room.

"Looks like it's unlocked," was all he said. If he were wondering the same thing she was, he wasn't going to tell her.

At the top of the stairs, he pushed open the trap door and lifted himself up into the room above them. He leaned down to pull her up behind him then shone his light around the tower. Other than a tarnished brass chest pushed up against one of the glass windows, the lantern room was empty.

Blake stood catching her breath. All around her, great glass windows stretched from floor to ceiling. The fog that encircled the lighthouse gave her the sense they were suspended above the ground, completely cut off from the outside world.

"So you weren't imagining things after all." Declan's voice was grim as he knelt to open the tarnished chest.

Whether he was speaking to her or to himself, she wasn't sure. Certainly, he didn't sound as surprised as she would've expected. Walking up behind him, she stared uncomprehendingly at the contents of the trunk. "What is all that stuff?"

Declan ran his fingers over what appeared to be three legs of a tripod, lined up in a row and secured to the inside of the trunk cover with canvas belts. At the bottom of the trunk, a large yellow object lay on its side. "A floodlight," he said, lifting a booklet encased in plastic and reading its title. "An AGA Fourth Order Portable Range Light, to be exact."

She studied the coil of a cable, the box of oversized clear class bulbs. "The sheriff said there wasn't a light up here."

"He was right, to a point. Originally, there would have been a Fresnel lens up here. That would've been taken out when they shut down the tower, years ago." Declan lifted a huge battery out of the trunk and studied it closely. "This looks like it was built later, maybe in the 1940's. They used lights like this to mark airstrips in World War II. And in lighthouses, as temporary fixes when there were problems with the main lenses."

"So you think they used it here back in the forties?" Blake knelt down beside him and ran her fingertips over the cool brass. "During the war?"

He nodded. "Maybe the Coast Guard tried to keep the station minimally functional for a while. When they auctioned it off, they probably didn't realize this was even up here. Or didn't care." He set down the instruction booklet, his expression darkening. "Or maybe somebody brought it up here."

"So what did I see last night?" she asked. "Don't tell me you think it was just some kids who got in and were fooling around with it."

"Maybe it was," he said without meeting her eyes. He set the heavy battery back in its place and carefully closed the lid. "Could be possible."

"What else could it be?" she persisted. There was something he wasn't telling her.

He stood up and crossed to the windows that looked out toward the sea. "Who knows," he said quietly, without turning around. "Maybe it was Lucy's ghost, manning the tower."

She watched the tension in his back, debating whether or not she should press him further. Whatever he thought was going on, he wasn't ready to share it with her. "I want to take a look outside," she said. "From in here you can't see anything below."

"No."

He turned around to face her, but not before she had opened the door to the catwalk and stepped outside. If she had thought the wind was strong before, she was nearly swept off her feet now. It whipped her hair across her face, making it difficult to see, and pinned her against the glass behind her.

She realized she was gripping the railing so hard her knuckles were white. She inched a few feet along the catwalk, wondering what had possessed to her attempt this. How easy it would be to fall. She imagined what it would be like, to feel her body tumbling through the empty air, to know death was unavoidable.

Forcing herself to the edge of the catwalk, she

looked down and experienced a rush of vertigo so powerful she nearly lost her balance. The crash of the waves below blurred as she fought down the nausea rising within her.

She had slumped back against the glass when Declan's arms wrapped around her. He pressed her head to his broad chest, holding her so close that for a moment she felt as though he would crush her. When he loosened his grip it was to take her chin between his thumb and his finger and force her to look into his eyes. "Careful," he warned, his other hand firm against the small of her back. "I wouldn't want to lose you."

The expression on his face was dark, unreadable. As he bent to kiss her she forgot everything but the warmth of his lips on hers. She stood on her toes to kiss him back, opening her mouth to let his tongue probe hers. She didn't care that she was standing exposed a hundred feet above ground. Safe in his arms, she wasn't afraid of falling. The only thing that mattered was his kiss, the exquisite happiness that welled up within her at the touch of his hands on her face, the roughness of his lips pressing into hers.

"We'd better get back inside," she said abruptly, pulling away from him. "Before we lose our balance."

Declan looked as if he'd already lost his balance—and she couldn't help wondering if something besides the hundred-foot drop scared him. As he guided her toward the door, one hand on the railing and the other firmly planted against her back, she found her thoughts returning to her past. What if she had met Declan five years ago instead of Henry? Would the chemistry between them have led to something more serious? The connection between them was undeniable—but his silence told her he was already pulling away. If their kiss scared him there must to be a good reason for it because he wasn't the sort of man who scared easily. What was he keeping from her?

Blake reached the door and managed to get it open fairly easily. She stepped over the threshold into the lantern room and blew on her hands. If she thought this was bad, how was she going to handle the winter? Not for the first time she wondered if she would stay in Eagle Point or end up selling the place and moving back to New York.

Stepping into the tower behind her, Declan shut the door against the wind. He stood beside her, pointedly not touching her. The fog was not quite as thick as it had been, though visibility was still pretty bad. They gazed out into the darkness for several minutes. Neither of them spoke and she was on the verge of asking him what he was thinking about but she couldn't bring herself to do it. Maybe she didn't have the guts. Whatever he might or might not say, she knew she was playing at something she shouldn't be.

She pointed at a wavering light not far from shore. "That's not a boat, is it?"

"It's a boat all right."

"Why would somebody risk being out in this?"

Declan didn't answer her. Instead he kept his eyes on the distant boat, a single speck of light in a sea of darkness. From the looks of it, the craft was anchored somewhere close to the granite cliffs to the north of the lighthouse.

"Probably just somebody doing some late night fishing," he said lightly, but when he turned to face her his expression was unreadable. "People here are struggling just like everybody else. Hard times drive people to do desperate things."

"Maybe some things are worth taking chances for." The words were out of her mouth before she could stop herself. Instantly, she regretted them. *One kiss and I'm a train wreck.*

"Maybe," he agreed, his eyes never leaving her face. But he didn't look as if he meant it.

Chapter 5

"If you ask me, there's a curse on that family." Maggie Smith shook her head as she stepped into the back room of the Eagle Point library. "Poor Lucy."

The only light came from the microfiche machine Blake had been poring over for the past hour. She looked up from the news article in front of her, relieved to have the chance to give her eyes a break. She had spent most of the morning scrolling through the 1922 reel of *The Eagle Point Register* in hopes of finding information on Lucy Stone. Though she couldn't say why, Blake was certain that understanding what happened to Lucy was the key to understanding the events of the day few days. "'Why do you think there's a curse?"

The elderly librarian frowned. "Three generations of women, all orphaned," she said. "All come to a bad end. My grandfather never believed it, but back in the day some used to say Lucy's husband made a pact with the devil—promised all his descendants to him in exchange for earthly riches."

Blake racked her brain for any mention of money in connection with Billy Stone. And what did she mean about three generations of orphans? "Wasn't he just a lighthouse keeper?"

Maggie Smith's eyes flared with something like excitement. "Oh, yes," she agreed. "That's how he got his money."

Blake smiled in bewilderment. "I'm afraid I'm not following you."

Her confusion seemed to please Maggie. Blake wondered if she didn't get the chance to tell the story much. After all, the library was a quiet place, even during tourist season. "You've got to remember what year it was when he disappeared."

Blake got the definite impression she was being toyed with, but steeled herself to be patient. Remembering the "Charleston" record she'd discovered on her first day, she took a guess. "Wasn't it in the twenties?"

Maggie's faced beamed, as if Blake were a particularly bright student. "Bingo. And what was going on in the twenties, dear?"

Blake was no expert in history, but she knew that one. "Prohibition."

The librarian nodded. "In 1919 Congress passed the Eighteenth Amendment forbidding the sale and consumption of liquor. That sparked all kinds of mischief around here. Men who never so much as thought of running a stop sign started smuggling liquor over the border. You couldn't blame them either. It might have been the roaring twenties but up here times were pretty tough. Men had families to feed—and with the Canadian border so close it was child's play to transport the goods into the U.S. They could make more money in a single night than they'd bring in all year from fishing. That's quite a lot of incentive to break the law, wouldn't you agree?"

"So Billy Stone was a smuggler." Blake furrowed her brow as she worked it through. "But if everybody was doing it, why did people say he was the one who signed a pact with the devil? Why not all of them?" She was the sort of person who followed the law compulsively, but after hearing Maggie's explanation she could understand why so many men got involved with smuggling back then.

"A rum runner, to be exact," Maggie corrected her. "Rum runners used boats. Though as a rule they weren't smuggling rum. Whiskey and champagne, mostly."

"But I'm still not following you," she said, "Did people say he was cursed just because of Lucy's suicide?"

Maggie walked over to the row of shades that blocked out the morning sunlight. Raising one halfway, she stood gazing out at the town green. "No, not that," she said. "Well, that was the beginning of the story of course. You're right though—most people didn't give two shakes about rum running. It was just a quick way to make a buck, for most. But what Billy was doing, well, that was a different story."

Blake willed herself not to get up and shake the story out of the older woman. Trying to prod her toward her point, she asked, "What was he doing?"

The librarian turned away from the window and folded her arms. "Not everybody smuggling was from Eagle Point. There were plenty of Canadian fishermen just over the border who wanted a piece of the action. They were hurting too. Every foggy night there would be Canadian boats crossing the border and stashing cases of liquor on this side. The difference was they didn't know the territory the way our boys did. Especially on bad nights, when they relied on the lighthouse to show them the way."

An idea was beginning to form in Blake's mind, but it still eluded her. "Did Billy not keep the beacon lit?"

"He did a lot more than that," Maggie said. "Though that was bad enough. But somewhere along the line he got the idea of making false lights. Some say he'd heard it from sailors who talked about the legends connected with Nags Head down in Carolina. Either way, the way my grandfather told it, Billy would tie a lantern to a mule and walk up and down the shores at night. With the lighthouse dark, the Canadians would see the false lights and think they were anchored ships. So they'd head for shore and run aground on the rocks. Billy would be there, waiting, and as soon as the ships got into trouble he'd board them and transfer the loot onto his own boat."

Blake was taken aback to see Maggie's eyes fill with tears. Clearly, this wasn't just an idle tale for the woman. "Was your grandfather a rum runner?" she guessed.

The librarian nodded then dabbed at her eyes. "He and his brothers. The money was just too good to pass up. One night they were out on a run and came across one of the Canadian schooners Billy lured off course. He'd already been on board and taken what he needed to by then, but the two smugglers were still there—they were screaming for help, begging my grandfather and his brothers to save them."

Blake said nothing. Billy was nothing short of a murderer—but was Maggie Smith's grandfather responsible for the death of two men as well?

"It was my grandfather who talked his brothers into

trying to save them." The librarian pursed her lips. "By the time they got there the schooner was almost completely submerged. The waves were twenty feet high and it was so dark you couldn't see your own nose. The smugglers on the other boat were clinging to the mast of the ship, afraid to jump into the icy water. My grandfather's brother threw them a rope but it kept falling short. So he plunged in and tried to swim to them. It wasn't very far to swim, but the current was too strong. Pretty soon he was drowning."

Tears leaked out of the corners of Maggie's eyes and she swiped at them absently. "As soon as he saw what was happening my grandfather's other brother went in after him. The current was too strong for him too. My grandfather tried to save them—he wanted to—but he was terrified. He knew he wasn't a strong swimmer, especially compared to his brothers. So he just stood there, watching them all drown. It was only a matter of minutes but it stayed with him his whole life."

"That must have been truly awful." The sight of the elderly woman's grief made Blake feel as if she might start crying as well. In an effort to lessen the tension, she turned to the microfiche machine and pressed the rewind button. The reel whirred as it picked up speed, but the high-pitched noise did nothing to alleviate the strain.

Maggie pulled a crumpled tissue out of her skirt pocket and wiped her cheeks with it. "My grandfather didn't know who did it, not at first. But he found out soon enough. One night he went to see Billy out at his place. Luckily for Billy, he wasn't there. Probably out counting his loot or luring another ship onto the rocks. When my grandfather saw Lucy and the baby he couldn't go through with what he'd planned."

Blake tucked the microfiche reel back into its case. "Was he going to kill him?"

"I don't know." She reached over and took the case from Blake. "He always said his intention was just to talk to him, man to man, about what he was up to. But he brought a pistol along with him and my grandfather had a pretty bad temper, once you got him going."

"But somebody did kill him, eventually," Blake said as delicately as she could. "Isn't that what they say?"

Maggie gripped the case so tightly Blake thought she would crush it. "If they did and I'd been around back then, I would've been the first to congratulate them. But nobody knows, not really. He disappeared one night and was never heard from again. Some say he drowned and I hope he did." The words held a trace of doubt.

"If he didn't drown, where did he go?"

Maggie's eyes sharpened, as if she were seeing her for the first time. "Plenty of places he could've gone to, if he wanted. People were starting to ask questions about Lucy's death. Though there were plenty of reasons for her to kill herself, not everybody believed it. The Coast Guard turned up at his house one morning to ask Billy some questions and the next thing he was gone. Just up and vanished. If you ask me, he took all that money he made and high-tailed it out West."

Thanking the librarian for her time, Blake grabbed her bag and rose from her chair. She hoped her trip to the library would help her unravel the mystery that surrounded Lucy Stone's death. But after talking with Maggie Smith, the truth seemed more elusive than ever.

****

When she rounded the corner and saw Cuppa Cafe's brightly colored flag dancing in the breeze, Blake had no intention of stopping. For one thing, she'd drunk more than her share of caffeine already. Earlier that morning she dug her coffeemaker out of stacks of unpacked boxes and brewed herself a full pot. If she were honest with herself she would have to admit she hoped Declan might show up in time to share it with her. But there had been no sign of him all morning. Blake half expected to pass his truck on her way to town, but the winding road remained empty for the entire drive. She couldn't help wondering if he were intentionally avoiding her. There were more than a few questions he would need to answer when he did show. What had he been doing out there? Why the gun— again? Why did he kiss her?

Maybe the real question was why did she kiss him back?

Sitting in an overstuffed velvet chair in an out-of-the way corner, Blake scanned the room for a sign of Angie. But the cafe owner was nowhere in sight, nor was anyone else who worked there. As she looked around the cafe it struck her that a number of customers hadn't been served yet. It was too late for breakfast and too early for the lunch rush so the cafe wasn't all that busy. Even so, customers at several tables looked as if they were tired of waiting for their food. After five minutes passed without any sign of Angie one man got up and walked out. Another followed a moment later.

As she watched them head out the door she noticed the man she'd seen at the general store seated a couple of tables away. Not surprisingly, considering the indecipherable name of the computer conference he'd mentioned, he seemed intent on the top-of-the-line laptop in front of him. *He does look kind of cute,* she conceded, even if he reminded her of Henry.

Extracting a copy of the article about Lucy Stone's suicide from her bag, she read through it again. She still wasn't sure what she was looking for or even why she was so sure Lucy's death was connected with the woman who fell from the tower. The woman you thought you saw fall, she amended silently. At the time she was convinced that what she saw was real, but now she wasn't so sure. Could Sheriff Santos be right about her overactive imagination? After all, she and Declan had talked about Lucy earlier that night. *And you certainly drank your share of wine.*

Banishing memories of that night from her mind, she returned her attention to the article. She ran her fingertip down the page as she read, willing the words to reveal their secrets. She finished the article then raised her eyes from the page in hopes of spotting Angie and found the man gazing intently at her.

It wasn't, she realized, a look that indicated any type of romantic interest on his part. If anything, he appeared slightly worried about her. Blake blushed, feeling as if she'd missed a button on her shirt or misapplied her lipstick. She tried a smile.

He smiled back. "Sorry, I didn't mean to stare."

"It's okay," she said. "I get that a lot. At least since I've moved here. I guess I don't exactly blend in."

"No," he agreed. "You're not the type to blend in. Here or anywhere. I'm Tyler Burke, by the way. I remember you from the other day, at the store. You're the one opening the inn, right? Out at the lighthouse?"

"Yep, that's me."

"How do you like it out there so far?" he asked. "Seen any ghosts yet?"

Blake debated what to say. Tyler might seem a bit nerdy, but there was something disarming about him. "I don't know," she said seriously. "I'm not going to rule out the possibility that ghosts exist just because they haven't been proven scientifically." As she said the words, she couldn't help thinking of Declan. *Occam's razor.* The most obvious explanation was almost always the right one. *Well, to hell with Occam, whoever he was.* "We believe in all kinds of things now that would have seemed like magic to people a couple hundred years ago. Maybe someday somebody will prove ghosts exist too."

"I agree completely," Tyler said vehemently, much to her surprise. "'There are more things in heaven and earth, Horatio, than are dreamt of in your philosophy."

"Hamlet." She nodded, more pleased than she wanted to admit. Declan was always so sure of himself, so grounded in the real world. Could she really see herself with someone so...definite? "Aren't you supposed to be some kind of computer genius, by the way? What's with the Shakespeare?"

He grinned sheepishly. "You got me. I confess to occasionally engaging in activities that don't relate to computers. Not much, though. I am kind of an addict. My dad bought me a beat-up PC for my tenth birthday and I've pretty much been in love ever since—" He seemed about to say more when his cell phone went off, making both of them jump.

Tyler picked up his phone and she turned away, not wanting to give the impression she was listening. Most of his side of the conversation was gibberish to her anyway, full of technical terms she'd never heard before. After a few minutes he gathered up his things. "Looks like I've got to head out," he said, catching her eye. "Do you come here often?"

Blake winced at the line without being sure why. Was he hitting on her? On the one hand he seemed as if he was trying to flatter her earlier in the conversation. But the look in his eyes was merely one of polite interest. And it wasn't as if he'd asked her out.

"It seems I do," she told him. "Though usually the service is a bit better."

Tyler slung his computer case over his shoulder and walked over to her table, lowering his voice. "It usually is. Angie seems a little out of her element today. And a bit understaffed."

As if on cue, the cafe owner burst through the swinging doors that led to the back room. In her arms, she carried a heavy tray of food that looked as if it might crash to the floor at any moment. Angie's apron bore several stains and her short black hair stood up in all directions, giving her a wild, untamed look. She crossed the room and slammed several plates down before a family of four seated near the window. Blake watched in fascination as the little boy at the table took one bite and spit his food back onto his plate, to the horror of his sister, who began complaining loudly. Another moment and the boy's father set his fork down and said something to Angie in a low voice.

If the man wanted to keep things calm, he was out of luck.

"Okay, I get you. Meal's on the house," Angie said so loudly her voice rang out across the cafe. "But if you ask me you're making a big deal out of nothing."

Angie's disheveled appearance and stormy expression weren't exactly winning her any prizes for hospitality. The last time Blake saw the cafe owner she seemed a bit domineering but certainly not insulting and petty. And not at all disheveled. As the disgruntled father headed out the door, Angie turned and saw Blake.

Unlike the Isabella Rossellini smile she gave Blake the other day, the owner barely acknowledged her presence this time. Smoothing her apron, Angie curled the corners of her mouth ever so slightly before disappearing again out back.

"Well, I think I'll be off before Angie bites my head off," Tyler said, pulling a few bills out of his wallet and depositing them on his table. "Maybe I'll see you again sometime. Good luck with your ghosts."

Blake laughed uneasily, remembering the events of the previous night. "Thanks."

With a parting nod, Burke headed out the front door followed by another disgruntled couple. When yet another woman got up and left, Blake wondered if she should follow their lead. The last thing she should be doing was buying a double caramel latte with whipped cream. She'd spent the morning chasing ghosts and there was more work than she could possibly imagine waiting for her back at the lighthouse. Every room in the house needed a good scrubbing, the kitchen and the living room needed to be painted, and layers of wallpaper had to be removed from the upstairs bedrooms. That last job alone would take weeks. And that was only the beginning. Declan worked hard the day before but he'd only accomplished a tiny portion of what needed to be done.

Declan. Blake sighed as she absently flipped through the menu. Wasn't he the real reason she was stalling?

Much as she wanted to deny it, she knew there was no real point in doing so. All morning she wavered between the overwhelming desire to see him again and the urge to avoid him at all costs. Again and again, she replayed the kiss in her mind until she could almost feel the sensation of his lips on hers. Part of her—a very big part of her—wanted nothing more than to let down her guard with Declan. Up until now she had pushed every man who ever loved her away. It had always been easy, just like it was with Henry. And just as she'd done before, Blake imagined herself pushing Declan away too. All day she'd been off kilter and she liked to be in control. But when she thought of Declan she wasn't in control at all. She was as vulnerable as she'd ever been in her life.

Even his presence—or his absence—was fraught with meaning now. Would he be there when she got back? If he was, did that mean it was business as usual? Or something more? And what if he didn't show? They'd agreed on projects to be completed, but hadn't discussed a schedule. Maybe he wanted to avoid her too. It had been a dangerous situation and he had been afraid for her. One thing led to another—but would Declan realize his mistake in the morning and try to distance himself?

Blake shook her head so vehemently the few remaining customers gave her odd looks. She smiled at their bewilderment. *Silly girl,* she told herself. *You're not going to get rid of Declan's ghost that easily.*

Ghosts, she thought with wry humor. *Back to Lucy again.* Forcing herself to concentrate on her menu, Blake decided to forego the latte and order green tea instead. She looked toward the back of the cafe, wondering again what had happened to Angie.

Something was definitely up. There was no sign of either Kelly or Jenna, and it seemed unusual that Angie wouldn't have scheduled at least one of them to work that morning. Blake remembered the marks she'd seen on Kelly's arm when the girl dropped her bag at the general store. She was no expert on drug use, but the fact that both arms were covered meant Kelly's problem was probably pretty hard core. Blake knew heroin needed to be injected, but wasn't sure which other drugs did.

Just as she decided it was none of her business, Angie emerged from out back with another overfilled tray in her arms. Placing the tray next to the table, the cafe owner slammed several plates down before a table of two married couples. Brushing into a glass of juice with her arm, Angie's face crumpled as the orange liquid splashed onto one of the men's shorts.

His wife tried to wipe up the spill with napkins then shot Angie a furious look. "If you would slow down," she lectured, "you'd be a lot more efficient."

Angie's smile was deadly. "And if you were a little less efficient," she replied, "maybe your husband wouldn't be cheating with his secretary."

The silence was deafening.

Blake watched in horrified fascination as the woman threw down the soggy napkins and stormed out of the cafe, followed by her husband. The remaining couple exchanged knowing looks before they too got up and headed out the door.

"Okay, that's it," Angie snapped, removing her apron. "Everybody out. Cuppa Cafe is officially closed for the day."

Nobody seemed particularly upset. If anything, people looked relieved. Blake pushed her chair back into place and debated whether she should say something to Angie, who crossed the room and flipped the OPEN sign to CLOSED. The day before Angie seemed hip and just edgy enough to be interesting, but now there was something almost frightening about the cafe owner.

Blake watched as the other customers filed out of the place, quiet as sheep in sight of a wolf. She was about to do the same when Angie moved to block her exit.

"You're the one who wants to turn the lighthouse into an inn, Blake, isn't it?"

Under Angie's intense gaze, she did feel very much like a sheep about to be devoured. "That's right," she said, a little more tentatively than she meant to.

"I figure if you're planning on opening an inn, you've got to be at least a half-decent cook." As if she realized just how intimidating she seemed, Angie tried a bright smile and stepped aside from the doorway. "I also figure—if you don't mind me saying so—that you wouldn't mind earning a little extra money."

Blake's temper flared. Just because her house was falling apart didn't mean she was desperate for money. And the phrase "half-decent cook" ruffled her ego. "What's your point?" she asked curtly.

Ignoring Blake's unfriendly tone, Angie sat down heavily in an overstuffed chair across from the one

Blake previously occupied. "I'm literally in hell," she said, turning imploring eyes to her. "This place was a zoo all morning and both my waitresses seem to have jumped ship. I'm a basket case—you saw what just happened. I know you've probably got a hundred other things going on, but I've got to get somebody in here fast. And it's got to be somebody reliable. I don't know you from Adam but you strike me as the reliable type. Unlike others."

Blake wasn't biting. She had far too much going on already and didn't see how she could possibly start cooking as well. Still, she felt some sympathy for the distraught cafe owner. "What happened to your other waitresses?"

"I have no idea," Angie said in exasperation. "First Kelly doesn't show for her six a.m. shift. I thought I'd be able to handle the early morning at least, but then it started getting busy. By mid-morning I was totally swamped. I was actually counting the minutes until Jenna's shift was due to start. Then no Jenna."

It was odd, Blake thought. From what she'd witnessed the other day the two waitresses were none too fond of each other. So it would make sense that neither of them would particularly want to go on working together. But would they both quit without any notice? It seemed unlikely. "I assume you tried calling them," she said.

"Calling them?" Angie gave a short guffaw. "Hell, I've been calling both of them every fifteen minutes since seven o'clock."

She eyed the comfy chair across from Angie then decided she didn't want to be any closer to her than necessary. "They wouldn't have gone someplace together, would they?" Even to her, the suggestion sounded far-fetched. "Maybe they were on their way here when their car broke down?"

"Maybe," Angie said doubtfully. "They used to be pretty tight, but that was before Jenna got involved with Chris—the father of Kelly's baby. Jenna's a few years older than Kelly and for a while she seemed be playing big sister. Then Kelly introduced Chris to Jenna and, well, to put it politely, one thing led to another. Can't say as I blame him—you've seen Jenna, right? Girl attracts men like bees to honey. Anyway, after that Kelly wouldn't have anything to do with her. It finally looked like things were gonna work out for those two when Jenna came into the picture. Too bad, too, what with him being Grace's daddy and all. Eventually Kelly and Jenna got to hate each other so much I started scheduling them so their shifts didn't overlap—which wasn't easy in a small place like this."

It was a familiar story but Blake still couldn't help feeling some sympathy for Kelly. It was bad enough to have her friend steal her boyfriend, but to have her steal the father of her child? Worse. Much worse. Though, to be fair, Blake didn't know all the details. Maybe Kelly tried to make her relationship with Chris something it wasn't. Or maybe the drugs...her line of thought broke off abruptly. For some reason the cafe owner's state of mind was starting to rub off on her. Though it wasn't uncommon for young girls to ditch work, something wasn't right. "Do you know where they live?" she asked.

"Jenna lives in town with her mom, but she's not the one I'm worried about. Truth be told it's Kelly—and the baby—that's got me worried."

Blake nodded in agreement. "Kelly lives by herself?"

"She hasn't got any family, at least not from around here. She rents a house on the other side of the cove. More like a shack, actually." Angie smoothed her stained skirt with her palms. "I know this is going to seem pretty weird, considering you just met me, but is there anything I can say that would convince you to take a ride over there with me? I'd go myself—I *will* go myself—but I'd rather not do it alone, if you know what I mean. Kelly's gone through a pretty hard time, what with the baby and Chris ditching her for Jenna and the drugs—"

She left the sentence unfinished, whether deliberately or not, Blake wasn't sure. Even with the words left unsaid, she had a pretty good idea what Angie was implying. More than anything, Blake didn't want to accompany the edgy woman out to some dump in the middle of nowhere. And once they got there and found out Kelly wasn't answering her cell because she'd decided to quit, did she really want to be present for the confrontation that would inevitably follow?

She nearly lost her balance when Angie touched her arm. Blake readjusted her shoulder bag and shifted uncomfortably from foot to foot. "I'm kind of busy," she said, when she remembered Grace laughing and clapping her hands as groceries rolled across the floor at Herrick's. "But I guess I could fit it in."

Angie shot out of her chair so fast Blake took a step back, fearing the woman was going to hug her. Instead she flew toward the front door and held it open for her.

Ignoring the knot in her stomach, Blake stepped

out onto the cement stairs that led up to the cafe. Luckily she had traded in heels for sneakers shortly after her arrival at Eagle Point.

"Check it out," Angie said quietly. "Two o'clock."

At the end of the street, Declan was leaning back against a black Corvette, deep in conversation with a stunning redhead in tight jeans and a low-cut top. A redhead who bore a striking resemblance to Jenna Campbell.

Chapter 6

Angie hadn't been exaggerating. Kelly Reilly's place really was a shack. As Angie's Subaru rounded yet another curve in the endlessly winding road, Blake spotted a small protuberance that jutted out from the cliffs up ahead. The dwelling hadn't been painted and the wood was a grayish shade that made it look even more depressing. The roof sagged deeply, as if it might collapse at the any moment, and in the yard was a paint-chipped swing-set minus all but one swing. Instead of adding a cheerful note, the blue sky above formed a stark contrast to the air of gloom that hung over the place.

What would it be like to live here? Blake thought first of Kelly, then of Grace. No wonder the waitress seemed so angry at Tyler that day in the general store. Who wouldn't be, when he was flitting around the globe and she was stuck raising her daughter in a place like this.

"I think that's it," said Angie, squinting through the glare hitting the windshield.

Blake braced herself as the car hit a rut in the road, making her bounce so high she nearly bumped her head on the roof. From the looks of it, the place was deserted. There was no garage and no sign of a car in the driveway.

Angie pulled up alongside the house and turned off

the car. Neither woman spoke as they climbed the rickety steps that led to the uneven porch. Not that either of them spoke much on the ride out. After Blake managed to convince Angie not to confront Jenna, the two women sat lost in their own thoughts for the twenty-minute ride. Angie, no doubt, was fuming about being blown off by Jenna—who looked as if she had no intention of reporting to work that day.

For her part, Blake couldn't bear to start a conversation that she knew would end with a reference to Declan. Angie really didn't seem to know who he was, which in a way was a relief. Somehow it would be even worse if the cafe owner understood that the man Blake hired two days earlier was flirting with a girl at least ten years younger than he was.

At the thought of Declan leaning back against the Corvette—his Corvette?—she bit her lip. She thought their kiss had meant something, but there he was with Jenna not twenty-four hours later. When he left her that night she hadn't thought to ask where he would spend the night. She hadn't even asked if he would be at work the next day.

She had trusted him.

If she was angry at Declan, she was even angrier at herself. After three decades spent in the most dangerous city on earth, she should have known better than to believe a stranger. And what had he even told her about himself? Next to nothing.

Yet despite her anger she couldn't help realizing she was being a bit irrational. Yes, what she saw on the street didn't look good. But she wasn't close enough to see what Jenna and Declan were saying. And after all, what did she really see? Declan leaning against a

Corvette talking to a sexy redhead. As she and Angie crossed the yard she had the uncomfortable feeling of being on the wrong side of an argument. Henry had gotten jealous a couple of times for no reason. Shouldn't she at least ask Declan about Jenna before condemning him?

Still, something about it troubled her. Something besides the thought of Declan staring at Jenna's all-too-revealing shirt. It was as if she were looking through the wrong end of a telescope. Her perceptions—of Declan, Kelly, Jenna, even Angie—seemed distorted somehow. The truth about all of them seemed small and out of focus. And she didn't know how to change that. Or if she wanted to.

Angie rapped her knuckle on the faded door once, then twice, but there was no answer. The lone swing whined an eerie metallic lullaby as the wind cut across the empty yard. Blake stood motionless by Angie's side, trying to ignore her growing sense of foreboding. Maybe the young mother took her child on a trip to Boston. After all, Kelly had talked about getting Grace into modeling. Maybe she ditched Angie for the chance to make better money, Blake thought without conviction.

"Nobody's answering," Angie observed darkly. "In case you hadn't noticed."

"Try the door to see if it's locked," she suggested, walking over to a dusty window and peering through the crack between the curtains.

Inside, all was dim, silent. Cupping her hands around her mouth, she shouted, "Kelly! Kelly, are you in there!"

No answer. With a shrug, Angie turned toward her.

"Do you think we should try to get inside?"

"Probably not," she said. "We should probably call the sheriff first."

"You're right," Angie conceded. "If we go in on our own, isn't that breaking and entering or something?"

Blake stood undecided. If they entered the house, it would most certainly be breaking and entering. You didn't need to be a lawyer to know that. Yet something was urging her on, pushing her to find a way inside.

"Wait," Blake said, holding up her hand. She pressed her ear to the door and made out a strange, tinny sound coming from somewhere inside. "Do you hear that?"

Angie stared at her in confusion. "Is that a...music box?"

"Or maybe some type of mobile, the kind that hangs over cribs." Blake pushed her shoulder against the wooden door. "We've got to try to open the door. Grace might be in there by herself."

Angie positioned herself alongside Blake and they both pushed, with no success. After five minutes, Angie stopped to rub her shoulder. "This thing's stronger than it looks," she said. "It's not going to budge."

But Blake was already running down the porch steps, heading around to the side of the house. "Maybe there's a window open," she called over her shoulder.

"Good idea," Angie called back, hurrying after her, then taking the other side of the house. "Nothing over here."

"Got one." Blake's voice was barely a whisper. When Angie rounded the corner to the back of the shack, Blake pushed the screen up and shimmied through the opening. "I can hear Grace," she said urgently, pulling Angie in after her.

After the blinding sunlight outside, the interior seemed nearly black. Feeling her way down the hallway, Blake tried to follow the sound of the music box. When she reached the end of the hall, she stepped into what looked like a nursery. Grace looked up from her crib, where she sat watching several stuffed butterflies circling above her head.

Blake's mind flooded with relief as she tried to pull down the crib gate, then gave up and leaned down to take the child into her arms. Hugging Grace, she whispered reassurances to her, not sure she believed them herself.

"Mama," Grace whimpered, then started to cry. Blake wasn't sure if was referring to her or to Kelly, who was nowhere to be found. Grace's diaper was soaked through. Switching on the light next to the crib, Blake looked around the room for the changing table. She laid Grace down and unsnapped her pajamas before she realized she'd never changed a diaper in her life.

Well, no time like the present to learn. She tried to hold Grace's legs still while she took off her soaked pajamas then used one of the wipes on the table to clean her up as quickly as she could. "Angie—" she called out nervously.

There was no answer. The silence of the place settled over her, making her skin crawl.

Angie had been right behind her. Hadn't she? And where was Kelly?

Blake finished changing the diaper and set Grace on her hip without bothering to dress her. Grace started whimpering again. "Mama," she cried again and again as Blake made her way back down the hallway, trying to shush her.

"Shhh," she said, holding her finger to her lips. "Angie! Kelly!" she cried out, half wishing she hadn't agreed to Angie's request, then hugging Grace more tightly against her. "Where are you?"

She'd reached the kitchen when heard Angie's voice, coming from somewhere at the front of the house. "In here," came Angie's muffled response. "You need to come see this."

The door to Kelly's bedroom was half open. Debating whether she should enter with the baby or not, Blake waited outside the threshold. "I've got Grace."

"It's okay," Angie said from where she sat at a small desk, typing on what must have been Kelly's laptop. "There's nothing in here she can't see."

Like the rest of the house, Kelly's room was a lot nicer than Blake had expected. Though it was obvious the girl didn't have much money everything was neat and clean. The bedroom furniture was cheap, mostly secondhand from the looks of it, but Kelly had painted it shades of turquoise and pale green. Bright curtains hung from the windows and the walls were decorated with framed posters of exotic places. On the bulletin board above the desk was a collage of pictures, mostly of Grace. She scanned the room for photos of family members or even friends and found none.

"It doesn't look like anybody's been in here," Blake said, leaning over the laptop, which was pink and high tech—not at all the sort of hardware Kelly would have been able to afford on her own. "How'd you get on that thing? Isn't there a password or something?"

"Grace." Angie sighed. "What's the point of

having a password if it's your kid's name?"

"She probably didn't expect anybody to be searching her stuff," Blake said, suppressing a twinge of guilt.

"Maybe," Angie said. "On the other hand, I'd bet she'd be pretty damn grateful we just saved her kid. Kelly had issues, but I'll say one thing for her—she was a good mother. In a lot of ways Grace may've been the best thing that ever happened to her. Got her to clean up her act. At least that's what I thought anyways. Take a look."

Blake peered at the email that filled the screen. "Was that already open?" she asked, readjusting Grace on her hip. Luckily, the child had stopped crying, seemingly as fascinated by what was on the screen as they were.

Angie nodded and hit the print button. A single sheet of paper fed into Kelly's printer, emerging a moment later with the strangest list Blake had ever seen. "This came up when I booted up the computer. Must've read it right before she took off."

Blake lifted the sheet of paper off the printer tray and studied it.

From Monk9277@monkeyfactory.net
Reply to 317296331@monkeyfactory.net
To Irisheyes21@yahoo.com
Date Wed, July 30, 2011 at 3:11 am
Subject Guest List #7
Mailed by anonymousemail.net
Cristy
Lucas
Henrietta
White Lady

Hitler's Dog
3172200100003X
0582400200000
Ruby E

To Blake, the email read like some sort of insane guest list—something the Mad Hatter would throw together for one his tea parties in *Alice in Wonderland.* She stared at the list until it blurred, trying to puzzle out its meaning. Cristy and Lucas sounded like ordinary people, but what about the White Lady and Hitler's Dog? Irisheyes21 might be Kelly, but who was Monk9277 at monkey factory? What was the meaning of the string of numbers at the bottom of the email? Why was "Ruby E" listed below the numbers and not above, like the other names? The more she studied the piece of paper, the more it eluded her.

"I don't get it," she said, handing the paper back to Angie. Grace reached her hand out for it, nearly tearing it in two. "It might as well be written in hieroglyphics."

Angie folded the paper and tucked it into her jeans pocket. "It's Greek to me too," she said. "But I don't think it's an invitation to the Church Social, if you know what I mean."

Grace started whimpered again. Blake scanned the room for a toy or a rattle but found none. Instead she held up her finger and let Grace wrap her small hand around it. The sensation of Grace's fingers clinging tightly to her own was so intense it made Blake dizzy. Sitting down on Kelly's bed, she positioned Grace on her lap. Grace still clung to her finger, almost as if she were afraid if she let go Blake might disappear.

Just like her mother.

Angie looked up from the paper. "If it is some kind

of invitation, 31-7-11 could be the date," she suggested.

"That makes sense," Blake agreed. "What numbers come next?"

"Two two zero zero," Angie read. "An address?"

Blake closed her eyes. "I don't think so," she said. "Could be 2-2-0-0 is military time. Sort of a code?"

"That's last night," Angie's eyes lit up triumphantly. "Maybe Kelly went to a party."

"And never made it home," Blake finished.

They looked at each other without speaking. If Kelly hadn't made it home from the party, where was she? There was no location listed anywhere in the email. "A party at the monkey factory?" Blake guessed, remembering the sender's odd email address.

"Makes as much sense as anything else" Angie turned her attention back to the screen. "I tried getting back into her email account but I'm locked out. Either the account timed out or she saved the email to her computer desktop and left it open."

Grace's eyes were glassy and half open. The child must have been up for hours, waiting for Kelly to return. Smoothing back Grace's platinum curls, Blake voiced what she knew both of them were thinking. "We've got to call the sheriff," she said. "Kelly might be in danger."

"I know," Angie said, switching off the computer. "The place will need to be searched—she might even be here somewhere. I took a look around while you were changing Grace, but it's not like I did a thorough search or anything."

"It's possible." Blake didn't really believe Kelly was in the house—the place was too quiet, too empty— but the sheriff's office would need to make certain of that. At the thought of Santos heading the search, her stomach tightened. Was the man really up for something heavy duty like that?

Grabbing a couple of tissues from a box next to the bed, Angie wiped the keyboard clean then shut the cover to the laptop and wiped that clean as well.

"What are you doing?" Blake asked, trying to keep the panic out of her voice.

Angie stuffed the tissues into her jeans pocket and regarded her cynically. "Not that Charlie Santos would ever think to dust for fingerprints," she said, "but do you want to explain to the sheriff why our prints are all over a missing girl's computer?"

Your prints. Not ours, she thought, but said nothing. What if somebody else's prints were on that computer as well? Well, they weren't anymore, and it was too late to do anything about it. "I guess that means you're not going to say anything to Santos about the email?"

Angie gave her a penetrating look. "Are you?"

Blake wasn't a lawyer anymore but the idea of tampering with evidence still seemed like the equivalent of swearing in church. On the other hand, Santos was no fan of hers. Telling him she searched Kelly's computer was going to make her life a lot more difficult. "I don't know," she said, taking a chance. "It seems wrong, somehow. That note may be the key to finding Kelly."

Angie averted her gaze, whether out of frustration or embarrassment, Blake wasn't sure. As Grace's eyes fluttered closed she shifted the child so that she was cradled in her arms. "Do you have your cell phone on you?"

"It's in the car," Angie said. "But there's no point in calling from here. No reception."

Blake sighed in exasperation. Back in the city, she always railed against the way people couldn't survive without their cell phones. Now she found herself wishing Eagle Point would get its act together and join the twenty-first century. "There's got to be a phone here somewhere," she said. "Her internet's got to be hooked up to a landline There's no cable out here, right?"

"Right." Angie scanned the room, then headed for the door. "I bet there's a phone in the kitchen."

"Hurry," she said. If Kelly were in trouble, every minute counted. Looking at Grace asleep in her arms, her heart contracted. Please let her be okay.

Angie hovered on the threshold a minute, her gaze coming to rest on the sleeping child. "I know this is going to sound naive," she said, "but I really thought she wasn't using anymore. I mean, sure, she had her problems in the past—for a while I thought she wasn't going to make it."

Blake nodded, remembering the track marks that ran up and down both arms. "Heroin?"

"Maybe," she said. "In all the time I knew her she never said one word about her problem. But her body said a whole lot. After the baby came, she seemed a lot more together—she used to shake, you know—dropped a few trays. I should've fired her, but I didn't. I guess I felt sorry for her. But then all of a sudden she seemed okay." Angie furrowed her brow. "At least until Chris started dating Jenna."

Blake fought the impulse to cut the conversation short. Still, she couldn't help herself from asking, "Do you think that was what pushed her back into drugs?"

"Could be," Angie said, turning to leave the room. "Even so, I'd swear on a stack of Bibles that girl was clean." She stepped out into the hallway and froze. "Somebody's here."

Blake heard it too. The unmistakable sound of tires on gravel. She was up off the bed and halfway toward the front door before she even realized what she was doing. "Is it Kelly?" she whispered, coming up behind Angie and peering onto the front porch from behind a curtain.

Angie pointed toward the sheriff's cruiser as it pulled up behind her Subaru. "Looks like the cops must've figured out Kelly's missing."

"That's a good thing, right," Blake said under her breath, pointedly ignoring the flutter of her pulse as she watched Santos and his deputy climb out of the car.

"Right." Angie's sarcasm was hard to miss.

Both women stood motionless as the two men approached. At the sound of their heavy steps on the porch, Angie backed up against the living room wall and braced herself for the worst. Blake held Grace as tightly as she could, debating what to do.

"We haven't done anything wrong," Angie whispered to her in a defiant voice.

"Not if you don't count breaking in, hacking into Kelly's computer and suppressing evidence," she whispered back. Deciding that the best defense was a good offense, she crossed to the door and pulled it wide open. "Thank goodness, you're here, Sheriff Santos," she said smiling broadly, with as much enthusiasm as she could muster. "We were just about to call you."

Well, at least that part was true. Sort of.

Charlie Santos stood on the other side of the screen

door with his fist poised in the air, as if he'd been about to knock. Blake watched with something like fascination at the parade of expressions that flickered across the sheriff's face. Shock first, then bewilderment, followed by anger. "What in God's name are you two doin' here?" he asked, shoving past Blake and Grace until he stood in the center of the living room. The deputy sheriff walked in behind him quietly, his dark eyes serious.

"I'd a thought it of this one," he said with a nod in Blake's direction. "But you too, Angie?"

The sheriff's reprimand irritated her to the point of fury. "If it hadn't been for us, Grace would still be here by herself," she told him, pulling herself up to her full height and switching into turbo-lawyer mode. "Kelly's been missing since this morning. You need to send out a search party."

If she hoped to intimidate Santos into backing down, she failed miserably. Taking a step forward, Santos was so close to her she could smell the tobacco on his breath. "There's no need to send out a search party," he said with quiet fury. "Kelly's dead."

A chill ran up her spine. Blake tried to think of something to say but could find no words. She said a quiet prayer of thanks that Grace was still asleep in her arms

A muffled sob came from the corner of the room. Angie stood with her fist in her mouth, trying to hold her emotions in check. "How—" she began, unable to finish. "What—happened?"

Santos actually smiled. "That's what I come to ask you two ladies about," he said, turning toward Blake. "Funny thing is, Kelly's body washed up on shore 'bout a quarter of a mile from the lighthouse. And her car's parked just around the bend from your place, Ms. Cartwright. Ain't that interesting?"

Blake fought to keep her composure. "How did she die?" she asked finally.

"I was pretty sure it was a suicide 'cause from the way that girl's body's busted up it looks like she musta jumped from the tower, but now I drive out here and find you two inside a dead girl's house and I have to wonder."

Beneath the smile was anger, real anger. Blake wondered what it was about her that made Santos dislike her so much. Was it the fact that she was an outsider? That she wasn't about to let him intimidate her? Whatever it was, his aversion toward her was all too evident—and might even be dangerous. If the sheriff wanted to make her life difficult, he would be able to do it.

The deputy walked over to them and laid a hand on the sheriff's arm. "Charlie, these ladies did help the baby," he said. "And doesn't Kelly work for you, Ms. Corelli?"

"We were only checking up on her." Visibly pulling herself together, Angie stepped forward so that she was standing next to Blake. "She didn't show for work this morning and I was worried. I asked Blake to take a ride out here with me."

Santos raised an eyebrow. "Sure you were. So I hope you gals won't mind coming down to the station and giving a couple of statements," he said. "Danny'll take you back while I search the place for evidence."

It was almost as if Santos was glad to be rid of his deputy. As if he wanted to do the search alone.

Somewhere in the back of her mind, an alarm bell rang. "I'd like to make a phone call," she told him. "Now."

"You can do that down at the station."

"As far as I know I haven't been charged with any crime," she said angrily, walking over to the phone in the kitchen. "So I don't believe I need your permission to make any number of calls."

Grace opened her eyes and began to cry loudly. Despite Blake's efforts to quiet the child, her screams rang across the room. "Shhhh," she said, rocking her in her arms.

"Tampering with a crime scene," Santos mumbled as Blake punched a number into the phone. "And shut that baby up!"

"This isn't a crime scene." She shot him a dangerous look. "Say another word and I'll file charges against you for intimidation."

Angie and the deputy said nothing, both of them content to remain spectators at a battle neither of them understood.

Blake crossed into the kitchen, shifting Grace onto her hip and lifting the receiver on the wall off its hook. As the number she dialed rang on and on without even clicking onto voicemail, her hand shook and she could only hope Santos was too dense to notice.

"Hunter." Declan's clipped, confident greeting rang out across the room.

For a moment she wasn't sure she could speak. "It's Blake," she said, struggling to make herself heard over Grace's shrieks, "I need you to do something for me."

Chapter 7

"What do you think?" Blake held up two tiny sundresses. "The yellow or the pink?"

Declan stared at the two outfits in puzzlement and tried to make a decision. He had no idea—they both seemed more or less interchangeable to him. He crossed his arms and tried to give the impression he was considering the plusses and minuses of toddler sundresses, when in reality he was wondering what he was doing in the middle of a department store during the most important investigation of his career. When Blake called him from Kelly's house he hadn't hesitated, even though it meant cutting off his boss in mid-sentence. By the time he got to the sheriff's office Santos was purple with frustration. Apparently the sheriff had latched on to his only "lead"—Blake and Angie's presence at Kelly's house—and he wasn't ready to let it go, not without getting something out of them. It took hours to convince Santos to let them leave with Grace and Declan doubted the man was through, not by a long shot.

The question was, did Santos truly believe they were involved? Or were his accusations against Blake and Angie little more than a fishing expedition? Even more to the point: would he have acted any differently if it was his own investigation?

Which, in a way, it was.

Yet here he was, smack at the center of the frilliest section in Macy's. Not counting the lingerie department, he amended. And at least that area held some interest for him. He had a sudden vision of Blake clad in nothing but black lace and sighed. Bad enough to be stuck shopping for baby clothes when he should be working. Even worse to be inches away from a woman he was finding it increasingly difficult not to think about bedding.

Focus. He needed to focus. Had to before the whole investigation was shot to hell and whoever was behind the operation was safe in the Caribbean or some equally remote location. The thought of to his opponent yet again riled him more than he dared admit. Almost against his will, an image of a figure sitting in a beach chair, Mai Tai in hand, rose up before him. The face was no more than a blur, never more than that.

He closed his eyes and counted to ten. When he opened them again Blake was staring at him with an odd expression on her face. He could see why the sheriff didn't like her. With her stunning features and her city-girl persona, she may as well have the word "outsider" tattooed across her forehead. That Santos allowed her to leave with Grace was downright shocking, even if it had taken him hours to come to that decision. He supposed the idea of having a baby underfoot while he was investigating the first real crime Eagle Point had seen in years must have been too much for the sheriff to handle.

With a start, Declan realized Blake was waiting for him to answer. He tried to look as if he had some clue as to why one dress might be better than the other. "Maybe the pink?" he suggested.

Seated in the front of their shopping cart, Grace pointed at the yellow outfit. "Pink," she echoed.

Blake tilted her head and studied the sundress.

"Not the yellow?" she asked him. "To be honest, I never really liked pink for girls. When I was little my mother always insisted on dressing me in pink and I hated her for it."

"The yellow looks nice," he said diplomatically. "It suits her coloring." He was particularly pleased with that last comment. It made him sound like he knew what he was talking about.

Blake held up the yellow dress, then replaced it on the rack and chose a green two-piece outfit with a duck sewn onto the front. "How about this one?"

Grace pointed to the green outfit. "Pink," she said happily.

"Or maybe something in blue?" Blake asked, sifting through the outfits on the rack. "Who says only boys can wear blue."

Declan pushed their shopping cart forward, trying not to think what his boss would say if he could see him. Was it possible that the workaholic curmudgeon might actually demote him? Maybe—if didn't get his head in the game. Kelly Reilly was dead and Declan was sure she'd been murdered. He was also convinced that she died because of her connection with his own investigation.

The trouble was, he had no idea how or why she was connected with it.

Even worse, the clock was ticking. Something was about to go down in Eagle Point. And soon. Everything he'd uncovered in the past few months pointed to that. But would he be able to get to the bottom of things in time?

"You know what," Blake said with a grin, gathering up all four outfits and piling them into the shopping cart. "I'm going to get them all. Who knows how long it'll be before the sheriff lets us into Kelly's place to get Grace's things."

"Sounds good to me." Her smile was infectious. In spite of everything—his loathing for shopping, the pressure of the investigation, the lies he'd been forced to tell—he couldn't help being caught up in the moment. There was something reassuringly domestic about shopping with Blake, something he found hard to resist. If he let himself, he could almost imagine it was their own child they were shopping for, not the indirect victim of a crime he should have prevented. What would it be like to be married to her? To raise a house full of children together and grow old sitting out on the front porch, watching the last rays of sun shining across the water?

Declan pressed his lips together. This was the problem. Or to put it bluntly—Blake was the problem. Ever since he'd met the woman he couldn't focus on the job at hand. Here he was spinning out fairytales when he should be sifting through the facts of Kelly's murder.

Focus, Hunter.

Normally, he was a pretty cut-and-dried sort of guy. In relationships that detachment hadn't worked out too well, but it was also what made him good at his job. Really good.

Up until now. For the past few days he'd been a mess of emotions. His mind kept going back to the kiss up in the tower, breaking his concentration and interfering with his instincts. Pressing his fingertips to the bridge of his nose, he tried to clear his head. Not to feel but to think. He'd been critical of Santos for questioning Blake, but could he rule her out as a suspect? After all, what did he really know about her? She seemed like the sort of woman he could fall in love with, but how much of that persona was genuine? Hadn't he made that mistake before, with devastating consequences?

"Hey, are you okay?" Blake turned away from the sales rack and stared at him again.

He couldn't help noticing the tiny line that appeared at the center of her forehead whenever she was worried. Why did she have to look so damn cute? He averted his gaze. "I'm fine."

Grace shook her rattle but Blake ignored her. "You don't seem like you want to be here."

"It's not that," he said, still refusing to meet her eyes.

Blake hesitated a moment before speaking. "Then what is it?"

Turning to face her, his sense of control slipped away. "Look, Blake—" he paused, not sure whether to go on then plunging ahead anyway. "I know your heart's in the right place, but we're an hour away from Eagle Point. A woman died fifty yards from your house and both of us were out there with the killer. What are we doing here, playing house with somebody else's baby while the sheriff is probably contaminating evidence as we speak?"

"I'm sorry," she said. "I needed...to get away. Just for a little while. After all those hours down at the station. Knowing Santos will probably be out there at the lighthouse when we get back." Blake sniffed. "And I thought—I mean I know Grace should be with her father—but I thought for now—"

The quaver of emotion in her voice was too much for him. Pulling her close, he took her into his arms and kissed her trembling lips. This kiss was softer, gentler, than the one they'd shared the other night. There was something intimate about it—something that bonded him to her in a way he'd never experienced.

The eyes of the other customers were on them but he didn't care. The thought of Blake in pain was almost unbearable. "I'm sorry," he whispered, caressing her hair with his hand. "You've been through hell."

"It's okay." Blake laid her head against his shoulder. "To be honest, I've been thinking the same thing. I knew you didn't want to be here, but I guess I wanted to pretend. At least for a little while."

Declan heard a gurgling sound behind him. Grace was sucking her thumb, calmly watching the two of them. "You're right though," he said, a little uncomfortably. "I don't think we can count on getting into Kelly's place anytime in the near future. I don't know about you, but my supply of diapers is pretty low."

She returned his smile, but her blue eyes were serious. "Now that Kelly's gone," she said resolutely, "Grace should be with her father. Once we finish up here, we need to take her to him."

He raised his brows. It wasn't their responsibility to handle the matter of Grace's custody but the thought of Santos dealing with anything related to the child seemed more than a little outlandish. Still, he forced himself to ask, "Don't you think you should let the sheriff deal with that?"

Blake gently pried Grace's thumb out of her mouth. Grace wrapped her fingers around Blake's again, ignoring the rattle she held up in front of her. "Santos has already called Social Services. If we don't act quickly Grace is going to end up in a foster home."

Grace clung to Blake's finger—almost as if her life depended on not letting go. On the surface, the child didn't seem all that upset. But now that he thought of it, it was a little bit odd, the way she hadn't once asked for her mother.

Probably some kind of coping mechanism. Grace might have designated Blake as a substitute for Kelly, but the longer the two of them were together the more difficult it was going to be when it came time for them to separate. "You're right," he admitted. "As usual."

"I know." Blake flashed him her classic grin, then headed toward the front of the store. "Let's get out of here. I think we've got enough to get her through the next few days."

If she noticed how Grace watched her every move, she didn't show it. As he followed behind her he couldn't suppress the feeling that handing Kelly's baby over to Chris McAllister might be harder on Blake than anybody else.

The sooner she did that, the better off they'd all be.

****

Chris McAllister watched Blake warily. His hand rested on a greasy beat-up table, loosely clutching a can of Pabst beer. "How many times do I need to say it," he said in exasperation. "She. ain't. my. kid."

"That's not what Kelly said." Blake absently rocked the portable carrier at her feet. Even though she doubted Grace would wake—it was nearly midnight—the rhythmic motion gave Blake some comfort. The trailer was small, not to mention poorly ventilated, and it certainly wouldn't win any prizes for cleanliness. But neat or not, Chris was Grace's father.

Chris took a swig of his beer and wiped his lips with the back of his hand. "I don' even know who you are, lady, but if Kelly told you I was that baby's daddy she was lyin' through her teeth."

Declan stiffened, but he remained silent beside her. On the way over to the trailer park she persuaded him to give her a chance to talk to Chris, who would likely be in an unsettled state of mind. The funny thing was, Chris didn't seem all that upset about Kelly's death. The only thing that did seem to bother Chris was the fact that she was trying to hand over his daughter to him.

Despite his protests, Grace certainly looked like him. Kelly had been dark, what Blake's mother would have described as "Black Irish"—dark eyes, black hair, pale nearly translucent skin. Chris, on the other hand, was blonde, with light blue eyes that matched Grace's exactly.

"I know you probably think this is none of my business," said Blake, ignoring the exhaustion deep in her bones. "But it is my business, in a way, because I'm the one who's been taking care of Grace since Kelly disappeared early this morning. When I was down at the station I heard the sheriff calling Social Services. If you don't step up and take responsibility for your daughter, she's going to end up with strangers. Is that really what you want?"

"If you don't want to take care of her," Chris said,

looking at her through bloodshot eyes, "then why didn't you leave her with the sheriff?"

She tightened her grip on the carrier to keep from screaming. "It's not that," she told him evenly. "I don't mind taking care of Grace. But she's already lost one parent." She leaned forward and forced him to make eye contact with her. "Your daughter needs you."

Chris's eyes darted to the clock on the wall. "Forgive me for being rude," he said flatly, pushing his chair back from the table, "but it's just shy of midnight. Now I don't know about y'all, but I have to work for a living and that means I got to be up by four a.m."

"We didn't think about the time," she apologized. "We thought you might be worried about Grace. But if you'd prefer, we could come back tomorrow, when it's more convenient. Or if the next couple of days are busy, we could even keep her for a little while, until you get the place fixed up for a baby."

Chris exhaled through his nostrils. "You seem to be missin' my point. To repeat, that baby ain't mine," he said in a warning tone. "Now I know there's a resemblance and that's probly why lots of people got it into their heads that she belongs to me. But hear me when I say this. Kelly was one messed up girl. Probly slept with half the men within a fifty-mile radius. Did I sleep with her? Hell, yeah. Does that mean I'm the father of her kid? Hell, no." Lifting the beer to his lips, he downed it in a single swig and set the empty can down in front of him. "Now if you don't mind, I got to get some sleep. I'm done talking about that whore."

Blake half raised her free hand to reach across the table him and slap him, then forced herself to stop. Rising out of her chair and lifting Grace's carrier, she nodded almost imperceptibly. "If that's what you want."

"Oh, believe me," Chris said. "That's exactly what I want."

Declan rose out of his chair as well. "The girl's dead," he said with quiet intensity. "There's no reason to speak ill of her."

From where he sat across from them, Chris looked up at Declan for the first time since they entered the trailer. Maybe he was intimidated by the fact that Declan had a good six inches—not to mention at least thirty pounds—on him. Maybe it was the simple fact he was a man. "I'll give you that," he said, crushing his beer can with his fist. "But for the past year and a half that girl's made my life a living hell. First, she goes around shooting her mouth off about me bein' Grace's father, then she sticks her nose in where it doesn't belong, and on top of everythin' else she goes and offs herself."

Declan's gaze flicked from the demolished beer can back to Chris. "I don't think Kelly did 'off' herself," he said mildly.

"Then you thought wrong," Chris spat out the words. "Even sent me a friggin' note."

Blake nearly dropped Grace's carrier. "She sent you a note?"

"No way Kelly'd kill herself without sticking it to me one last time."

"Did you give the note to the sheriff?" Declan asked.

Chris leaned all the way back so that the front of his chair tipped off the floor. "Do I look like some kinda fool?"

Neither Blake nor Declan answered him. Balling up the crushed beer can, Chris attempted to shoot it into the trash and missed. He swore in frustration, then got up off his chair and stumbled toward the back of the cramped trailer. After a couple of minutes he returned holding a wadded-up piece of paper, then threw it down on the table. "Take a look for yourselves if you don't believe me."

She set down the carrier and peered at the wrinkled note, which Declan was smoothing out across the table. The overhead light shone down onto it, making the carefully formed cursive seem even sadder than it already was. The stationery was pale green, with a border of tiny butterflies running along the edges of the paper. Though Blake had never seen Kelly's handwriting, something about the lettering was distinctly feminine. July 31, 2012

Dear Chris,

Im writing to tell you Im going to kill myself tonight. Theres no point in living anymore. I tried as hard as I could to make things work for me and Grace but I cant seem to do it. I'm back on drugs again and cant break there grip. Grace is better off without me. Please dont blame yourself for anything. I was the one to blame. Your an awesome guy and I dont want you to feel you have to do anything to uphold my memory after I'm gone. Please dont try and stop me. Its already too late.

K

Blake reached out her hand and ran a fingertip along the edge of the letter. She didn't know what to think. Had the woman who fell from the lighthouse been Kelly? Had she really gotten back into drugs again? Looking up from the girlish script, she asked, "Where did you find this?"

Chris stood at the other end of the table, arms crossed. Clearly, he felt he had more than enough to convince them of the dead girl's insensitivity toward him. "Folded up under the windshield of my truck."

"I suppose it didn't occur to you that she might not have killed herself yet," Declan said dryly.

"As a matter of fact, it did," he snapped. "I didn't notice it till I got up to drive down to the marina this morning. She musta left it there when I was sleepin."

"But you didn't tell anybody," Declan said leaning forward, resting his hands on either side of the note. It wasn't a question.

"What difference would it'da made?" The fisherman's chin jutted upward.

The steel in Declan's tone was unmistakable. "You might have been able to save her."

"Maybe." Chris shrugged. "Maybe not." With his tangled curls and bloodshot eyes he looked like a cornered animal with its fur standing on end. "Or maybe she wasn't worth it."

Declan rose from his chair and the two men faced off on opposite sides of the table, their faces inches apart. Declan seemed wound so tightly his control might snap at any moment. As for Chris, he looked as if he were itching for a fight.

Fearing what might happen, Blake stepped forward and clasped Declan's hand in her own. "Thank you for your time," she said as politely as she could manage. "Now that we know your feelings on the matter, you don't have to worry about us bothering you."

Chris turned his attention to her, then to Grace

sleeping in her carrier. For an instant, she thought she saw something like emotion flicker in his pale eyes, but it faded so quickly she might have imagined it.

"You stay outa my business," he said. "And I'll stay outa yours."

She could feel Declan radiating anger. She squeezed his hand as tightly as she could, willing him to think of Grace. Willing him not to escalate the situation any further.

Without turning his back on Chris, Declan leaned down and gripped the carrier handle with his free hand. When the three of them reached the trailer door, he swung it open and guided Blake through, handing the carrier down to her.

Chris watched them, looking as if he wanted nothing more than to beat the living hell out of Declan, though he remained quiet. Whatever his reasons were, he seemed to want nothing more to do with any of them.

Declan paused in the doorway before stepping out into the night. "As for minding my own business," he said, "I'm afraid I can't make you any promises. I only make promises I intend to keep."

Chapter 8

"That went well," Blake said.

It was the first time either of them had spoken since leaving the trailer park. As she fought off sleep Declan's pick-up bumped along the hilly dirt road that led to the lighthouse. Paved roads were another modern convenience Eagle Point seemed to lack, she thought groggily. Not to mention streetlamps. As they climbed yet another hill in a series of steep inclines the butterflies in her stomach did somersaults. "Worse than a rollercoaster," she mumbled.

"I guess you're going to be babysitting for a few more days," he said, casting a sidelong glance in her direction.

His headlights cut through the night but beyond their reassuring glare all was black. No moon shone in the sky, and even the stars seemed unnaturally dim, little more than pin-pricks. She wondered if she should be afraid, but the truth was she was just too tired for fear. Too tired even to worry about Grace, who lay asleep between them, strapped into her car-seat with a yellow baby blanket tucked snugly around her. Smoothing the blanket, Blake said, "I don't mind."

He kept his eyes on the road, saying nothing. Up ahead, a car appeared around a turn, its headlights tangling with theirs. It was moving fast, too fast for the unpaved road. "Wonder who that is."

She roused and stared at the headlights. "Probably Kelly's killer, coming from the scene of the crime," she said, stifling a giggle. After everything she'd been through that day, her composure was beginning to fray at the edges. "That's how it always happens in movies."

"Luckily for us," he said, "this isn't the movies." His gaze followed the car as it moved closer. "It looks too beat-up to be an official vehicle. My guess is Santos and his sidekick are probably gone by now. And I wouldn't worry too much about it being whoever murdered Kelly. Kelly's killer probably has a nicer car."

Despite his light tone, something about his remark got her attention. It didn't surprise her that he doubted the suicide theory. She wasn't buying it either. But why did he sound as if the killer was somebody he knew? And whose Corvette had he been leaning against earlier that day? The scene outside Cuppa Café came rushing back and suddenly she was wide awake. Sitting up, she watched as the car hurtled toward them at an alarming speed. "I never thought murderers were known for their taste in cars."

"You'd be surprised," he said in a low voice. "But I wouldn't worry about it. It's probably just a couple of teenagers fooling around. Rushing home before their parents notice they missed their curfew."

"Probably," she said vaguely, trying to remember the last time she'd made out with a guy and rushed home after curfew. *Must have been in high school*, she guessed, wincing at the memory of how unhappy she'd been then. When people met her they assumed she had always been attractive and had her pick of guys, but that hadn't been the case. At 5'10" she'd towered over most of the boys in high school and her thinness only made her seem awkward, not fashionable. She hadn't had the slightest sense of how she should dress to emphasize her best features or what to do to tame the mass of blonde curls that reached the middle of her back. The final blow had been when she had gotten braces. The only guy who wanted anything to do with her was a computer geek more interested in playing Nintendo than in kissing her. At the time she'd been in love with the starting quarterback, a three-letter captain who never walked down the halls without a posse of girls trailing behind him.

The car appeared again on the ridge immediately ahead of them then began its descent. As it roared past them, she breathed a sigh of relief. Maybe it was just teenagers, but she got the distinct impression that Declan was playing down his misgivings. On the other hand, considering what they were dealing with, there was no such thing as being too careful. Or too paranoid.

"Looks like whoever it was isn't interested in us," Declan said.

"Guess you were right."

"Guess so."

The two of them drove on in silence. Her mind was still far away, roaming the halls of Vanderbilt High. Like her, Kelly must have believed she was unworthy of love. Maybe she turned to drugs because they made the pain and the insecurity stop, even for a little while. "I don't think Kelly wrote that note," she said quietly, more to herself than to Declan.

"The writing looked like it belonged to a teenage girl," he remarked, digging into his pocket and pulling out a small square of paper. "It's only a signature, but it looks nothing like the writing in the letter. I don't think Chris could've faked that."

Blake stared at the crumpled credit card receipt. Someone had written Chris McAllister across the signature line in labored cursive. "When did you take that?"

He shrugged, but didn't reply.

She switched on the overhead light and held the receipt close to her face. Though it was difficult to see in the dimness of the cab, it was clear the signature bore no resemblance to the handwriting in the note. "It's very different," she said. "Can't people disguise their handwriting though?"

"Only to a point. There are similarities a writer can't hide, even if he wants to."

"Or she," Blake pointed out. "Maybe a woman wrote the note."

Declan's pick-up crested then began its final descent. Further off, the shadowy outline of the lighthouse loomed against the darkness. She half expected to see lights in the tower or another body tumbling through the air to the surf below. Or even a ghost, wandering the grounds for all eternity.

"Almost a hundred years ago Lucy Stone killed herself and left her daughter an orphan," she said, thinking out loud. "Last night, Kelly Reilly might have done the exact same thing." A wistful feeling took hold of her as she looked out the passenger-side window at the lighthouse. "It almost makes me believe in ghosts. Maybe Lucy really does lure people to their deaths."

"Almost." The doubt in his voice was unmistakable.

Blake cast a disgusted look in his direction. "I

know, I know," she said. "Occam's razor."

"You got it."

"Sometimes things aren't all that obvious."

"Maybe so," he agreed, "but even then it's a matter of uncovering what's hidden, not spinning fairy tales about what *might* be true. All that does is allow the realists to keep exploiting people."

She smiled wanly, a little taken aback by his resistance to anything that couldn't be detected with the five senses. "Maybe sometimes fairy tales come true."

"Not in my experience."

Declan pulled up alongside the keeper's house and turned off the ignition. He got out of the truck without speaking then reached into the cab for Grace's carrier. Lifting it off its base, he gently maneuvered it out of the truck and headed for the house. Clearly, the conversation was over. "I'll get her inside," he said over his shoulder. "Then we can figure out the sleeping arrangements."

"Sleeping arrangements?" she asked, unsure if she was pleased or annoyed. She couldn't ignore the jolt of anticipation that shot through her at the thought of Declan spending the night. But another part of her registered the arrogance in his assumption and railed against it. At least the man might have asked.

She tried to recall if she'd gotten around to unpacking any sleepwear besides torn t-shirts and baggy sweats. When she realized she hadn't, in fact, "gotten around to it," she experienced a second epiphany. *Am I the same woman who hasn't missed a manicure in an entire year?* After all that had happened since her arrival, the things she'd considered important in the city didn't seem to matter all that much.

Reaching into the backseat of the cab to grab the Macy's shopping bags, she wondered if she could really have changed after such a short time. Could it be the woman she thought of as the "true" Blake Cartwright didn't bear much resemblance the woman she was turning out to be? By the time she gathered up the packages, Declan was already on the porch. He pushed open the door and maneuvered through the threshold with the carrier, setting it down just inside the entryway.

She had locked the door, she was certain of it. Hadn't she?

Adjusting her grip on the shopping bags, she remained motionless in the driveway, uncertain what to do. Should she let him stay the night? And if she did, what did that mean, exactly? If he meant to answer her question once they were inside the house, his actions gave no indication of it. The living room lights flashed on and Declan disappeared inside, the screen door swinging shut behind him. .

Had she offended him by asking about sleeping arrangements or was he simply too arrogant to consider her feelings? Despite the fact that she'd spent the entire day with Declan she was no closer to understanding him than she was on the first day they met. Did he ever open up to anyone? She doubted it. It was hard to imagine him ever letting his guard down that much. Always, always, he needed to be in control.

Whatever the cost.

She set down the bags on either side of her and was about to slam the passenger-side door when she heard the familiar pulsing sound of a cell phone vibrating. Instinctively, she rummaged in her pocket for her phone before she realized the sound was coming from inside the truck.

Not her cell phone. Declan's.

She stood shivering outside the truck, telling herself there was nothing wrong with grabbing his phone for him and bringing it into the house. With a guilty glance toward the front door, she watched Declan walk back out onto porch and peer into the darkness. Would he call out to her?

Not Declan. Instead he would go on shutting her out, just like he had been all day. A ripple of anger surged through her. Why shouldn't she bring in his phone, she told herself. Why did the simplest things make her feel as if she were violating his privacy? Even more infuriating was the fact he was getting cell phone reception. Why did such a small thing seem momentous all of a sudden?

The phone vibrated again. Before she could change her mind she set down the packages and reached for it. She scrambled to fish it out from the gap between the bucket seat and the beverage holder. By the time she grabbed it, she didn't give a second thought to pressing the OK button at the top of the keypad. The screen cast a strange glow as an envelope icon appeared on the screen.

You have three new text messages.

Declan stood in the open doorway, his arms folded across his chest. "Everything okay?" he called to her.

Because she stood on the other side of the truck, he couldn't see what she was doing. She knew she shouldn't go any further. If she opened even one of those messages she would be crossing a line, and Declan might not forgive her. Then again, she'd witnessed a murder the night before—she was sure of it—and he appeared in her doorway just minutes after she watched Kelly fall to her death. And, he hadn't so much as mentioned his conversation with Jenna that morning.

Taking a deep breath, she pressed the OK button a second time to open the first text.

Though she shouldn't have been surprised, she was. She was floored.

"Hey, are you okay?" Declan repeated, walking to the edge of the porch. "Need some help?"

Had fun today. Off tomorrow night...drinks at your place? Or should we do it someplace else? ☺

She stared down at the text message, forcing herself to read it a second time. Not that she doubted what she was looking at. But she reread it anyway, partly to convince herself that the man who kissed her out on the catwalk was nothing but an illusion. She didn't know him—would never know him—but some silly, romantic part of her had wanted him to be mysterious.

Because unlike Declan Hunter, she still wanted to believe in fairy tales.

The only problem was this one wasn't turning out so well.

"Hey," he shouted, a trace of worry in his voice. "What are you doing?"

When she looked up again he was standing a few feet away from her, his mouth open.

She regarded him icily. As her eyes came to rest on his mouth she found it hard to believe she'd kissed those same lips just hours before. Whoever Declan Hunter was, she wanted nothing more to do with him.

"You've got a message," she said with supreme disdain, walking over to him and holding out the cell phone at arm's length.

She expected him to be angry. To yell at her for violating his trust. Instead he remained perfectly still, watching her with a look of pain on his face. "Blake, listen to me—"

"Let me guess," she said, cutting him off before could say another word. "You can explain."

"You don't understand."

"Right." She brushed past him without so much as a second look. When she reached the porch, she turned back, unable to resist the urge to see him one last time. "Do me a favor, okay? The next time you decide to kiss somebody, make sure she's as a much of an unfeeling son of a bitch as you are." Even as she said it, she understood the anger that washed over her just moments before was already dissipating. *Do Not Cry,* she told herself as she fumbled in her purse for the key then remembered she didn't need it.

He followed her, but he hung back, waiting a few feet from the porch. "I don't blame you for being mad." His face was lost in shadows, but his voice was shakier than she'd ever heard it. "Hell, Blake, part of me even wants you to kick me to the curb. But before you do just take sixty seconds and listen to what I have to say. If you let me inside, I promise I'll try to explain as much as I can."

To her surprise, she found she could actually laugh. "Not good enough," she said, stepping though the open door and lifting Grace's carrier with both hands. She turned back toward him and forced herself to finish it. "I'm going upstairs and then I'm putting Grace to bed.

When I look outside again, I want you gone."

****

Declan hadn't gotten very far when he stopped the truck. He sat with his hands on the wheel then leaned his head forward. There were no other cars on the winding road and outside it was so quiet he could almost imagine he was the last man on earth. He wasn't so selfish that he didn't realize any future for himself and Blake wasn't viable. And it wasn't as if his intentions were wholly dishonorable. Sure, the thought of staying the night at her place suggested certain possibilities to his sleep-deprived brain—he was a guy, after all. But his main instinct was to keep her and Grace safe.

Which they weren't, not anymore. They were alone in a house fifty yards from spot where a murder had occurred less than twenty-four hours earlier. He had played down his fears about the car that passed them on the road. Maybe it was only a couple of horny teenagers racing back to town. Maybe not. Even if hadn't been the killer, it could have been somebody connected with his investigation. Because after three months in Eagle Point he was pretty damn sure Blake's property was somehow at the center of the organization he was investigating.

He didn't know how, not yet. But he was getting closer to finding out. Not much had happened in Eagle Point since his arrival. Had his cover been blown? Did whoever was running things suspect who he really was? It seemed unlikely, but on the other hand over the past few weeks the town had been as quiet as—well, as quiet as he would've expected a remote fishing village to be. Aside from the usual surge of seasonal tourism, the town seemed exactly what the guidebooks described it as: "A picturesque seaside escape untouched by the commercialism that has marred some of Maine's better known vacation getaways. Eagle Point offers a peaceful respite for those seeking a little R & R." He nearly laughed aloud as he recalled the blurb. Picturesque maybe. But definitely not peaceful.

Why did Kelly Reilly have to die?

He kept going back to that. And kept coming up with a blank. Did she know something? Was she involved in some way? He was pretty sure she was. But after reading the suicide note he wasn't quite so sure. Maybe she had killed herself and her death was diverting him from something far more important. Was she merely in the wrong place at the wrong time?

The wrong place being the lighthouse. Blake's place.

And Blake's door hadn't been locked. Maybe she'd forgotten to lock it earlier that day, though he doubted it. She hadn't been away from the city long enough to quit thinking like a New Yorker. If so, it meant somebody had been inside the house. Santos? Possibly. It wouldn't surprise Declan to learn that the sheriff had taken full advantage of Blake's absence, regardless of whether he had a search warrant. Nor would it surprise him if Santos left the place unlocked. Even after a couple of hours spent with the man, Declan had seen enough to know he was more or less incompetent. Hell, maybe the sheriff even left the door unlocked on purpose. He seemed to want to do anything he possibly could to annoy Blake, whose sophisticated manner clearly ruffled his feathers

He swore under his breath. Blake had no idea what

she'd inadvertently gotten herself into. She wanted to escape the corruption of New York, but now she was in even greater danger than before.

He should be out there. With her. And with Grace.

He raised his eyes and stared ahead of him without really seeing anything. Should he go back? She'd made it abundantly clear that she didn't want him there. He supposed he could spend the night in the oil-house again. Granted, if Blake found out she would probably contact the sheriff. And maybe fire him to boot. What would happen to his investigation then? Before her arrival he'd had free run of the place. Now he was forced to sneak around, searching for evidence when she wasn't looking.

But at least he still had access. Did he really want to jeopardize that?

He pursed his lips. Yeah, he did want to jeopardize that. He couldn't leave them out there alone. If Blake fired him, he'd find another way to continue the investigation. And to keep watch over her and Grace.

The realization was more than a little unnerving, but he didn't question the truth of it. He couldn't guarantee his presence would protect them—but he knew damn well they'd be a lot better off staying with somebody who was trained to deal with this kind of thing. Somebody good at hunting killers. And God only knew he fit the bill on that count. He'd been doing exactly that for most of his life and he wasn't about to stop now.

Unfortunately, that was the problem.

He wasn't going to stop. No matter what his feelings for Blake might be—and he wasn't at all sure he knew what they were—he would be moving on.

Maybe it would take weeks to accomplish his goal. Or even months. But whether it was sooner or later, whether he won or lost this round, at some point he was going to wrap things up in Eagle Point.

And when he did he was going to move on to the next location. The next job.

He envisioned Blake back at the keeper's house, rocking Grace then laying her gently down to sleep. They should have bought a crib, he thought, wishing he'd set one up for her. They would need one, at least for a while. Chris wanted nothing to do with Kelly's child and God knew how long it would take to get Grace into a foster home. Well, Blake could set up a crib on her own. She could take care of herself—and Grace.

Even so, how long would it be until Social Services got involved? He knew all about Social Services, more than he ever wanted to. After spending six years being bounced from foster home to foster home, he decided he'd had enough and ran away the night of his sixteenth birthday. He never looked back.

Until now.

He thought this case would be no different from all the others. Sure, he knew he would be returning to Eagle Point after more than two decades spent avoiding the place. But all the years of shutting out his emotions gave him a false sense of confidence about the impact being back would have on him. Every corner he turned seemed to evoke a new memory. Meeting Blake somehow multiplied the effect tenfold. The problem was, they were memories he didn't want to confront. Not when he was involved in the biggest drug investigation he had ever been a part of. Though he wasn't sure exactly how extensive the operation was he'd uncovered enough to convince him that it was supplying heroin, methamphetamines and a host of other drugs to much of New England. From Maine, the organization's tentacles spread to Boston, New York, Newark, Detroit and a host of other cities. While most of the drugs that came into the United States arrived via Mexico, the U.S.-Canadian border was more or less an untapped frontier. With more than 5,000 miles to guard, there was no way to prevent contraband from entering the country. Then there was the not-so-small matter of the Atlantic and Pacific Oceans. The only thing that surprised Declan was that not many drug lords took advantage of the opportunities the porous border presented.

Of course, that wasn't the case anymore. For the past couple of years somebody had been taking full advantage. If his guess was right, it wasn't someone new to the business either. Something about the way it was being run was unnervingly familiar. He couldn't say exactly why or even specifically how, but neither could he rid himself of the idea that he was looking at a fingerprint he'd seen before. A face he knew. But he could never bring it into focus.

If he could just stay on track. But too damn many things kept preventing him from doing that. Blake, for one. After so many years spent suppressing his emotions, his control was dangerously close to cracking. And once that happened he didn't know if he'd be able to regain it. He hardly knew her but the feelings she brought to the surface seemed so real he was beginning to have a hard time functioning. Maybe he didn't need to leave because it was what she wanted.

Maybe he needed to do it for his own sanity.

He stared at the road ahead. He could honor Blake's request and keep driving. He could return in the morning, after she had time to cool down, and try to talk her into at least keeping him on as a contractor. He could make up some new reason for Jenna's texts, one that wouldn't require him to level with her. Or he could do the foolish thing and turn around. He could try to explain the truth and watch her get even angrier when she realized why he agreed to work for her. Then she would tell him, again, to get the hell out of her life.

Which would make his plans infinitely more difficult. While it wouldn't be impossible to go on with the investigation without access to her property, it wouldn't be easy. Hell, he may even be pulled off the case if he couldn't gain access. But even if his boss did pull him off he could go on with his life, such as it was, and never return to Eagle Point again. There would be new investigations, new dealers to bring down. Nothing needed to change.

Or he could take a risk.

****

Blake padded down the stairs in bare feet, her pink terrycloth bathrobe wrapped tightly around her. Her hair was twisted into a messy knot at the back of her head and her face was free of make-up. She held a flashlight in one hand, just in case. The power was on, thank God, but the lights had flickered a couple of times and she wasn't taking any chances. Not after what had been going on.

She wasn't tired, not anymore. She had pushed her bed up against the corner of her room and tucked Grace in, worrying about the lack of a crib. Despite her fears

Grace curled up in a fetal position and closed her eyes. After watching her for several minutes Blake decided she could risk going downstairs to make herself a cup of tea.

When she saw him a flash of rage ripped through her. Still, she couldn't ignore the twinge of happiness that accompanied it, like the sun peeking out from behind a mass of storm clouds. He stood at the center of the room, his dark eyes on her. "How did you get in?" she asked.

Declan held up a tiny black object. "Skeleton key."

Well, at least that explained how he opened the door earlier. She stepped into the living room, still holding the flashlight. Bad enough that he deliberately flouted her command to leave. Even worse that he did it when she looked about as sexy as a ratty gym towel. She knew she wasn't sizzling hot like Jenna, but she at least wanted him to regret losing her a little bit. "So I tell you I never want to see you again and you break into my house?"

He nodded. "Guilty as charged, counselor."

"I should call the sheriff on you."

"Maybe you should." He deposited the key into his shirt pocket. "Anything might happen. Only I don't recall you having a phone."

She indicated the darkened kitchen with a tilt of her head. "As of today I do. I had one installed before I left this morning," she lied, willing herself not to look away from him.

He gestured toward the entryway magnanimously. "Don't let me stop you then."

Was he calling her bluff? Or just playing with her, like a cat pawing a very angry mouse? "Of course, if I did call the sheriff he'd probably hang up on me."

"He's not a fan," Declan agreed, a smile tugging at the corner of his mouth.

Should she order him out a second time? Turn around and rush back upstairs? She knew the absolute worst thing she could do was to go on standing there looking into his dark eyes. Like staring at a cobra. Every rational bone in her body was telling her to push him out the door, but the desire he sparked was hard to resist. Beneath his plaid shirt was a rock-hard six-pack and broad shoulders that rippled when he moved. Even his slightest gesture exuded strength—and danger. Not to mention sensuality so intense it was all but impossible not to want him.

Damn the man.

She looked down vaguely at the flashlight and tucked it into her bathrobe pocket. With a start of horror, she realized her half-open robe revealed not skin but polka dots. If there was an award for frumpy she'd win hands down. Much as she hated herself for it, some crazy part of her wanted to believe he came back because of her. Surely he'd been with his share of gorgeous women. And of course there was Jenna, whose erotically charged texts left no question about her intentions when it came to Declan.

She exhaled slowly in an effort to calm down. She was not going to let a man like Declan Hunter get to her. She ordered him to leave her alone and yet here he was, ignoring her wishes yet again. He had deceived her and he might well be sleeping with another woman. To hell with him.

Declan stood a few feet from the door, his face unreadable. The only lamp in the room stood next to the couch, its cone of yellow light in stark contrast with the dimness of the room. Yet even with his face lost in shadows he looked as intense as she'd ever seen him. She wasn't afraid, exactly, but she wasn't about to allow herself to let down her guard either. Her attraction toward him was so strong now it was almost too much to bear. But could she trust him?

He took a step toward her. "Those texts weren't what they seemed to be."

"They seemed pretty convincing to me. And today in town," she continued, not bothering to keep the skepticism out of her voice. "I suppose the conversation you and Jenna were having wasn't real either. Or the Corvette? Was that a figment of my imagination, too?"

"Don't pull away from me, Blake," he said, crossing toward her until he was so close she could smell the spicy aroma of his aftershave. "I can't tell you everything but I promise I'll level with you, as much as I can without putting anybody else in danger." He took a breath, as if he were steeling himself to do the hardest thing he'd ever done. "I'm not just a guy who renovates houses."

"Thanks for the news flash," she said but her heart flickered with some unnamable emotion. Triumph? Satisfaction? Anger? She wasn't sure.

"This is probably a mistake, maybe the biggest mistake I'm ever going to make. If you betray me I could lose my career." He paused then ran a hand through his hair, making it even more unruly than it already was. "I do renovate houses—or at least I have in the past. I wasn't lying when I told you that. But that's not my job."

Wanting to put some distance between them, she

walked over to the faded sofa and sat down without saying a word. Instinctively, she knew her silence was worse than all the accusations she could have made. Her heart was beating so hard she clenched her fists. Anything to stop herself from blurting out her feelings. Not that she was even sure what her feelings were.

"I work for the DEA," he went on. "I've been a special agent for their narcotics unit for ten years. I specialize in maritime drug trafficking, which is why I'm in Eagle Point. I'm in the middle of an investigation that involves a U.S.-Canadian smuggling operation that's more extensive than anything we've seen before."

She stared down at her fists, which were balled in her lap. "So renovating my house is just your cover."

"Yes."

"And you've been lying to me more or less from the second I met you," she said, keeping her eyes downcast. She couldn't look at him, not yet. If she did she wasn't sure if she would punch him in the face for lying or throw herself into his arms for finally telling her the truth.

"I'm sorry," he said quietly. "I didn't have any other choice—the people I deal with aren't very nice, in case you haven't already guessed that. If I told you who I really was I would've been putting in you in more danger than you're already in."

His last sentence hung between them. The idea that she was in danger didn't bother her as much as she would have expected. She supposed it was because he wasn't telling her anything she didn't already know. But she didn't like the idea that Grace was in jeopardy too. Maybe if Blake had known his real mission all along she could have done more to protect them both. Would she have brought Grace back to the keeper's house if she understood what they were at the center of? Even the sheriff's office seemed preferable to the danger the child might be in now.

The grandfather clock against the far wall struck midnight and she nearly jumped out of her skin as its doleful chimes resounded across the room. Much as she hated to admit it, Declan's presence did offer some comfort in such an isolated spot. "So why are you telling me now?" she asked when the ancient clock fell silent again.

"I don't know."

It was the uncertainty in his voice that made her finally turn to look at him. A muscle worked in his jaw, as if he were making a supreme effort to control his emotions. "I guess you're not going to be starting any long-term projects," she said with a half-hearted smile.

"Probably not," he said. "The intelligence we've gotten indicates something is going to happen soon. Very soon. After that—"

"After that you'll be gone."

"Yes."

Which was worse, the old lies or his terse version of the truth? Blake wished he would offer her something else. Even a lame attempt to convince her he might not have to leave right away might be preferable to this. But on the other hand at least he was leveling with her. He had no intention of hanging around for her sake or any woman's—he'd made that all too clear. "And the texts from Jenna?"

"I'm not sure how she got the impression I'm interested. I'm not. As far as I'm concerned, she's just part of the investigation," he said. "Jenna used to be close to Kelly. We believed Kelly got mixed up in something connected with the smuggling ring. I tried to approach Kelly directly a couple of times but she wouldn't have anything to do with me. Maybe she suspected something? I don't know. If I'd managed to get through to her, she might be alive now." At the mention of the dead girl's name, his expression grew thoughtful.

Their eyes caught and held as the silence lengthened. "You can't blame yourself," she said after it became clear he wasn't going to make any attempt to justify what he had—or hadn't—done.

"I don't," he said quickly. "That kind of thing comes with the job. I do what I have to do and try not to think about it anymore than I need to."

"Is Declan Hunter even your real name?"

"Yes," he said. "That much at least is true."

For a full minute or so, they remained quiet. Her gaze traveled around the dim room, from the sagging bookshelves to the shabby, overstuffed furniture to the Victrola in the corner. Anything to divert her thoughts. But every time she let herself look back at him, his eyes were on her. She half expected him to plead for forgiveness—or to walk out the door. By now she knew that wasn't his style though. If anything, he seemed to be waiting for her to tell him to go.

Which she should do. Not because he'd deceived her. Now that he had explained what he was really doing in Eagle Point, she could forgive him for not being straight with her up front. Hadn't she always known he wasn't who he said he was? Yet she still let him into her life. If she were honest with herself she'd have to acknowledge that she knew he wasn't a house renovator the moment she'd brought down that bookend onto his shoulder She hired him without so much as checking a reference. Come to think of it, the only other decision she'd made so impulsively was to buy the lighthouse. And look where that had gotten her.

No, she didn't want him to walk out the door because he'd misled her. She wanted him to leave because that was exactly what he was going to do once he finished his investigation. If she let Declan into her heart, would she be able to watch him move on in a month or two?

He shifted uneasily from one foot to the other. "Do you want me to go?"

"Just answer me one question."

"Shoot."

"Did you deliberately mislead Jenna about your feelings to get information out of her?"

"No," he said. "I talked to her a couple of times, that's it. We took a drive in her Corvette and I gave her my number then told her to call me if she ever wanted to talk about Kelly's problems." He shook his head. "I said I was Kelly's uncle. Who the hell would want to date her ex-friend's uncle? I've got fifteen years on her at least."

When she thought about it afterward, she supposed it was his bewildered expression that convinced her. He really didn't know how sexy he was. As the realization sunk in, her anger toward him began to fade. Maybe he wouldn't be around much longer. And maybe there wasn't any future for them. But he came back. He said he didn't want Jenna and, to her surprise, she believed him. Against all odds, she trusted him.

She rose from the couch and stood on tiptoe, wrapping her arms around him. He was so hard it was impossible for her not to feel him, even through her robe. Their faces were just inches apart, her lips brushing against the stubble on his jaw as she whispered into his ear, "That's all I need to know."

Chapter 9

Taking a step backward, Blake untied her robe and let it slip to the floor. She gave him a slow smile and began fumbling with the buttons of her flannel polka dot pajamas. Wisps of her hair escaped from the knot at the back of her head and two crimson spots darkened each cheek. At last she stood breathless before him, clad in nothing but white cotton panties.

It was the hottest thing he'd ever seen.

Declan had been with his share of women but he'd never wanted anyone the way he wanted Blake at that moment. She was the most beautiful woman he knew, passionate and real, nothing like the statuesque ice goddess he'd taken her for when he first met her. He grew rock hard, his erection straining against the front of his jeans. He could think of nothing besides his desire to place his hands on her skin, to feel his lips on hers. He didn't care that she hadn't bothered to put up curtains, exposing them to anyone who might be watching. He didn't care that it was going to be pretty damn difficult to leave her when it was all over. But if he went one more second without touching her he would lose his mind.

Fortunately, he didn't have to wait.

In a single motion he took her into his arms and pressed his lips to hers. She met his kisses with a ferocity he'd only glimpsed up on the tower. His hands slid over her shoulders, caressing her arms, her hips, the small of her back. She fumbled at the snap on his jeans but he couldn't wait. When she couldn't get his zipper down, he let go of her and pulled it down himself, stepping out of his jeans and boxers then pulling his t-shirt over his head and casting it down next to her robe.

Blake caught her breath. His chest heaved with desire as he pulled her to him again, cupping her bottom with his hands. His erection pressed into her belly, pulsing with heat. She ran her fingertips around the tip and an electric thrill coursed through him. His mouth traveled down her neck, branding her throat with hot kisses before descending to the valley between her breasts. He leaned down and took her hardened nipple into his mouth, flicking his tongue over it then suckling it with a steady rhythm.

When her moans became frantic, he released the nipple and cupped the other breast, circling the nipple with his thumb and his forefinger then closing his mouth around it. She gasped as he took it into his mouth, laving and sucking. Leaning her head back, she ran her hands through his tangled hair. Never in his life had he felt this alive, as if his nerves were turned inside out.

"Don't stop," she breathed.

Releasing her nipple, he raised his lips to hers once more and slid his tongue over her teeth. He groaned as she bit his lower lip. "I'm not sure I can stop," he said, snapping off the light and leading her to the couch, "not if we keep this up much longer."

He laid her down and knelt beside her, removing her panties and letting his hand stroke her belly a moment before lowering it to the pale tuft between her thighs. She lifted her hips to him, opening her legs to allow his fingers to slide into her. As he continued stroking her, moving his fingers in and out, he felt her tighten around them. With one hand she grasped his bicep, gripping him hard as the fire inside him threatened to burst into flames that would consume him.

"I want you inside me," she murmured, meeting his eyes. "Please."

"Maybe we should slow down—" he said. "There's no going back."

Blake ran her hands over his chest, arching her hips to him. "I don't want to go back."

At the touch of her fingertips he lost what little restraint he had left. He lowered himself onto her, crushing her mouth with his kisses and pushing himself deep inside her. Blake wrapped her legs around him and he reveled in the dark sensation of her inner muscles clenching around him. He was wild for release, hungry for completeness. She cried out as he plunged into her again and again, increasing his speed to a frenzied pitch. He'd never experienced a connection so dangerous, so intoxicating. As he thrust into her she met him with her hips, matching his rhythm. Their bodies were slick with sweat, feverish with need. He was at the edge of a cliff and falling was not only inevitable but the thing he desired most. With every thrust, he drowned in the seductive darkness washing over them.

Declan stiffened then uttered a stifled cry as he reached orgasm, pumping into her until there was nothing left in him. He closed his eyes as he rode her hard, riding wave after wave of sensation as her muscles clenched around him. She arched her back under him and the sweet, dark release of orgasm flooded every part of her, leaving him with a feeling so sharp that it was almost too much to bear. He buried his face in her hair as she clung to him, murmuring words he couldn't catch. The current between them was electric, unbreakable.

He collapsed on top of her, still inside her, as the tremors rippled through him. Planting a messy kiss on her forehead, he rolled to the side and wedged himself beside her on the narrow couch. "That," he said, stroking her hip, "was the best make up sex I ever had."

Blake pushed up on one elbow. "I don't think I like that."

"Don't like what?"

"Being compared to all your other women."

He pulled her back down so her face was a few inches from his. Raising his lips to her, he planted a kiss on the tip of her nose. "You don't need to worry about other women."

"I've got to get back upstairs," she said, jumping up abruptly and grabbing her robe off the floor. "I should check on Grace."

"I've never felt this way before."

The words were out before he could take them back. What happened between them was unlike anything he'd ever experienced but he didn't want to allow himself to take things too seriously. After all, he was going to leave sooner or later. Did the timing really matter? He didn't regret making love with Blake. When they joined together it was as if a bond formed between them that would never wholly dissolve, regardless of whether they were in contact. Whether he stayed another month or even another day he would always be linked to her, almost as if an invisible thread ran between them.

She tied her robe tightly around her waist and bent down to scoop up her discarded clothing. "You don't need to say that."

His eyes locked onto hers. "I know."

Did he feel guilty about what they had done? Had he said what he had in a clumsy attempt to make everything okay? An unfamiliar sensation tugged at his heart. If he meant what he said then his emotions were as much of a danger to him as they were to her. Because emotion mattered only to a point. He wasn't the sort of man who would back out of his responsibilities. He had a job to do—and reasons of his own for doing it. The last thing he wanted was to mislead Blake about their future. *So why did you say it then, Hunter?*

Blake crossed the room and paused at the bottom of the stairway, her hand resting on the banister. Moonlight spilled into the room, illuminating her pale face. Framed by wisps of ash blonde hair, she looked like some sort of ethereal being—too cold and too beautiful to be real. Already she was pulling away from him, retreating into the distant woman he knew now was nothing more than a way to protect herself from getting hurt by guys who wanted to sweet-talk their way into bed. *Guys like you.*

At least until he met her.

"Look, Declan," she said a little hesitantly. "It was fun. I haven't had sex like that in—well, actually I've never had sex like that. But please don't think you've got to say all kinds of flowery things so I won't get mad at you. I don't expect anything more from you, that's the truth. I'm not going to melt because you don't get down on one knee and propose we spend the rest of our lives together. "

"I've never had sex like that either," he said, noting the look of skepticism on her face. "And as for getting down on one knee—" He broke off, unsure what he meant to say. That he was the type of guy whose heart iced over at the mere mention of marriage? That if he spent more than six months in one place he got so stir crazy he was willing to do just about anything to escape?

Yeah, that was exactly what he planned to say. But he didn't want to hurt her.

"I should check on Grace," she said briefly, almost as if she were reading his thoughts. "Goodnight."

He watched her ascend the stairs, half hoping she'd at least glance over her shoulder before she disappeared down the dark hallway. She didn't. He'd been dismissed, that much was painfully clear. Did she want him to stay the night? For that matter, what did he want to do? Spend the next eight hours on a sagging couch or take off for the cottage he'd been renting on the other side of town? It wasn't a palace but it did have a bed. A nice, warm queen-sized bed. From the looks of it, the couch was only a short step up from the proverbial bed of nails. If he did stay, he doubted he'd sleep at all. Not on that old antique. Not with Blake overhead. Not with a potential killer nearby.

Who the hell do you think you're fooling?

He wasn't going anywhere and he knew it. At least he wasn't going anywhere yet. He laid back with his hands clasped behind his head and tried not to think of

Blake upstairs in nothing but panties. She was smart to keep her distance—and apparently she was more than capable of doing so. All things considered, she was doing a better job of it than he was. He'd never had a problem separating sex from emotion in the past but now he wasn't finding it all that easy. Because all he wanted to do was mount the stairs and crawl into bed beside the woman he'd just made love to.

****

The house went dark just as he was about to leave. He tucked his binoculars into his satchel and straightened, stepping out from his hiding spot. For the past hour he had watched their disgusting display, hardly able to stomach the sight of the two of them. What was even worse was that she was the one who started it, throwing off her robe and kissing him on the mouth. Things got worse, much worse, after that. When they disappeared from sight he was almost relieved.

Of course, he knew what that meant.

The mere thought of him entering her made him almost nauseous. He wasn't even sure why their union had such a strong effect on him. It certainly wasn't because he gave a damn about either of them. They were nothing to him, merely obstacles that threatened to undo everything he'd worked for over the past year. Yet he wanted her dead with a fervor unlike anything he'd ever known before. He wanted to kill Declan as well, though for other reasons.

It irritated him, knowing that the man thought he could outwit him. He hated that Declan Hunter was too dense to realize he'd been found out almost the moment he returned to Eagle Point. Appearing in town as if he'd simply been sightseeing, ingratiating himself with the woman then manipulating her for his own purposes.

Why didn't she realize Hunter was using her? She was little more than a pawn in his game, a way to gain access to her property, yet that fact seemed lost upon her. Either that or she didn't care. The image of her kissing him forced itself onto his consciousness before he could swat it away. God, she was a whore. As he wove his way through the dense pines that encircled the house he considered his options. Now that the girl was out of the way he had a little more leeway, but only a little. There was no room for error, not anymore. The first time things nearly went wrong and that scared him.

This time everything had to be perfect. Otherwise all his planning would have been for nothing. And now there was the baby. Bad enough he needed to deal with the blonde and her macho boyfriend. But the baby made things even more complicated.

He didn't want to kill the baby.

It was not a rational thought. What difference did it make whether he murdered a baby or an adult? A life was a life. People died every day and would go on dying till the end of time. Death was a fact that could not be avoided—a fact that allowed him to justify what he was about to do.

Still, he didn't want to kill the baby.

But in the end he would do what he must. If he listened to his conscience where would he be? He knew where—working in a factory like his father, with a pack of kids and a whining bitch of a wife to go home to every night.

Pine needles crunched beneath his feet as he made his way along the winding path that led back to the spot where he was parked. From somewhere far off an owl hooted, an eerie sound that made him think of death. For all his brilliance, he was still superstitious. It was a silly, feminine weakness, and he chided himself for it. He was far too intelligent for that sort of hocus pocus. But as many times as he told himself that, he still couldn't rid himself of his illogical beliefs.

Though maybe he could use them to his advantage.

****

The sound of the Charleston floated up the stairway. Its melody cast a net over her soul, summoning her with a power she couldn't explain. As she rose out of bed and crossed to the stairs she knew she had stepped into an enchanted world, a magical place where anything could happen. In the living room someone was cranking the Victrola, humming along to the tune. His back was to her but when she called out to him and he turned she knew he was the man she was meant for—the one she'd dreamt of since she was a girl. He held out a hand, beckoning her to the center of an imaginary dance floor.

Lights shimmered across the floor in a circular pattern. When she touched the back of her head she understood with a shock that her dark hair was cut in a sleek bob. A long string of pearls hung from her neck and her dress was a sheath of red satin. The music went on as they danced side by side, roaring with laughter as he taught her the steps. She fell back into his arms and he bent down over her to touch his lips to hers. When she opened her eyes he was gone, dissolved into the dream that caught her in its spell.

Outside a snowstorm raged, blotting out everything but the silence of the empty room. She stood alone in the chilly darkness, shivering in her flannel nightgown.

Wind rattled the windows and screamed through the pines, making her think of the dark stories her grandmother used to tell her when she was a child. She walked to the window and gazed out at the storm. The light from a lantern swayed up the path as her husband stumbled home through the blinding whiteness. He stood a few feet from her on the other side of the glass, cursing and stamping his feet to get off the snow.

Blake opened her eyes and saw Grace sleeping with her curls falling across her face and her thumb in her mouth. The room was dark, her thoughts tangled and incoherent. After a moment things sorted themselves out and she rolled onto her back, trying to remember the dream before it faded. She thought of the Victrola downstairs and the record she played on her first day at Eagle Point. Had it been Lucy's? Was the man who danced with her the one who gave it to her?

Was any of it even real?

She sat up and listened. All was silent. She swung her legs over the side of the bed and stood as quietly as she could. Grace stirred and for a moment Blake feared she'd woken her, but the child settled back into position.

She crossed to the window and looked out at the darkened lighthouse. Beyond its shadow a sprinkling of stars shone in a cloudless sky. In 1922 Lucy Stone stood at this same window, looking out at a view that probably hadn't changed all that much. Standing where Lucy had with a baby sleeping a few feet away, just as Lucy's baby would have slept. Blake was certain the lighthouse keeper's wife hadn't committed suicide. Whether the dream was the product of her overwrought imagination or something beyond explanation, she knew now that Lucy would never have left her daughter alone in the world.

Someone had pushed her.

At the thought of Lucy's fall from the tower, she remembered the death she'd witnessed the other night. But the figure that fell was a woman not a ghost. *Kelly.* Closing her eyes, she forced herself to bring into sharper focus the image she saw that night. Had there been lights? Another person on the catwalk?

Try as she might, she couldn't make the image any clearer. All she could see was the same figure tumbling through the night, replaying over and over in her head like a movie-clip endlessly repeating itself. Maybe that was all there was to see. Kelly letting herself out onto the catwalk then climbing up onto the balustrade and flinging herself into the churning sea.

No. Though no one was there to see her, she shook her head. Kelly wouldn't have taken her life either. Without being able to say precisely why, she knew it was true. Like Lucy, Kelly had loved her daughter. She may have struggled with drugs and that may have led her to get mixed up in something she shouldn't have. But when Blake thought of the collage of baby pictures tacked onto Kelly's bulletin board, she was sure the girl hadn't taken her own life. Even if she wanted to, she wouldn't have done it because of Grace. Kelly would never have left Grace alone in the world. *Not unless someone forced her to.*

She pressed her palm against the window pane, wishing the lighthouse could tell her its secrets. If Kelly hadn't killed herself, who had done it? And what of the suicide note Chris McAllister showed to her and Declan? If her theory was correct then it followed that the note had to be a fake. Declan said Chris couldn't have pulled something like that off but he was basing his conclusion on an illegible signature scrawled across a credit card receipt. Even if Chris didn't write the note he might have an idea who did. Maybe he killed Kelly himself and then tricked somebody into writing it. It was possible.

Blake leaned forward, feeling the coolness of the glass against her forehead. *That's the problem*, she thought. *Anything is possible*. Anyone could have written the note. Jenna hadn't disguised her dislike of Kelly and might have written it at Chris's request. Or maybe she killed Kelly herself. And what about the names on the list? Could "Henrietta" or "Cristy" or "Lucas" have done it, whoever they were? If they were involved with drugs, it might make sense.

Her mind flicked back to the way Angie shoved the print-out of Kelly's email into her pocket and wiped the keyboard clean. Angie seemed grief stricken when she learned of Kelly's death, but what did Blake really know about the cafe owner? Maybe Angie took the note because she'd been one of the guests. Kelly and Angie did work together, after all. And it was Angie who insisted on driving out to Kelly's place. Maybe the reason she wanted her there wasn't that she was afraid of what she might find, but to make her visit seem less suspicious.

But Angie wasn't the only one acting strangely. Why did Santos seem almost eager to get rid of his deputy out at the house? When the sheriff returned to his office nearly an hour later he seemed even more agitated than he had when he first arrived. Did he have something to hide as well?

She sighed in frustration. In some ways, she'd never been so confused in her entire life. In others, she felt oddly at peace. Making love with Declan, smoothing Grace's hair, even scrubbing the dusty rooms clean again after so many years of neglect—these things gave her a sense of simple joy that sprang from somewhere deep within. It had been many years since she'd known that kind of happiness.

Walking back over to the bed, she laid down and placed her head on the pillow so that she was facing Grace. The child's expression was deceptively peaceful, as if she were caught up in the gossamer web of a dream. But whatever Grace was dreaming of, her reality would never again be the same. Blake only hoped she could protect her from the dangers that seemed to be gathering round them.

Chapter 10

She woke to the smell of bacon and eggs. Stretching her arms over her head and yawning, Blake glanced at the clock on the bedside table. 6:00 a.m. Apparently Declan wasn't the sort of guy who believed in sleeping late.

Resisting the urge to duck back under the covers, she got out of bed and lifted Grace onto her shoulder. Her eyes opened as soon as Blake picked her up. She looked at Blake as if she didn't understand why it was Blake, not Kelly, who was laying her down and unfastening her diaper.

"Mama," Grace said determinedly, pushing Blake's hand away from her. "Mama."

Unlike the other day, when she hadn't been sure who Grace was referring to she had no doubt now. Grace wanted her mother. After more than a day away from Kelly, the child was beginning to get upset.

"Mama!" Grace said, raising her voice and kicking her legs wildly as Blake struggled to clean her up and fasten a new diaper. The word unnerved her, making the task of changing the diaper seem nearly impossible.

"Stay still, Gracie," she told her in what she hoped was a soothing voice. "Be good for Blake, okay?"

"No!" Grace said over and over. "NO NO NO NO NO NO NO!"

Blake grabbed onto Grace's foot, then caught the

other, unsure of what to do next. Why was taking care of a baby so much more complicated than she'd realized? Even something as simple as changing a diaper was becoming a major production. "Are you willing to come to a settlement?" she asked in an exasperated voice.

"NO NO NO NO NO NO NO!"

"Need some help?" Declan stood in the doorway, already showered and dressed. "There's scrambled eggs and bacon downstairs. And coffee."

"Please don't tell me you're a morning person."

"What's wrong with being a morning person?"

"Nothing," she said, "if you get to bed before four a.m."

"Couldn't sleep?"

"Nope."

Declan wagged his head. "Hmmm," he said. "I was pretty worn out myself. It's not every day I get to see a hot woman naked."

In spite of her mood, she couldn't help grinning. Grace stopped kicking momentarily and seemed to be following the conversation. "You don't think she understands what we're saying" she remarked. "Do you?"

"I hope not." He laughed and walked over the make-shift changing table on top of her dresser. Without missing a beat he took Grace's feet into his hands and pushed Blake toward the door. "Let me take care of this. You go eat. Then shower," he told her. "And no, that's not a comment on your appearance. You look beautiful."

"Shower first," she amended, trying not to look pleased at his compliment. "Then eat."

Declan gave her a slight bow. "As you wish, m'lady."

****

When Blake emerged from the shower twenty minutes later she found Declan downstairs in front of the stove. He seated Grace on a couple of pillows and pushed her chair up to the antique pedestal table at the center of the kitchen. An array of cheerios was scattered before her, matched by an equal number on the floor.

"Coffee?" he asked. "I looked around for a dustpan but couldn't find one."

She wrapped both hands around the mug and sat at the table. "I still haven't even unpacked most of my stuff," she said. "Or gotten a phone installed. With everything going on there hasn't been time." At this last admission, she bit her lip.

"So you were bluffing about calling the sheriff?"

"I wouldn't have called him either way." She took a sip of coffee. "I just wanted to scare you."

"I'll remember that," he said, pulling his cell phone out of his jeans pocket and handing it to her. "Oh, and before I get into any more trouble I thought I'd show you this."

sorry 4 all the msgs. not crushing on you i swear :) need 2 tell u s/t about kelly. important i think. can u meet at 9 out at Boho Chic? DONT show up at cuppa cafe.
PLS.

Blake studied the message a long time before looking up. What surprised her wasn't her absolute lack of reaction, but the irrational surge of jealousy that possessed her the previous night. "Well, I'm glad to hear she's not crushing on you," she said with a grin.

146

"When did you get that?"

"It was there when I woke up this morning."

"How the heck do you get phone reception out here?" she asked. "That's what I'm really jealous of."

"I'm hurt," he said, smiling back at her. "But don't get too jealous. All I can do is text. I tried calling my boss this morning. No such luck.

"Apparently you can receive them too," she said, raising an eyebrow.

He cut her off before she could say another word. "Don't even think it. After last night—"

She blushed to her roots. "I'm not," she said quickly, wondering how she had morphed into a secure person overnight. On the other hand, she wasn't so secure she wanted to launch into a discussion of their relationship, if it could even be called that. "What's Boho Chic?" she asked, changing the topic.

"Angie's competition." If anything, he seemed relieved at the shift. "It's a couple of streets down from Herrick's general store. From what I hear it's a pretty dull place, at least in comparison to Cuppa Café. Which I suppose is exactly why she suggested it."

"Do you think Jenna's message is legit?"

"I don't know," he said, handing her a plate filled with scrambled eggs and bacon. "But I have to take it seriously."

"I guess it makes sense that she wouldn't want to meet you at Cuppa Cafe." The bacon was slightly burnt but Blake put a slice into her mouth anyway. In all the years with Henry, he had never once burnt a slice of bacon. Now that she thought of it, she couldn't recall him ever eating bacon. *Too mainstream,* he would have said. Whatever Henry was he was definitely not mainstream. As she watched Declan pouring himself a cup of coffee she had to admit he wasn't mainstream either. Far from it. The difference, she supposed, was that Henry was pretentious. Declan on the other hand was probably the least pretentious person she'd ever met.

He sat across from her, sipping his coffee thoughtfully. "I can see why, especially if she doesn't work there anymore."

"I suppose so." Even so, something about the urgency of Jenna's request struck her as odd. "Angie doesn't seem like the type who would be willing to forgive and forget. She isn't somebody I'd want to cross."

At the mention of the cafe owner's name, Blake remembered the email they found on Kelly's computer. She hesitated only a moment before deciding to tell Declan about it. If she was in this far she might as well take a complete leap of faith. "Yesterday, on Kelly's laptop, we found an email. There were a bunch of names on it—and a couple of numbers that didn't seem to make any sense."

He stopped short, his coffee cup poised in mid-air. "What kind of names?" If he wondered what they were doing on Kelly's computer, he didn't mention it.

She shook her head. Everything from the day before was such a blur. "I can't remember all of them. There were some normal names—like Chris and Luke and Kim—but then there were these weird names too. There was a list, then a long string of numbers, then a name—I think it was Ruby—and another long string of numbers, then another name. It was weird."

Grace chose that moment to throw a few more

cheerios onto the floor. Though she knew she shouldn't encourage her, Blake couldn't help laughing. "I'll get them," she said, kneeling down and gathering the fallen cereal into her palm. "I don't want you making me look bad."

"Not possible."

"You're quite the ladies' man, aren't you?"

Declan laughed but there was a seriousness to his tone. "Actually, no."

She had the sudden urge to kiss him then forced the idea out her head. Last night was amazing—but she didn't want to fool herself. This morning it was as if they were playing house, pretending to be a family when they were anything but that. Straightening up and depositing the cheerios into the trash can, she turned to look at Declan and Grace. Declan was playing airplane with one of the cheerios to keep Grace amused, and from the look on her face it was working. "You're pretty good with her," she said, keeping her voice neutral. "Do you have kids?"

If she meant to shock him, it worked. "Kids?" he asked incredulously. "Hell, no. I barely have time to take care of myself."

She didn't know if she was relieved or saddened. "It's just that you seem pretty sure of yourself around them," she said. "Like you've done it all before."

He flew another cheerio into Grace's mouth. "I have done it all before," he said without looking at her. "I was a foster kid. You probably don't know much about that kind of thing, but not everybody's in it because they love children. There are a lot of parents out there who do it for the money. More kids equals more money. It's a pretty simple equation, unfortunately."

"That must have been rough."

He shrugged. "It was what it was. My dad took off when I was around three and my mom died a few years later. My grandmother raised me but she died when I was 10. Afterward there was nobody left to take care of me so Social Services got involved. For a while, at the beginning, they tried to find me a permanent home, but after a while they gave up Nobody's going to adopt a twelve-year-old boy. So I got bounced around a lot. In my travels I met my share of babies that needed their diapers changed."

His eyes darkened with pain. She stood at the center of the kitchen, unsure what to do. Or say. The last thing he would want was pity. "Well, I'm sure it will come in handy one day," she said, wincing at how cheesy she sounded.

"Maybe," he remarked noncommittally, lifting Grace out of her chair. "I don't really see kids in my future. Like I said, it doesn't exactly come with the territory. Anyway, it's good of you to offer to take care of Grace. Not everybody's as generous."

She wondered how much of Declan's resistance to having a family sprang from with his upbringing. Why would he want to bring a child into the world when his own experience was so awful? But he might meet the right woman one day and settle down. Much as she wanted to daydream about it being her, she couldn't allow herself to do that. The outcome would be too painful. "I wish I could remember more about the email," she said, changing the subject again. "I have the feeling it's connected with Kelly's death."

"Don't worry about it," he said. "I'll get a copy

from Santos. The man hates my guts too, but he has no choice but to cooperate. He doesn't know who I am. But that's going to change real soon."

She felt some satisfaction at the image of the sheriff's expression when he learned of Declan's true identity. Then she realized she hadn't told Declan what happened to the email. "He doesn't have a copy," she said nonchalantly.

He stood Grace on the floor and grasped her hand in his. She took an unsteady step, then another. As he watched her clumsy attempt at walking he smiled but when his eyes met hers he was deadly serious. "Why doesn't he have a copy?"

Blake's face grew hot, as if she'd been caught cheating on an exam. "Well, we kind of, um, decided not to mention it."

"Why not?" he asked, looking genuinely surprised. "Santos may be incompetent, but he is the law. Holding back evidence is obstruction of justice. You could go to prison for that. Especially if this turns out to be a federal case."

Why on earth had she listened to Angie? "It just kind of happened."

"Do you have the email here?"

"Angie has it," Blake said. "She printed it out then stuffed it into her pocket."

"Stuffed it in her pocket," Declan repeated quietly.

If she been nervous about keeping silent before, the effect was multiplied tenfold. Clearly, he was frustrated—and worried. "What if we give him the email now?" she asked. "Would that make a difference?"

He released Grace's hand and watched her take a

few steps before falling onto her bottom. Picking her up off the floor and handing her to Blake, he said firmly, "I doubt it. Either way you need to get it. The killer's name could be on that list."

"I'll try."

He sighed then leaned forward to kiss her. To her surprise, he planted a quick kiss on Grace's forehead too. "I've got to get going or I'm going to miss Jenna," he said, taking her chin between his forefinger and his thumb. "But do me a favor and take a ride in to see Angie. I don't want to be baking you any cakes with nail files in them. And be careful—if that email means anything and I have a damn strong suspicion it does— then you and Angie need to keep quiet about it."

"My lips are sealed." She flashed him what she hoped was a rakish grin as he hurried out onto the porch and drove off. Grace's fingers played with Blake's hair as she listened to sound of the pick-up truck's tires fade into the distance. Already her hip had adjusted to the baby's presence.

Despite her good mood, a tremor of fear prickled her skin as she turned back to the breakfast dishes. The night before her mother passed away from cancer, she raised her head off the hospital pillow and told her someone was "walking on her grave." The next morning she was dead.

Blake didn't believe in premonitions. But as she gathered the dishes from the table, she understood for the first time what her mother meant.

****

In spite of her misgivings, things at Cuppa Cafe were almost normal. The place was as crowded as it was on her first visit and Angie seemed contained, if not exactly calm. A steady stream of orders flowed from the back of the cafe and there was a new waitress behind the register, a fortyish woman with blunt-cut hair and a solid build. Everything about her screamed responsible. Whereas Kelly and Jenna were young and hip—the waifish sort of girls who blended seamlessly with the eclectic decor—the new woman stood out like a bull in a china shop. As Blake sat with Grace at a table at the window, the woman cast a sharp look in her direction but it didn't faze her. Somehow the fact that she didn't fit in at Eagle Point wasn't all that important anymore.

Well, at least the new waitress didn't look like the type to get into a fight over a man, especially not Chris McAllister. Blake bit her lip to keep from smiling. Not that anyone in their right mind would want to date McAllister. Try as she might, she couldn't understand what Jenna—or Kelly—saw in him. Aside from his rugged good looks, there was nothing redeeming about the fisherman. He was rude, uncaring and his views on women certainly left something to be desired. Why anyone would fall in love with the man was a complete mystery to her.

Though there didn't seem to be a whole lot of choice in Eagle Point. That was something she'd probably need to get used to, she supposed, pretending to wonder why she wasn't more concerned about the lack of men in town. She knew damn well why. *But that doesn't mean I have to dwell on it*, she told herself, pointedly scanning the room for eligible men.

There weren't many and most of them looked like tourists. A smattering of husbands with wives and kids filled the booths and a few men sat before laptop computers, typing or talking on their cell phones. A couple of gray-haired retirees sat in front of the large plate-glass window playing chess. Off in a corner, Blake thought she recognized Tyler Burke but his back was to her so she couldn't be certain. Though he couldn't have been much less than thirty, he was probably the youngest guy in the cafe. His nerdy, quirky personality would appeal to some women. But from what she'd heard at the store that day, she doubted he actually spent much time in town. He probably flew in for August and was bored out of his skull by September.

Slim pickings, she thought, though she knew most of the men in town were out on their fishing boats and wouldn't be back until late in the day. Aside from tourism and fishing, there wasn't much in town that allowed people to make a living. And even the tourism wasn't all that spectacular. Eagle Point was too far up the coastline for most people. The majority of visitors preferred to spend their vacations in more sophisticated places like Bar Harbor and Wells Beach. Usually people who drove this far north were the rare few who really did want to "get away from it all." More often than not Eagle Point was a stop on a longer trip, one that ended in Nova Scotia or Quebec City. Blake remembered one realtor who tried to talk her out of buying an inn so close to the Canadian border. "If it's an inn you want, there's lots better places than that. I can show you some property down by Ogunquit that'd be perfect for you."

She was right, of course. But something about the photos of the lighthouse rising up against the cliffs resonated deep within her. After the madness of the city it offered her the kind of peace she'd always dreamed about.

The lighthouse was perfect. Except for the fact that it was haunted. And that someone had been murdered there. And that it might be at the center of a drug ring.

She'd only been in town a couple of days and the situation had gotten so preposterous she suppressed the impulse to burst out laughing. Extricating her finger from Grace's grip, she waved Angie over to their table. Resplendent in a flowing indigo sundress, Angie looked as if she hadn't a care in the world. If Blake hadn't seen her sobbing at Kelly's place the day before, she would never have guessed that anything could be wrong. The woman should have been an actress. *Was Angie even better at acting than she realized?*

"Hey, lady," Angie greeted her, a pot of coffee in her hand. "How are you holding up? I see you've taken on a sidekick."

For a second, Blake thought Angie was talking about Declan. "Oh, you mean Grace," she said a little self-consciously, glancing at the baby seated in the high chair across from her. Though she hadn't asked for Kelly again, Grace seemed unusually subdued. The child sat perfectly still with her eyes fastened on Angie. "I'm watching her for a few more days, I guess. Chris says she's not his."

"Well, if she's not she sure is the spitting image of him," Angie said sarcastically. "Though maybe he'll come around. Fatherhood takes getting used to for some men. I just hope he doesn't get Jenna knocked up too."

Blake pursed her lips recalling the way Chris virtually ejected them from his trailer. "Looks like Jenna quit after all, huh?"

Angie's mouth curved into a cynical smile. "No such luck. She gave me a song and dance about coming down with the flu. I don't know why I can't bring myself to fire her. God knows she deserves it, but somehow I can't get the words out. Thank the Lord I was able to convince my cousin Mary to help out until I can get somebody new in here. 'Course Jenna's driving her nuts and they've spent all of five minutes together. This morning she shows up late again, then before she's half-way through filling the sugars she tells me she's got a doctor's appointment and will be back in a half hour." Angie looked at her watch. "That was two hours and twenty minutes ago."

Well, at least Jenna's absence probably meant she kept her appointment with Declan. At the thought of him, a pang of guilt prodded her conscience. Covering the mug Angie set down in front of her with her hand, she lowered her voice. "None for me," she said. "Actually, I'm not really here to eat. I was wondering if you've still got that email?"

There was no need to mention which email. As soon at the words were out of her mouth, Angie's face darkened. "I thought we agreed we weren't going to show that to Santos," she said quietly, glancing around the cafe as if to see who might be listening.

"I'm not going to show it to Santos." That much at least was true. "I'd like to take another look at it, if you don't mind. I think it might be important."

"And I think you're barking up the wrong tree," Angie said. "For one thing, I'm not even sure I still have it. For another, if Kelly did get back into drugs and it somehow led to her killing herself, that's not something she would've wanted splashed across the newspapers. Because that's what'll happen and you know it."

"I don't believe she did kill herself." Blake pursed her lips, wishing Angie wouldn't keep mentioning Kelly by name. Grace would have known her mother as "mama" but her gaze was riveted on Angie, almost as if she knew Kelly was the topic of conversation.

When the cafe owner spoke again her voice was strained. "Look, I know you just got here, so you don't know how this town works," she whispered, leaning so close one of her dangly earrings brushed Blake's cheek. "This place is a gossip mill of the first degree—which is kinda funny since there's not a whole heck of a lot happening around here. So the way I see it, there's some things better left unsaid. You didn't see Kelly when she was so strung out she thought spiders were crawling out of her ears and laying eggs in her skin. When she'd phone me in the middle of the night to come get Grace 'cause she'd had a bad trip and was afraid of what she might do. I thought she was clean, but the more I think about things the more I'm thinking she'd hadn't kicked her habit." Angie straightened and stepped back from the table, signaling that the conversation was at an end. "In a way I hate Kelly for what she did to that child sitting beside you. But at the same time I don't want to see her name dragged through the mud all over again. If we—" she broke off in mid-sentence to stare through the front window.

Blake followed her gaze and saw Jenna tearing down the sidewalk, just inches ahead of Chris McAllister. Before she could even process what was happening Jenna burst through the door and attempted to slam it shut behind her. "You crazy bastard!" she screamed. "Get the hell away from me!"

Jenna wasn't fast enough though. Chris lunged after her, inserting his shoulder into the crack between the door and its frame. In a moment of incomprehension, Blake watched customers screaming and shoving their children onto the floor.

That was when she realized McAllister had a gun.

Chapter 11

Blake had seen it a thousand times on television: the moment when time slows down and every movement, every gesture, seems to spin out endlessly. She'd always thought it was a special effect—a kind of gimmick that allowed filmmakers to flaunt close-ups of the actors.

Until McAllister showed up.

She watched in horror as he stood blocking the cafe's front door, holding his pistol at arm's length and aiming it directly at Jenna. Women screamed and tried to hide behind the tables as fathers shoved their children behind them and crouched on the floor. From all directions came the sound of sobbing and dishes crashing as furniture was overturned.

For what seemed like minutes but must have been no more than a few seconds, Blake sat frozen in place, unable to move or even cry out. *Grace.* She couldn't form a coherent thought, couldn't figure out what it was that she needed to do. *Grace.* There was only the one word—the same mantra repeating itself in her head, pulsing through her veins like a heartbeat.

Using her body to block the baby from McAllister's view, she lifted Grace out of the high chair and pressed her tightly to her chest before turning the table on its side and scrambling behind it. Immediately, Grace began shrieking, ignoring her attempts to quiet her. Fortunately the sound of her cries was lost in the chaos and didn't seem to catch McAllister's attention.

From where the two of them lay behind the small table, she couldn't see either Chris or Jenna. Several other customers were crouched nearby, scattered behind overturned tables and chairs. Angie was positioned behind a small round table a few feet away, surreptitiously dialing her cell phone. Angie looked up and caught Blake's eye, her face pale. For the first time since she her arrival, Blake was truly happy about the prospect of seeing Sheriff Santos.

She just hoped he got there in time.

"Everybody shut the hell up!"

McAllister's command rang out across the cafe and an ominous silence settled over them, broken only by muffled sobbing and Grace's cries. "Time to be quiet," she told the child under her breath, holding her finger to her lips. "Please, please be quiet."

"I said shut that kid up," McAllister repeated, more loudly this time. His voice quavered, as if he realized he'd gotten himself into a situation that was spiraling out of control.

In desperation, Blake inserted her forefinger into Grace's mouth. The baby took it immediately, sucking on it as if it were a pacifier. She breathed a sigh of relief, hoping Grace wouldn't get bored with her finger. Though from the intensity of her suckling, she doubted the child was going to stop anytime soon.

"Listen, Chris, I told you already—there's no one else. I swear to God." Jenna's voice rang out across the cafe, nervous but adamant. "Just put down the gun."

"Jesus, I'm gettin' tired of this shit," Chris spat out the words. "First Kelly, now you. You'd think I'd learn my lesson the first time around."

"You know you're the only one I love," Jenna assured him. "Please, Chris, put down the gun. For me."

Jenna's attempt to defuse the situation enraged her boyfriend even more. Blake heard the sound of dishes smashing against the wall and a chair skittering across the floor. A few seconds later came the unmistakable sound of plate glass cracking. "That's rich," McAllister snapped. "That's really goddamned rich. I'm such a chump I'd almost believe 'ya too, except for one little problem. I saw the texts with my own eyes."

At the mention of texts, Blake winced. Had McAllister seen the messages Jenna sent to Declan? It sounded like it—unless Jenna had a habit of sending flirtatious texts to men who weren't her boyfriend.

"Listen, you jackass, I don't know what you think you saw, but I stand before you now telling you I never sent any texts to anybody but you. And to be frank, I'm gettin' damn tired of your bullshit."

Blake was impressed. Jenna was a pretty convincing liar, not to mention a gutsy one. Here the girl was standing not three feet away from a gun and she actually sounded annoyed with him for finding her out.

McAllister snorted with disgust. "You're good," he said. "But not that good. I saw him, *Irish Eyes*." He spat out the nickname, as if the mere sound of it on his tongue sickened him.

"Where do you get off followin' me," Jenna shot back angrily. "I'm not your possession. I have a right to my own life. I wish I never got involved with you in the first place—I wish I'd never gotten involved with any of your bullshit. I wish—"

"Shut up, you goddamned whore," McAllister yelled, lunging toward her and grabbing her by the throat. "I loved you."

Jenna's sputtered cries echoed across the cafe, sending chills up Blake's spine. Even more frightening was McAllister's use of the past tense. Where was Santos? And his deputy? The sheriff's office couldn't be more than a couple of miles away. Angie must have texted him minutes ago—and other customers were doing it now too. Surely the sheriff wasn't so incompetent he wouldn't respond to a barrage of 911 calls. And where was Declan? If he'd met with Jenna why hadn't he seen McAllister chasing her afterward? Her heart knocked against her rib cage. What if Chris had already done something to Declan? What if he'd been waiting outside for their meeting to end?

Blake deliberately slowed her breathing. She couldn't think about that now. What she needed to think about was keeping Grace out of danger. That was all she could manage. If she let herself start worrying about Declan she would fall apart entirely. Biting her lip so hard she thought she would draw blood, she tried to consider the situation calmly.

Was there a way out?

No. The front door was blocked. The back door was too far away. She'd never make it, even without Grace. With Grace...her heart twisted at the scenario the thought conjured up. If she so much as made a move in that direction he'd shoot her dead first and ask questions later. Of that, she had little doubt.

Could she try to talk to McAllister?

Again, she knew the idea wasn't plausible. McAllister already disliked her intensely. Trying to use her negotiating skills on him could backfire—and that meant Grace would be in more danger, not less.

She was still casting around for a plan when a vaguely familiar voice addressed McAllister. "You don't want to do this. Your girlfriend said she loves you and I think deep down you know she's telling the truth. Deep down you know you're making the biggest mistake of your life."

Risking a peek over the table, Blake saw Tyler Burke rise to his feet and walk over to the shattered window, about ten feet from the wall Chris was backed up against. Jenna stopped struggling and was perfectly still with his clamped around her neck, the barrel of the gun pressed to her temple. Her eyes were large and panicked.

Tyler took a step toward them. "If you give me the gun before the sheriff gets here," he said as reasonably as if he were making a remark about the weather, "it's going to go a lot better for you in court. You might even be released on bail. But if you kill her, you're going to spend a long, long time in prison."

McAllister aimed the gun at Tyler without releasing his grip on Jenna. "Take one more step and I'll blow your fuckin' head off."

"I know you're bluffing." Tyler took another step.

"Stay the hell away from me!" McAllister shouted. "One more step and I'll show you who's bluffing."

Tyler took another step. And another.

"I'm warning you."

Blake shut her eyes, waiting for the shot. When none came she opened them and saw that Tyler move even closer to McAllister, close enough that he might be able to grab the gun if he were lucky. The hand that held the gun was shaking now, so much that it looked as if McAllister were making a supreme effort to keep it trained on Tyler.

Tyler took another step.

He was definitely close enough to grab the gun now. With everything in her, Blake wanted him to lunge forward and wrestle it out of McAllister's hand. She glanced down at Grace, who was still busily sucking on her finger. Then, inexplicably, Grace smiled at her. Tears welled up in Blake's eyes.

How was it possible that the worst and the best moments always seemed to happen at the same time? Brushing her fingertip against Grace's cheek, she smiled back at her. "I'm always going to take care of you," she whispered, realizing with a shock that it was true.

If the two of them made it out of there, Blake was never going to give Grace up. Whatever battles she had to fight to gain custody of her, she was ready to fight them. She didn't care how much it cost or how difficult it was going to be raising a baby on her own. Grace needed her. And she needed Grace.

If they made it out of there.

Turning her gaze back to McAllister, she saw him cock the gun.

He was going to shoot.

She watched as he raised the gun and aimed it squarely at Tyler's chest. "It's too late," he said wearily. "It's all over."

Now, Blake thought, willing Tyler Burke to read her thoughts. *Do it now.* Before it's too late for all of us. She heard Angie breathing jaggedly, then turned to see the cafe owner's left hand clutching at her heart.

For a moment Blake wondered if Angie were having a heart attack, but the cafe owner must have read her thoughts, because she smiled at her shakily and mouthed "I'm okay."

Where is Santos? she mouthed back.

Angie shook her head. *I don't know.*

Almost as if on cue, the sound of distant sirens wailed. McAllister heard them, too. Glancing nervously over his shoulder at the empty street, he had the look of somebody who realizes he has no escape. Bursting into a stream of some of the worst language Blake had ever heard, he released Jenna, who scrambled across the cafe and burst into broken sobs.

McAllister watched her take refuge behind an overturned armchair, then raised the gun to his own temple.

"Put it down."

Tyler took a final step and wrapped his hand around the gun. "You don't want to do that," he said evenly. "You have too much to live for."

"I'm not so sure about that anymore," McAllister said, his voice little more than a hoarse whisper. Breaking into sobs himself, he let go of the gun and fell to his knees. When several men in the cafe wrestled him to the ground he didn't resist. By the time Santos arrived, followed by a slew of police cars from nearby towns, the situation was more or less resolved.

Hanging his head, McAllister held out his hands for the cuffs and allowed himself to be lead out of the cafe. Hardly able to belief the situation hadn't resulted in anything worse than a few overturned tables and a shattered plate glass window, Blake dusted herself off and rose to her feet. Grace held both arms up and Blake took her, letting tears spill down onto the little girl. Rocking her back and forth, with her head pressed against Grace's, she regained her sense of balance, if only a little.

When she was steady enough to walk she glanced over at Tyler Burke. She wanted to thank him, but apparently everybody else had the same idea. He stood at the center of a swarm of customers and police officers, nodding and shaking hands. Angie pushed her way to the front of the crowd. She ignored his outstretched hand and wrapped him in an enormous bear hug. When she released him, he was grinning sheepishly. He looked pleased, if a little embarrassed, by his sudden celebrity.

Jenna was crying softly, a solitary figure in an overstuffed chair near the cracked window. A large hole gaped at its center and a network of spidery lines radiated outward from that. In the bright sunlight, the broken glass shone, sending prisms of reflected light onto the tiled floor. It struck her as oddly beautiful.

Blake headed in Jenna's direction, wondering whether or not she should ask her about Declan's whereabouts. Would alluding to their meeting put him at risk in some way? Suppose he was already hurt?

Before she could push through the swarm of people, the deputy sheriff approached Jenna and said a few words to her. The girl nodded without looking up, then rose from her chair without uttering a single word. The deputy sheriff placed his arm behind her back, guiding her through the crowd and down the front steps.

Strapping Grace into her carrier, Blake debated what to do. If Declan was nearby he would have shown up by now. It was impossible to be downtown and not hear the cacophony of sirens and raised voices that rang out along Main Street. Should she go to Boho Chic and try to find him? Surely if he were there he would have made his way to the cafe. Especially because he knew Blake planned on going there.

Had he gone home? Followed a lead that came up as a result of his meeting with Jenna? Or was he hurt? McAllister was out of control long before he arrived at the cafe. Blake doubted he would have hesitated to hurt Declan given the chance.

She had reached the front sidewalk when a hand closed around her arm, just above the elbow. Whirling around, she found herself face-to-face with Charlie Santos, who looked none too pleased.

"Not so fast, Ms. Cartwright." the sheriff told her, drawing out the word *Ms.* as if to emphasize his contempt for her. "You and I need to have a word."

****

The crib directions were useless, but Declan couldn't have been happier about that. He sat on the floor at the center of Blake's bedroom, surrounded by an array of unassembled parts, wishing the investigation was one tenth as simple as putting together a piece of furniture. Though he'd misled her about the nature of his work, he hadn't been lying when he told her about his love of restoring old houses. He'd always loved building things with his hands. It gave him the kind of satisfaction he could never fully experience in his line of work.

Like bringing criminals to justice, making things took effort and skill. The difference was that at the end of an investigation he could never really feel good about what he'd accomplished. Much as he wanted to believe justice was black and white, cut and dried, it never was. Case in point—his own mother. As a kid Declan watched her battle her addictions, willing her to beat them. Even when she started dealing to pay for heroin, he forgave her—at least until one of the teenagers she was supplying turned up dead one crisp fall morning. Even now, he couldn't decide if he loved or hated her.

On the other hand, a crib or a chair or table were objects he could touch, simple things with a concrete purpose, not to mention an innate beauty that his hands knew how to bring out almost instinctively.

Drug dealers were another matter entirely. After more than a decade as a DEA agent Declan still felt he was finding his way in the dark most of the time. He was good, no question about that. He'd seen other agents killed in more ways than he cared to remember. Sometimes—not often—it got to him and he would toy with the idea of getting out. But he knew he never would. He couldn't. Something inside drove him to keep going—to make one more arrest, bust up one more ring of dealers. It was as if something beyond his control were compelling him to go on pushing himself.

If he weren't so good at his job, maybe he could justify making a change. The trouble was, he wasn't just good at his job. He was the best. Though his boss never said the words outright, both of them knew it was true. So did everybody in his unit, for that matter. When younger agents looked at him there was a kind of reverence in their faces, almost as if he were some kind of legend.

Some legend, he thought, staring at the directions before crumpling them up and tossing them across the room. He slid the metal crib rod into the compression spring then screwed it onto the headboard. His hands worked effortlessly as he replayed his conversation with Jenna.

There was something off about the girl, but he couldn't say what. Declan had the distinct sense that she wasn't telling him all she knew, but he was used to that. He was also convinced Jenna was protecting someone, but again, he couldn't say who. McAllister? Maybe. When she spoke about him he sensed something else, something he couldn't put a name to. Contempt? Fear? Maybe just plain dislike. But if Jenna didn't like her boyfriend why was she with him? Was she addicted to drugs like her ex-friend Kelly? Was McAllister her supplier? It seemed a likely explanation, but something about it didn't fit. For one thing there were no track marks on Jenna's arms. For another, she didn't strike him as someone with drug problem. If his mother taught him one thing it was how to recognize an addict.

At least the harbormaster had been helpful. After his futile meeting with Jenna he headed down to the marina and had a conversation with Ethan Larsson, who had been overseeing Eagle Point's waterways for nearly three decades. With his red suspenders and salt-and-pepper hair, Larsson looked like the quintessential fisherman. He even had the Maine accent to match.

Larsson was tight-lipped at first, offering no more than monosyllabic answers to his questions. Even when Declan flashed his badge the old man seemed unimpressed. It wasn't until he mentioned the lighthouse that Larsson reacted at all.

"By-the-Jesus, that place is 'a haunted," Larsson

said, tapping a pinch of tobacco into his pipe. "Saw her ghost, back when I was a kid. Went out there one night on a dare. Broke into the towah and climbed all the way up to the top while my buddy was waitin' at the bottom. Lots of kids said they did it, but not many of 'em had the guts to make it all th' way up. When I got up to the lantahn room I look out and see this white lady drifting along the shore. And may God strike me down if I'm lyin' but don't I hear a baby cryin'?" Larsson leaned all the way back in his chair and puffed on his pipe until the tip glowed. "Folks thought I was pullin' their legs, but it's God's honest truth."

Declan reached for one of the sides of the crib and began securing it to the headboard. Another couple of turns of the screw and the crib would be finished. He smiled, anticipating the pleased look that would appear on Blake's face when she walked in and saw it. As he worked, his mind ran over the conversation with Larsson. Something about it troubled him but he couldn't say exactly what. According to Larsson, Chris McAllister hadn't been out much at night, but there was a strange pattern to the dates he did his "midnight fishing." Perhaps even more importantly, he'd taken his boat out on the night Kelly died.

As for his story about Lucy's ghost, surely the old man was playing some kind of game with him—the naive flatlander. But now he wasn't sure. Maybe Larsson really did believe he saw Lucy's ghost. People usually saw what they wanted to see. At least he'd gotten what he needed from old man.

He tightened one last screw then stepped back to inspect his handiwork. With its dark wood and elegant, old-fashioned look, the crib was bound to please Blake.

Setting the mattress into it, he removed the fitted sheet he'd purchased that morning from Herrick's and fastened it onto the mattress.

At the sound of the door opening, he tensed. His hand tightened around the screwdriver, ready to defend himself against any threat. He knew it was probably Blake but after so many years he couldn't control his reactions. Suspicion was second nature. Or maybe first.

It wasn't until he heard her voice that he allowed himself to relax. She was talking to Grace about nothing in particular, laughing at her babbling as the two of them climbed the stairs. He wasn't sorry he'd told her who he really was, even if it meant his career might be put in jeopardy. It felt right to tell her the truth. Whatever happened, he had no regrets

Declan set down the screwdriver and looked toward the empty doorway, hungry for the sight of her. Before last night it had taken a supreme act of will to keep himself focused on the investigation. To his surprise, he actually managed better after making love to her. Knowing what was between them steadied him, not the reverse, as he had feared. All day he found himself imagining the moment when he would see her again. He wanted to kiss her badly. Needed to kiss her.

When Blake appeared in the doorway and saw him her smile faded. He stood up, wondering why she looked so upset, even angry. Cutting him off before he could form a coherent sentence, she sat down hard on the bed and settled Grace on her lap. The worry in her eyes was unmistakable. "Where the hell have you been?"

Chapter 12

Blake hated herself for the anger in her voice. She hated watching Declan's expression change—seeing him close off from her. He hadn't moved since she sat down on the bed, but she could feel the distance between them stretching out. Part of her wanted to rush into his arms and beg him for forgiveness. But another part remained aloof.

She couldn't permit herself to give free reign to her emotions, not after what had happened. She had done that with Grace and look where it had led her. Settling the child into the newly assembled crib, Blake turned glassy eyes toward Declan. "Chris McAllister showed up at the cafe," she said, gripping the crib railing with both hands, "with a gun. I think he saw you with Jenna and got jealous. He also mentioned something about texts. He must've thought she was cheating on him."

He exhaled slowly, as if he were using every bit of willpower to keep himself under control. "Did he use it?"

She shook her head. "This guy named Tyler talked him out of it, so nobody got hurt. The sheriff and the police got there after it was already over. But that's not the worst part." Smoothing Grace's curls, she forced herself to say it before he asked. "They're going to take Grace."

Declan was at her feet, kneeling before the two of

them. "I'm sorry," he said taking her hands in his. "Do you know when?"

She noted the lack of surprise in his voice. He probably expected it all along, she realized. After all, he'd been through it himself. "I want to adopt her," she said, gaining strength from the warmth of his rough hands. "I told that to Santos, but he wouldn't listen. He said Grace wasn't safe in Eagle Point—not after what happened with Chris—and that she'd be better off someplace else."

"Since when did Santos become an expert on child psychology?"

Blake smiled in spite of herself. "He said she needed a real family. Not some incompetent flatlander who'd probably be moving back to the big, bad city before Christmas."

"Did he actually say that?"

"Not in so many words," she said. "But his meaning was crystal clear."

Declan got up off the floor and sat down next to her on the bed. The nearness of his presence made her skin tingle with anticipation, even though she knew making love again was out of the question with Grace just inches away. With his fingertip, he traced the side of her face before letting it come to rest on her lower lip. "You can fight him on this," he told her firmly. "We can fight him."

She wasn't sure who kissed who first. She only knew the sensation of his lips on hers blotted out the pain. His tongue parted her lips, twining with hers, gently probing. Holding his face between her hands, she savored the rough feel of the stubble that shadowed his jaw. Her heart beat wildly and when his hand cupped her breast she lost any desire to hold back. Her body seemed to have a will of its own. At the root of her was a need that only he could fill. All she wanted was to open her thighs to him and surrender to the bliss of him entering her again and again.

"We've got to stop," she told him breathlessly. "The baby."

"Right," Declan agreed, adjusting his shaft beneath his jeans. "The baby."

When their eyes met, it was all she could do to keep from bursting into laughter. The pained look on Declan's face was nearly irresistible. He stood up and tucked a strand of hair behind her ear. "Come on," she said, tugging at his hand. "Let's go."

He looked at her uncomprehendingly. "You mean downstairs?" he asked. "Want to have some coffee?"

Her lips curved into a smile. "Not coffee," she whispered as she pulled him to her led him into the spare bedroom at the end of the hallway. "But I do want something hot."

****

From her perch on the porch steps, Blake stared out at the sea and tried not to wonder how Declan had gotten to be so good at sex. Not that she was complaining. After a blissful hour spent on a thin cot upstairs she felt like she'd just run a marathon. At one point the mattress springs were creaking so loudly she was sure Grace would wake.

Declan came through the door and sat down next to her, handing her a steaming mug of coffee. "Something hot for you."

She cast a sidelong glance at him. "Been there, done that."

He grinned, looking altogether pleased with himself. "You know I'd like to try out a real bed sometime," he said, wrapping a strand of her hair around his finger. "I don't mind couches and cots, but it would be interesting to see what happened if there was a bit more room to maneuver."

"You make it sound like a military engagement," she said merrily, sipping her coffee.

"Believe me," he said, leaning forward to kiss her yet again. "That's not the kind of engagement I'm talking about."

Silence hung between them. Even though he wasn't serious his banter stung a bit. She knew anything long-term was out of the question, but having him joke about it made what they did have seem trivial. Unless he was serious. *Enough with the fantasies already*, she told herself, fixing her gaze on a group of seals sunning on the rocky shore.

"When I was a kid we came here once," she said meditatively. "Well, not here, but it was somewhere in Maine. Further South, I think. After spending my whole life in the city the sea cast a kind of spell over me. The sky was so blue, the same color as the water. When my family returned to Manhattan I used to lie in bed and imagine I was floating away on the waves."

"Maybe that's why you came back."

"Maybe you're right." She turned toward him and studied his face. "Funny until now I never gave it any thought."

His gaze came to rest on a parcel wrapped in brown paper that was propped next to the door. "Looks like you got a package." He reached behind him and picked it up. "They must've come when we were 'napping.'"

"I don't remember hearing a truck."

Declan raised his brows. "I'm not sure I would've heard a train pull up."

"I wasn't that loud."

"Uh-huh."

With a start, she grabbed the package from him. "Oh no."

"What?"

"The guy I was seeing—the one I mentioned before—he sent me this for my birthday. He texted me the other day and I completely forgot." At the thought of what she'd been doing for the past hour, her conscience niggled at her. She hadn't heard from Henry since his text—the least she could have done was to text him back. "I wish he hadn't sent it."

Declan set down his coffee and leaned forward on the porch step. Crossing his arms over his bent knees, he turned toward her and gave her a searching look. "Are you sure it's over between you two?"

"Absolutely," she said, turning the package over in her hands. "At least it is for me."

"Maybe you should let him know that."

She stared at the neatly typed label, the extra postage stamps. It was so like Henry. Would the card inside be typed too? If there even was a card. Henry wasn't one for displays of emotion. Maybe if he had been, their relationship might have been different. But even as she considered the idea, she knew nothing could have changed things between them. They had been compatible in so many ways, but she had never loved him. Without thinking, she said, "Why does love have to be so important?"

He averted his gaze. "I don't know," he said. "But it is."

Blake studied his profile in the afternoon light. The strong jaw, the shadow of stubble she loved to trace with her fingertips, the dark eyes. When she looked at him she knew he tapped into a part of her that no one had ever reached. A part of her she hadn't even been sure existed.

But so much had happened in such a short time she was afraid to trust her feelings. She had turned her life upside down by leaving the city. Then she watched a woman die. And now she was planning adopt a one-year-old. Could she trust what her heart was telling her about Declan? It was probably better if she didn't. He's going to leave, she reminded herself.

Setting the package down next to her, she stood up and smoothed her jeans. "I'm going to check on—" She stopped in mid-sentence and inhaled sharply. "I just remembered something."

He looked at her guardedly, almost as if he expected her to reveal something about her feelings for Henry. "Everything okay?"

"Yes, yes," she said, jumping up and disappearing inside the house. She emerged a few minutes later with a notebook and pen. "When we were in the cafe today, McAllister called Jenna "Irish Eyes." That was the name on the email we found on Kelly's computer. At the time I just assumed we were looking at Kelly's email account. But what if we weren't—"

"You mean you think Kelly got into Jenna's account somehow?"

"I don't know," she said. "Angie wouldn't give me the copy we printed out. She said she didn't want to destroy Kelly's reputation. But I can remember some of it, I think."

"Close your eyes," he suggested. "Maybe that will help."

"Okay," she said, closing her eyes. "I'm trying."

"Maybe if you—"

"Shhhhh." Blake tapped the pen impatiently against the notebook, willing herself to call up the image of the email print-out. She summoned a memory of Kelly's bedroom and tried to envision the way the screen looked that day. When she opened her eyes she began writing, quickly at first, then more slowly. She stopped and looked down at the paper. "I can't remember all of it." She shook her head.

"That doesn't matter," Declan said. "Read what you have."

She handed him the notebook and showed him what she'd written so far. "I know I remember more," she apologized. "But at least it's a start. Maybe I'll remember more later."

He took the notebook in both hands and held it in front of him. He studied her handwriting for a long time, saying nothing. After several minutes, she edged toward him and peered over his shoulder. The only sound was the call of seagulls mixing with the crash of the waves breaking against the rocky shore.

From monk (something) @ monkey?.net or com
To irisheyes @ ?
Date July thirty (the day before Kelly died)
Subject Guest List
Luke?
The White Queen (or Lady?)
Christine (or Christy or Krista or Cristy)

Ruby (was this at the bottom?)

Hitler's Dog

two strings of numbers—one started 31711—the date Kelly died.

"I'm sorry," she said at last. "I know it doesn't make much sense. I'm pretty sure the heading said it was some type of guest list. There could have been a number, but I can't remember what number it was. Do you think those are real names mixed with code names? Maybe it was some type of party where there would be drugs?"

"You're sure about those," he said, pointing to the spot where she'd written the list of names. "You're sure it said Luke and Cristy?"

"No," she said, "that's the problem. I'm not sure. I only looked at the list for a few seconds before Santos showed up. I don't know why Angie won't give me the list—she seemed really evasive about it."

"Hitler's Dog," he read aloud. "How about that one? That's fairly unusual."

Blake nodded. "That's the one name I am sure of. It's not the sort of thing you forget."

He frowned, but when she looked into his eyes she saw that there was a kind of fire in them.

"Do you know who that is?" she asked.

"Not who," he told her. "What. Hitler's Dog is a street name for heroin. White Lady stands for cocaine. Cristy is probably crystal meth. This isn't a guest list, it's a list of narcotics."

Her jaw dropped. "So if the email was sent to Jenna, not Kelly—"

"You said the first date was written 31711—or July

31st—that was the same day you saw Kelly fall from the lighthouse tower. My guess is that date was a code telling somebody a drug shipment was coming in," Declan said. "Maybe Jenna and Kelly were working together."

"But they hated each other."

"Maybe that was for show," he mused. "Part of the act?"

She shook her head. "No way," she said emphatically. "I saw the two of them at the cafe, the first day after I got here. If they were acting then they should've both gotten academy awards. What did Jenna say when you met with her this morning?"

"Not much," he said, pressing his lips together. "She kept going on and on about what a terrible tragedy it was. After half an hour, she bolted out of her chair and said she was late for work."

Blake doubted Jenna's grief was real. She also suspected Jenna had simply pretended to have information as a pretext to spend time with Declan. He might think it unlikely that she'd be interested in Kelly's "uncle," but it wouldn't surprise her at all if it turned out that Kelly was infatuated with him. "Well, at least the part about her being late for work was true. Angie wasn't too happy about it either. Do you think she meant to tell you something else and got cold feet? Or was she just after you?"

"Very funny," he said, tousling her hair playfully.

Clearly, the man didn't know how attractive he was. Jenna was younger than him, but that didn't mean she was immune to his charms. Declan might be pushing thirty-five but he was still sexy as hell. In his jeans and plaid shirt he looked like the quintessential cowboy. Suppressing her growing sense of apprehension, she tried to focus on the issue at hand.

"Okay, let's try to think it through," she said matter-of-factly, pushing his hand away and tucking her hair behind her ears. "If we backtrack maybe six months or so, Kelly has a serious drug problem and she's dating Chris McAllister. Then he dumps her for Jenna and she's more than a little upset about it. Then—if we can believe what Angie told me this morning—Kelly cleans up because of Grace. At least for a while, anyway."

"Then she turns up dead," Declan finished.

Despite Blake's efforts to sort things out, she wasn't any closer to seeing the truth. "Do you think she was up in the lighthouse because of a shipment?" Remembering the pacifier and the crying baby, she admitted it seemed likely. "I know this sounds incredibly naive, but I just can't believe Kelly would involve Grace in all this. But she must have."

He ripped the page out of the notebook and folded it thoughtfully. "It's not naive—we usually can't believe things of other people because we're not capable of them ourselves. This is the perfect location for smuggling—and Kelly and Jenna and whoever else is mixed up in this aren't the first ones to figure that out. Billy Stone was involved in rum-running way back in the twenties." He stuffed the paper into his shirt pocket. "With the Canadian border a stone's throw from Eagle Point it makes perfect sense."

He didn't smile at his unintentional pun, nor did Blake. Kelly, and maybe even Lucy, may well have died because of Eagle Point's proximity to the border.

"But what about the suicide note?" She knew

Declan was right about the likelihood that Kelly had involved Grace, but for some reason she didn't want to give up on the idea that Grace's mother had done what she could to protect her daughter. She wasn't even sure why it mattered. After all, she'd hardly known Kelly. "Do you think somebody faked the note to divert the sheriff's office?"

He stood and brushed off his jeans. To the west, the sun slanted through the pines, casting long shadows across the sea grass that stretched all the way to the lighthouse.

"Maybe," he said doubtfully. "But if that was the plan, why not leave the note somewhere where they'd find it? Why give it to McAllister?"

She rose as well. Surely Grace should be waking up by now. "Maybe whoever it was thought McAllister would give it to the sheriff?" The more the two of them tried to sort things out, the less clear they seemed.

The cell phone in Declan's jeans pocket vibrated, the unexpected noise making both of them jump. Retrieving the phone, he broke into a sardonic grin as he read what was on the screen. "Looks like the girl who got cold feet is ready to commit."

Blake leaned close to read the text. On the other side of the yard the sun dipped below the trees, deepening the shadows and casting an eerie chill over the scene. As she looked at what Jenna had written, the cold settled over her. The warmth of Declan's body did little to lessen her fears.

Need 2 talk 2 u. IMPORTANT
At Otter Bluff now. Waiting 4 u.

Walking over to the screen door and pulling it open, she turned back toward Declan. "What makes you think she'll actually tell you something this time?"

"Nothing," he said. "But I can't risk not going on in case she really does want to talk." He bent down toward Henry's package and held it out to her. "You wouldn't want to forget about this. Sure that's not a ring?" he teased. "Looks like it's about the right size."

The thought of Henry doing anything that romantic was inconceivable. Wasn't it? Once more, she tried to banish her doubts. Even if Henry had done something dramatic she was more certain than ever that leaving New York had been the right choice—whatever happened with Declan.

"Trust me," she said, with more certainty than she felt. "It's not a ring."

She took the package as Declan grabbed their coffee mugs in one hand and held the door open for her. From upstairs, she heard he faint sound of Grace singing nonsense words to herself. She was halfway to the kitchen when it occurred to her to wonder why the package bore an unreadable postmark.

Chapter 13

As Declan passed Blake on his way to the upstairs bedroom, he pecked her cheek. "My keys must've fallen onto the floor when we were getting naked" he said. "Either that or you swiped them to keep me prisoner here."

"Busted," she said, smiling automatically. As the sound of his footsteps echoed overhead, she stood frozen at the center of the braided rug in the living room. Lifting the brown compact package to eye level, she studied it curiously. Yes, Henry had sent her something. And yes, it was like him to print an address label rather than writing one out. But the extra postage seemed wrong somehow.

She stared at the package uneasily. To others, Henry appeared lavish with his money but Blake knew better. He did spend money but he never wasted it. Slathering on unnecessary postage would strike him as the equivalent of buying a new car at sticker price.

Then again, maybe she was reading too much into the extra postage Overanalyzing every last detail had always been one of her faults. With a slight shrug, she crossed to the kitchen and set the package down on the table. Grabbing a pair of scissors from one of the drawers, she settled in a chair and cut through the thick wrapping. Once it was removed, she lifted out a box.

Well, at least the box itself didn't seem all that

ominous. It was small, but not small enough for a ring, as Declan had suggested. Earrings, maybe? Even that seemed a bit of stretch for Henry. More likely an IPod Nano. Either way, she would have to return it. Declan was right. Henry at least deserved an honest conversation. Just because she assumed it was over didn't mean he did as well.

The name of a well-known department store was blazoned across the top, which was secured to the bottom with clear duct tape. Holding the scissors open, she sliced through the tape. When Declan appeared in the entryway, keys in hand, she broke into a grin. "Guess you foiled my plan."

His smile dissolved as his eyes came to rest on the heavily taped box.

"Stop!" he shouted, lunging toward the table and ripping the box from her grasp. The scissors clattered to the floor, skittering to a stop at the foot of a nearby chair.

"What's wrong?" Blake rose from the table, backing away as he sped toward the kitchen door, clutching the box to his chest. Throwing his shoulder against the kitchen door so that it sprang open, he sped outside and hurled the box away from the house in a high arc.

She watched in shock as the box struck the ground, detonating on impact. The explosion rocked the backyard, plumes of fire spreading out across the air. Smoke billowed across the sky, and Declan's arms wrapped tightly around her from behind. Sparks danced above the licking flames, rising upward then disappearing into the twilight.

She fell back against his rippled chest, letting his

strength envelop her. "I guess it wasn't a ring," she said with as much calm as she could muster. Which wasn't much.

"And I don't think Henry sent it either," he said without releasing his grip. "Somebody wants you out of here."

A nod was all she could manage. The idea that someone wanted her dead was almost impossible to comprehend. In all her years in the city she never came close to being killed. "Thanks for saving my life."

Turning her around to face him, Declan raised her face to his. He wore an expression she hadn't seen yet. Confusion filled his eyes, as if he were struggling with an equation he couldn't solve. "So why do I feel like I'm the one who almost died just now," he said roughly.

"Because you almost did," she said with a tremulous smile. "You risked your life to save mine. I'll never forget that. No matter what happens."

Declan wasn't smiling though. "I think I might be falling in love with you," he said, removing his hand from her face and stepping away. He pulled his Glock from its holster, pressing it into her palm and wrapping her hand around it. "I'll be back as soon as I can. Lock yourself and Grace in the house and use this if you have to. Don't let anybody in, not even Santos."

Blake stared down at the gun and decided not to tell him she didn't know how to use it. When she looked up he was already at the kitchen door, his eyes dark with an emotion she couldn't read. "Grace and I will be fine," she said, feeling as if she were telling him the biggest lie of her life.

Declan took a step toward her, then stopped. "Just be careful," he warned before disappearing inside the house. A moment later the front door slammed shut.

She stood outside, watching the licking flames die down then flicker out. "I might be falling in love with you too," she whispered as she listened to the sound of his pick-up fading down the road.

****

Declan's truck hurtled toward Otter Bluff, a rocky stretch of cliffs that jutted out over a thin ribbon of beach fifty feet below. A sliver of a moon rose over the ocean and next to it Venus shone brightly. Further to the East, the lighthouse rose up against a mass of thunderheads.

How long did he have until the storm broke? An hour? Two at the most, by his estimate. More than enough time to talk to Jenna and head back to the keeper's house, where Blake and Grace would be waiting for him.

Blake and Grace. He didn't want to think about them, about the expression on Blake's face when he told her he was falling in love with her. Or the way he thrust a gun into her hand and told her to be careful then walked out on her without even saying goodbye. He remembered how she'd sat on the porch in the hazy afternoon light, gazing out to sea as she talked about her past. What had she been like as a kid? An image of Blake as a child, scrambling across the rocks as she collected shells, lodged in his brain. She would have been just as beautiful, he was sure, and just as stubborn. Now that he'd gotten to know her he realized she was nothing like the cool-headed lawyer he first imagined her to be. She was soft and warm, not sleek. And she was vulnerable. Of course by now he knew it was a mistake to think of her that way. There was toughness in her too—something that refused to back away from a fight or a challenge. If anything, he was the vulnerable one.

He wanted to make love to her again more than he ever wanted anything in his entire life. He'd wanted women before, but not like this. For the first time he wondered what it would be like to stay in one place for more than a few months at a time. What would it be like to spend his nights next to someone he truly cared about instead of lying awake with his gun on the nightstand of yet another cheap hotel?

He couldn't think about that, not now.

Forcing himself to consider the task at hand, he scanned the cliffs for a sign of Jenna's Corvette. She hadn't said exactly where she expected to meet him and she hadn't responded to his texts. The remoteness of the location made him think she really did mean to give him some information this time. Several times that morning she seemed on the brink of opening up to him. But every time, a look of fear crept into her eyes and she pulled back, twirling her hair and giggling in a way he guessed she thought was sexy.

At the end of the road, a solitary figure emerged out of a copse of pines. It looked like a woman but from such a distance it was impossible to tell if it was Jenna or not.

It had to be Jenna. He needed it to be Jenna. If only she hadn't changed her mind.

He was unarmed, but that at the moment was just about the only thing that didn't bother him. It was unlikely she would be carrying a weapon, but even if she was he was fairly certain he could disarm her. Much as he hated to admit it, Blake was right—to a point. When they met earlier that day Jenna repeatedly reached out to lay her hand over his. On the surface, it was nothing more than a gesture of sympathy. But something in the way her eyes lit up every time he used her name made him wonder if maybe there was more to Jenna's interest in him than he wanted to believe. He was none too pleased to be the object of her desire, but it did give him a certain sense of security.

She wouldn't harm him, at least not willingly. Or even lure him into a situation where he might be in danger. *My protector*, he thought wryly. At the thought of Jenna doing anything for him, Declan suppressed a powerful rush of nausea. Women had always fallen for him and while he'd never consciously tried to use that fact he hadn't done much to discourage them from telling him what he needed to know.

Had he used their feelings to manipulate them for his own ends? *Maybe,* he admitted. *Make that probably.* He grimaced at the repulsiveness of the idea. For his entire career he'd told himself the ends justified the means. Sure, he played by the book when it came to following the law, but if a drug lord's girlfriend wanted to open up to him then who was he to turn her away?

Somehow he doubted Rita Gonzalez would agree with him. He still dreamt of the betrayed look in her eyes just before her pulse stopped underneath his thumb. She had loved and trusted him. In return, she got a bullet to the head from her boyfriend. Did it matter that the information she gave him led him to one of the most dangerous dealers in Colombia? He wasn't sure, but didn't think Rita would see it quite the same way. Luckily for him the dead couldn't speak.

He eased the truck to the side of the road, parking

it as far toward the edge as possible so that it would be relatively inconspicuous from a distance. When the woman emerged again from the shadows he immediately recognized Jenna's long red hair and skin-tight Nirvana t-shirt. *So she showed after all,* he thought. *If only she doesn't bail on me again.* She watched him climb out of his pick-up without moving from her spot among the pines, holding herself still as a cat about to pounce in the deepening twilight.

Suddenly he regretted not bringing his gun. *Blake needs it more than you do,* he chided himself. Anyway. he never believed she was involved in dealing drugs. He didn't doubt she knew something—hell, maybe she even suspected who killed her former friend. But according to his sources, there was nothing to suggest she was working with the smuggling ring. *Just another Rita Gonzalez,* he thought grimly. The only difference was that this time McAllister had already tried to shoot her in the gut. Lucky for her the guy was in custody for the unforeseeable future.

Was it possible McAllister was behind everything?

Declan dismissed the idea outright. He might know something, just like he believed Jenna did. Maybe he was even involved in some way. But McAllister wasn't the ringmaster, not in the crazy circus he'd stumbled across. It would take brains—not to mention balls—to pull off something of this magnitude. McAllister had the latter in spades but he was sorely lacking in the brains department. At most he was a pawn in somebody else's game, a functionary who would be sacrificed the moment he made a misstep.

Which he'd already made. A pretty big misstep.

"I wasn't sure you'd be here," he said, crossing

toward her and doing his best to keep his tone neutral. She'd run twice before and there was no reason she wouldn't do the same thing yet again. It was already past sundown and darkness was settling rapidly. He could hardly make out her face.

"I wasn't sure you'd come," she said, motioning him to follow her onto a path that led deeper into the woods. When he opened his mouth to speak, she touched a finger to her lips. "Not here."

Declan hesitated. He didn't know the area at all and he was unarmed. "Hang on a sec," he told her. "Let me get my flashlight."

Jenna shook her head. "No," she said. "No light. I don't want anybody to spot us."

"All right," he conceded, falling into step behind her as they headed down the narrow path. "We'll do it your way." *This better be worth it,* he nearly said aloud, but kept silent. The sooner he heard her out the closer he would be to finding Kelly's killer—and hopefully the person who was behind the largest drug smuggling ring on the East Coast. As he watched Jenna's narrow back a few feet ahead of him Declan tried not to listen to his gut, which was telling him to turn back.

As if on cue, a peal of distant thunder echoed across the cliffs.

****

Blake sat in the rocker, watching Grace play with some colored wooden blocks at the center of the braided rug. Outside, the darkening sky was thick with clouds. Blake switched on a couple of lights even though it wasn't all that late. The lights cast a yellow glow over the living room, giving everything a warm, homey feel. She glanced around its perimeter, taking in the antique furniture and the ancient-looking wallpaper and the scratched hardwood floors. She'd spent the entirety of Grace's nap scrubbing and unpacking, if only because it got her mind off Declan. After nearly two hours of frenzied cleaning she hardly made a dent. But at least she cleared away much of the old decor, substituting her own things for the out-of-date knick knacks that littered every available surface. The Victrola she wound up and played on the day of her arrival stood on an antique table in the corner of the living room. For some reason she didn't want to get rid of it.

The house was beginning to feel like home. The idea struck her as strange. She had only been in Eagle Point for a short time but as she watched Grace piling up the blocks then gleefully knocking them down again, she knew she'd finally found her place in the world. It would probably take her a year of work—hard work— before she could even think about opening the inn. Even then, she would be busier than she ever. Running an inn and raising a child by herself wouldn't be easy.

It was what she wanted though. She'd always dreaded hitting thirty because she believed it meant that life was passing her by. That she wasn't successful enough—or married. That she didn't have children of her own. She understood now that none of that mattered. Sitting in the small room while she watched Grace laugh was the only success that counted. Only one thing would have made it better, but she wasn't going to let herself think about that. Even if Declan's claim was true and he was falling for her, his abrupt departure made his intentions clear. He was going to leave her. Not because she didn't mean anything to him, but because he couldn't give up his career.

She sighed. Why did she always end up with the wrong guys? First Henry, now Declan. Add to that a string of relationships in her early twenties that flickered out as quickly as birthday candles. The difference was Declan sparked something in her no one else had. She'd only known him for a matter of days but she was going to miss him far more than she missed Henry. It was almost enough to make her believe in soul mates. She had never put much faith in the idea, in part because her parents' decades-long marriage was more of a business arrangement than a love affair. As far back as she could remember she hadn't seen them display any more emotion toward each other than the occasional peck on the cheek. When she was in middle school Blake would visit her best friend's tiny apartment, full of laughter and shouting, and secretly wish for a brother or a sister of her own. Not long afterward, her mother ordered twin beds to replace the queen-sized one she shared with her husband. By that time Blake was old enough to know what that meant but she never stopped wishing for a sibling. "We're lucky we got one," her father often joked. Her mother always smiled at his teasing, but the smile never traveled to her eyes.

When she was in high school Blake wondered if there was someone else. Unlike most teenage girls, she saw her mother as a romantic figure—a woman with a mysterious past, someone with a packet of love letters stashed in a secret drawer. Now she wasn't sure what she thought. Her parents seemed happy enough in a placid sort of way but she wasn't under any illusions when it came to their feelings for each other.

Maybe love isn't all that important, she thought. Except it was, at least for her, anyway. Declan was right when he said it mattered. She would rather spend the next ten years as a dateless single mother than one day as Henry's wife. As for her own parents, she wasn't like either of them. She wasn't willing to settle. She wanted the real thing—a mad, crazy running-through-the-streets-on-New-Year's kind of love. A wildly impractical, heart-pounding bond that would last a lifetime.

And if you can't have it?

Blake left the question unanswered. All she could do at the moment was concentrate on what she did have. Declan might not be staying but he would be back later that night. And he cared about her, she was sure of it. Those were the things she needed to focus on—the things that happened in the present moment. After a lifetime spent planning, she was going to do her damnedest to live for what she had now.

There was just one slight problem.

Somebody didn't want her to live.

Looking down at her lap, she smoothed out the brown paper the bomb had been wrapped in.

IF YOU LOVE THE LITTLE GIRL GET OUT NOW

The message was a crooked line of pasted letters cut from magazines. Every time she looked at it she got the urge to strap Grace into her car seat and drive as far away from Eagle Point as she could get. Especially when she dropped her eyes to the bottom of the paper, where a final mismatched sentence screamed its warning at her.

ACCIDENTS HAPPEN

Did the sender intend the note to be a warning? Was it possible they simply meant to scare her, not blow her to bits? If so, why not send the note first? More likely it was Plan B—an extra dollop of terror just in case the bomb didn't do its job. She didn't doubt the person who sent the bomb and the ominous message was Kelly's killer. She also believed whoever sent the email to "Irish Eyes"—the person who went by the name of Monk—was the one who was behind the threats. The whole picture was still hazy but parts of it were beginning to come into focus.

When she bought the lighthouse it had been on the market for three years. Aside from the former owner's children, who made yearly pilgrimages to Eagle Point, and a cleaning woman who occasionally tidied up the place, the lighthouse and surrounding buildings had been deserted. Which gave anyone free reign to use the place for whatever purpose they desired.

Clearly, her unexpected arrival shook things up. Now someone wanted her dead.

Well, she wasn't spooked that easily. She thought of Declan's Glock shoved into a drawer in one of the side tables next to the couch. She probably should have found a way to secure it to her waist but she didn't like having the gun out in the open around Grace. If anybody showed up all she needed to do was pull open the drawer and cock the gun.

At the thought of shooting a gun her mouth went dry. The closest thing to a weapon she owned was a can of pepper spray and she'd never used it. Hopefully Declan would make it back before any unexpected visitors showed up.

A bolt of lightning snaked its way across the living

room window, followed by a crash of thunder. Before she rose out of her rocker, the sky opened and a deluge of rain began falling. It hit the roof with deafening intensity and she rushed upstairs to shut an open window.

Grace called out to her from the spare bedroom.

"Hang on, Grace," Blake shouted back. "I'll be right there."

Apparently "I'll be right there" wasn't the response Grace wanted. She burst into loud cries, ignoring Blake's reassurances. Blake was halfway across the room when a stream of water fell through a hole in the roof. Another series of drips started up behind her, followed by an echo in the hallway.

"Dammit," she cursed, casting around for something to use for the leaks. Hurrying down the stairs, she picked up Grace in mid-stride and ran into the kitchen. She grabbed a few pots in one hand and tried to soothe Grace as she headed back toward the stairwell.

She couldn't do it.

She couldn't manage to hold Grace and carry the pots without dropping one or the other. When she set Grace down onto the floor in front of her blocks the child started shrieking immediately. Ignoring her raised arms, Blake mumbled a few lame words of comfort and headed up the stairs. "I'll be right back," she called down to screaming child. "Mama, will be right there."

She wasn't her mama. Kelly was. But somehow it seemed like the right thing to say.

Again, Grace didn't seem to agree. If anything, her crying reached a higher level of intensity. Combined with the storm's fury, Blake felt as she had when she was a child and the boy next door tortured her dolls relentlessly—claustrophobic, totally helpless, with no way to make the feeling stop. At the top of the stairs, she paused and gripped the handrail tightly with her free hand, willing herself to stay calm.

It was just a storm. Nothing was going to happen. She'd locked all the doors and she had Declan's gun. They were safe.

So why didn't she believe it?

A loud thud echoed from below, as if something had crashed to the floor. Dropping the pots at her feet, she raced down the stairs calling Grace's name. She reached the living room just as the lights flickered out.

Chapter 14

Grace's cries echoed through the darkness. Feeling her way with her arms out in front of her, Blake followed the sound until her foot hit the edge of the braided rug. A flash of sheet lightning lit the interior and she saw Grace on the other side of the room, at the divide between the kitchen and the living room.

"Stay there, Gracie," she called out to her as she stumbled through the blackness, trying to keep the image of Grace's location sharp in her mind. Another flash of lightning illuminated the room and she saw Grace crawling toward the kitchen.

"Not that way," she told the child, willing Grace to stop moving away from her. "Stay right there, okay?"

Grace was still crying. It wasn't the wild shrieking of the past fifteen minutes, but an even keening. Saying a prayer of thanks that the child's level of fear seemed to have subsided slightly, Blake edged toward the sound, running her hands over the bookshelf as she made her way toward the kitchen.

"Just one more minute," she said, realizing she was speaking as much to herself as to Grace.

Her foot hit an uneven dip in the floor and she nearly fell, but caught herself just in time. She was in the kitchen now and Grace's cries were close. The child must be only a few feet away. In the next flash of lightning she was able to lean down and sweep Grace into her arms.

"It's okay now," she murmured, holding her close. "I've got you."

Grace's crying faded to a low whimper as Blake rifled through the drawer for a flashlight and candles. Her breath came in ragged gasps and she consciously slowed it down. *So much for not being spooked*, she thought as the match in her hand flared to life. She lit a candle and placed it on the counter, then lit another and put it in on the kitchen table. The room came alive in the shadowy glow, giving the place a frightening, haunted feel.

A glance around the kitchen told her that whatever fell must be in the other room. With Grace balanced on her hip and the flashlight held out in front of her, she headed back along the hallway. The worn floor creaked and groaned beneath her as she edged her way forward, step by step, until she emerged into the living room. What seemed homey just an hour before looked eerily unfamiliar as she aimed the flashlight into the room.

The light traveled over the furniture and into the corners but nothing seemed amiss. She held her breath and tried to shut out the sound of the storm, listening closely. Outside, the wind raged but the interior of the house was quiet. In the corner, just past the bookshelves that lined the far wall, the Victrola lay on its side. The horn jutted up at a strange angle and the record on the turntable had shattered.

Making her way over to the spot where it lay, she knelt down and lifted a dark shard off the floor. She knew without looking which record it was. She hadn't touched the Victrola since her arrival and the memory of the Charleston's jaunty rhythm filled her mind. How had it fallen? Did someone push it off the table? Did Grace somehow manage to pull it off when Blake was upstairs?

As she shone the light onto the broken Victrola, a rush of sadness flooded her heart. The story of Lucy Stone pressed in upon her. Surely Lucy listened to that Victrola on nights much like this one, cranking the record player so its music could shut out the harsh landscape on the other side of the glass.

Grace reached out her hand to grasp the piece of record Blake held.

"Oh no you don't," she said, placing the shard onto the antique table. Setting the flashlight next to it, she stared at the broken player. She didn't know why it seemed wrong to let it stay where it was. It would be easier to clean up when the power came back on. But for some reason leaving the Victrola shattered across the floor seemed like a violation. She set Grace down beside her and used both hands to heft it back onto the table. The back panel of the gramophone had come loose as a result of the crash. Bending closer, Blake saw that a dark rectangular object was lodged in the crack between the frame and the panel. Prying the panel further open, she tugged on the object until it was free.

She grabbed the flashlight and aimed it at the object, though she already guessed what it was. The leather-bound book was worn with age and bore no writing on the exterior. Carefully lifting its cover, she saw that it too was blank. No name, no title or author. She wasn't looking at a book but at someone's diary. Page after page of eloquent cursive slanted across yellowed paper, penned decades earlier and hidden in the one place her husband would never think to look.

Lucy's diary.

She ran her fingertips over the pages, barely able to contain her excitement. Training the flashlight onto the dates, she saw that her guess had been right. Bringing a page close to her face, she struggled to make out Lucy's script. Sitting down next to Grace, she began to read.

January 3, 1922

My darling baby girl's second birthday. Hazel wakeful all night—as if she knew today was a special day. Several times I feared Billy would wake and that frightened me very much. He has never laid a hand on Hazel and I doubt he would, but sometimes there is a look in his eye that would frighten the devil himself.

Up at dawn to bake the cake and get everything prepared. Have only invited a few guests. Harriet Beacham and Mimi Powell along with their children, and two or three wives from church. I fear none of them will find it very hospitable here. My New Year's resolution was to bring beauty and happiness to our home and I'm sorry to say I've done neither. It is Hazel, not I, who imbues this place with joy. Were it not for her, I could hardly bear it here. I cannot imagine my life without her beaming face, her constant babble of half-songs, her curious nature. Sometimes it seems as if all I do is clean and iron and mend with nothing to show for it. Billy very unhappy yesterday morning, still recovering from his New Year's binge. I did what I could. Cleaned and polished the lens, as well as the insides of the tower windows, then took the weather readings and recorded them in the log book. Billy drinking again after sunset and soon passed out. Went up and lit the lantern and stayed as long as I could, then returned to find Hazel awake and out of her crib! It's going to be much more difficult now that she has mastered the skill of climbing. Have resolved to speak to Billy about the need for him to limit his liquor, for the baby's sake if not my own.

Officer Reston from the Lighthouse Bureau stopped by while Billy was still indisposed. When I came back and told him Billy was too ill to speak, his countenance was grave. One of the survivor's from last month's shipwreck reported seeing no light in the tower, as well as lights along the coast where no lights should have been. Understandably, Reston is highly suspicious. To make matters worse none of the liquor aboard the vessel was recovered. Of course, it may well have sunk with the ship but I think Reston suspects the truth. "These people are guilty of breaking the law, it's true," he told me, "but they don't deserve to pay with their lives." The tower logs of course report no such oversight. In addition, Reston asked me to copy out a recipe for fish chowder and when I handed it to him his eyes held a peculiar triumphant light. I fear he suspects how many nights it has been I, not Billy, who has performed the keeper's duties. As he stood at the door I waited for him to speak to me about the matter but he remained silent, only stooping to salute

Hazel—a   gesture   she   found   highly entertaining.

How lonely Lucy must have been, Blake thought, trying to imagine her life as wife to a drunken lighthouse keeper. From the sounds of it Lucy had taken on most of the keeper's duties in addition to her own responsibilities as a wife and mother. Pulling Grace onto her lap, she flipped forward through the pages to an entry dated two months later.

March 15, 1922

Ides of March, a day to be on guard. As well I might be, considering Billy's behavior as of late. He's withdrawn even further into solitude, shutting himself up in his study for hours on end. What he does in there I cannot begin to guess. Or don't want to. Last week during the storm another ship sank just miles away. It was too large a vessel to be involved in rum-running but I fear its captain saw the false lights and steered his ship toward what he thought was safety. Mimi told me there were no survivors and remarked on the unusual number of ships that have sunk in recent months, giving me a pointed look. Her words chilled me to the core. I checked the log as soon as she departed and found it written in Billy's handwriting. Try as I might, I cannot remember if the lantern was lit or not. I cannot remember if he was home either. He is so seldom home at night now I hardly notice his absence. If I probe my conscience perhaps I shall be forced to concede his absence was a relief. Have I been deliberately blind all this time?

    Colin came immediately after the wreck and met with Billy for a long time. When I asked about it, Billy lost hold of his temper. Colin came again yesterday, this time when Billy was not at home. He stayed rather a long time—in excess of two hours—in hopes that Billy would return. At the end of his visit he presented me with a small gift—a phonograph recording of a new song called the Charleston. He says it's all the rage in New York City. He spotted it in a Boston shop and thought it might amuse me, being so solitary here. When he left his eyes went to the bruises on my arms and then met mine. I blushed with shame, knowing he guessed my secret.

    He is quite handsome. Though it was terribly vain of me, I went to the mirror after he left and tried to see myself through Colin's eyes. The results, I'm sorry to say, were not encouraging. Even without the bruises I am quite hideous. No wonder I provoke Billy as I do.

As she reached the bottom of the page, Blake fought down her disgust. Not only was Billy Stone an abusive drunk, he was a murderer as well. How many men died as a result of his rum-running? She doubted anyone would ever know, but the number must be in the hundreds. Reading what Lucy had written about Colin Reston, she found herself rooting for the handsome Lighthouse Service officer. Though Lucy hadn't come out and said so directly, Blake was sure the keeper's wife cared for him. Without being able to explain why, she found herself longing for a happy ending for Lucy. If only her brute of a husband hadn't damaged Lucy's self-esteem to the point where she couldn't even look in the mirror without shame.

Grace reached out for the diary, wanting to touch its rough pages. Gently pushing her hand away, Blake turned to the final entry. Unlike the other entries it was written in a jagged script that bore little resemblance to Lucy's neat cursive. In several spots there were splotches of black, where ink had pooled without being blotted. She held the flashlight over the faded words and read.

September 19, 1922

This morning I received a brief note tucked into a stack of ironing I'd left in the laundry room. "Please tell me what you know. There are lives at stake. You are a noble soul and I know you will not continue to let innocent people die."

Needless to say the ironing remained where it was. After such a note any attempt to go about the ordinary business of the day was unthinkable. How can I tell him what I know? It's not the thought of betraying my husband that holds me back. It has been a long time since I thought of Billy with anything resembling fondness. But how I can summon up the courage to tell the truth when doing so would place Hazel and myself in grave danger? Colin thinks I am better than I am. I am not noble, not one bit, or I could never have allowed things to go on as long as they have. But perhaps I can yet redeem myself.

Perhaps Colin's faith in me can help me overcome my natural cowardice and spur me to act.

Might it be possible to escape from this place—and at the same time put an end to Billy's horrendous activities? Though I have been thinking just such a thing for months now, I do not know if I can bring myself to something that requires such bravery. I do not know if I shall act. Colin is correct about one thing though. If I continue to stand by while innocent people die, am I not as guilty as Billy?

The entry broke off and continued further down the page. Juggling the flashlight, the journal, and Grace, Blake struggled to make out the nearly illegible writing. If it was difficult to read before it was doubly arduous now. She should probably set the diary aside and return to it after she got things settled. But she couldn't stop, not when she was so close to understanding what happened the night Lucy died.

I did act! The other night after Billy fell into the usual drunken stupor I snuck into his study and searched his desk. There is a large shipment due to arrive tonight (how he learns of these things, I can only speculate) and I have little doubt that Billy plans to keep the tower dark then lure the vessel onto the rocks with his "ghost lights." But I shall do my best to ensure he never gets the opportunity.

I've packed my bags and Hazel's too. Tonight shall be our last at Eagle Point and I am not sorry. I only pray I can prevent Billy from discovering my intent. As soon I finish this entry I shall post the map of the tunnels leading to the caves, along with a full confession detailing my knowledge of the goings on here over the past two years, to Colin. Without it, it is unlikely the entrance to the caves should ever be discovered.

Despite my resolve I fear for Hazel's safety and wish we could leave this very moment. But if I depart now, there will be no one to light the lantern once Billy takes his horse to the cliffs above the coast. I cannot allow those people to die. But as soon as I light the lantern and know its beacon shall keep them from drowning, Hazel and I shall leave this place behind forever. I have stolen only the funds I need, enough to pay for our train fares to New York City and to tide us over for a brief period of time. In such a great city, Billy will never find us. I expect there shall be plenty of work there and I hope to find a place as a typist or a file clerk or perhaps even a switchboard operator. But even if I'm forced to seek a position as a maid or a factory worker I shan't complain. Though I shall miss the sea greatly, anything is preferable to remaining here in fear for our lives. Already I dream of cutting my hair short and renting a small apartment.

Though I doubt I'll ever have the chance to tell him I want to write it here, to see it on paper just once and thus imbue the sentiment with a trace of reality—I love

The writing broke off in mid-sentence and the remaining pages in the diary were blank. Blake flipped through to the end. A folded piece of paper fluttered to the floor. Reaching to pick it up, she saw that it must have been the map Lucy intended to post to Colin Reston. Had she failed to stop her husband then?

In her lap Grace quieted and watched the storm with wide eyes. Gathering the child into her arms and rising to her feet, Blake stood deep in thought. After reading Lucy's words she was certain she'd been murdered. Lucy hadn't been suicidal, she'd been on the verge of escaping to a better life. Before someone stopped her. Did she hear her husband and shove the diary back inside the Victrola? Was that why the entry ended so abruptly? Why hadn't she finished it later? If her husband showed up, she may have just had time to shove the diary and the map back into the Victrola without being caught. Whatever the case, if Billy Stone knew of the map and the diary he would undoubtedly have destroyed them.

Blake wished Lucy had gotten her happy ending, even though she knew that hadn't been the case. She and Hazel never took the train to New York City, Lucy never cut her hair into a bob or found a job as a typist. Instead she died a horrible death, forced to abandon her child and her dreams. She hadn't even been able to finish her sentence—to write just once the name of the man she loved.

She closed the journal and tried to put Lucy out of her mind. Despite the fact that the lighthouse keeper's wife died so long ago, she felt a strong bond with her—perhaps because their fates were so oddly similar. Like Lucy, she'd found new life through a child. And she had met a man she could love, just like Lucy. Neither of them had been expecting it, neither had gotten the chance to live out her romance.

As she stood watching the chain lightning illuminate the night sky, Blake made a vow that she would tell Declan of her feelings. Lucy hadn't gotten the chance, but she would. She wasn't going to let Declan go without telling him the truth.

There was something else she needed to do as well. In her final entry Lucy mentioned the tunnels that ran from the oil house to caves along the shore. Blake had always believed Lucy was the key to solving the mystery of the strange goings on at Eagle Point. And the diary was the key to Lucy.

If somebody was smuggling drugs over the border, wasn't it possible that they were using the old rum-running caves? How easy it would be to store shipments in those caves and transport them South afterward, just as the smugglers did during Prohibition.

The keeper's house had been vacant for three years. Whoever was behind the smuggling operation would have had the opportunity to use the lighthouse and the caves whenever and however they wanted to. No wonder they wanted her out. Her presence made the entire operation so much more difficult.

She could hardly wait to tell Declan. In the morning he could find the entrance to the tunnels and begin to map out the caves, hopefully with the help of his buddies at the DEA. Surely that would allow the agency to put a stop to the illegal smuggling. In the meantime, she would wait out the storm with Grace. Maybe she would even have time to read through the other entries in Lucy's diary. Idly she wondered why

Declan wasn't back yet. He must have left more than four hours ago.

Was Jenna leading him on another wild goose chase?

Or was it more than that? She was halfway to the kitchen for candles when it occurred to her that something might have gone wrong. Declan claimed Jenna wasn't dangerous, but how could he know that for sure? And even if she wasn't, suppose somebody got wind that Jenna was talking to a federal agent. Blake's stomach clenched, forcing her to set Grace down and brace herself against the wall. Declan knew what he was doing. So why did she feel sick?

And why wasn't he back yet?

Outside, a bolt of lightning struck one of the pines in the yard. Sparks flew out in every direction as the tree swayed then fell, missing the house by a few yards.

Blake stood mesmerized in front of the window. Unlike Grace, she wasn't watching the flaming tree. Her eyes were raised to the arc of light shining from the lighthouse tower. It swept out and across the roiling sea, cutting across the thick layer of fog that blanketed the shore. Lighting the way.

She understood why Kelly had died.

Chapter 15

"Let me guess," Declan said, stooping as they made their way into an abandoned stone building at the end of the winding path they had followed for the past hour. "There isn't any important information."

"No shit, Sherlock," Jenna said, reaching up on the window sill behind her. She pulled the gun on him so fast he barely had time to register that he'd been wrong about her.

Dead wrong, he thought, not smiling at the silent pun. "So why am I here?"

"You know for a federal agent, you're kinda slow on the uptake."

His eyes darted toward the door, which she bolted shut. Whether he admitted he worked for the DEA or not made no difference at this point. Obviously he'd underestimated her. "How did you know?"

"Does it matter?" She lifted the trap door in the corner of the room and beckoned him to climb down into the dark opening. "Either way you die."

"I misread you," he said without moving. "I took you for someone with a conscience."

Jenna laughed, though there was sadness in her eyes that belied her youth. "A long time ago," she said, "I was. But that was before my brother's best friend offered me a line of coke for my sixteenth birthday. Things kinda went downhill from there, you might say." Gesturing with the gun toward the hole in the floor, she flashed him a cat-like smile. "Now either you climb down there and start walking or I have to shoot you here. Personally, if I were you I'd take my chances in the tunnel."

"Why not kill me now?"

She cocked the gun and aimed it at his heart. "Because I'd have to clean up afterward and that would annoy me," she said matter-of-factly. "But I will if I have to."

Reluctantly, Declan climbed into the shaft and found himself in a narrow tunnel lit with electric torches. The damp smell and the narrowness of the passageway fed into every claustrophobic dream he'd ever had. Cobwebs hung at regular intervals and from a distance he heard a peculiar screeching. Probably bats, he thought dispassionately, stumbling forward through the labyrinthine corridors that twisted ever deeper.

As if to assure him that she really would kill him, Jenna kept the barrel of the gun pressed into the small of his back. Jumping down after him, she fished a pair of handcuffs out of her pocket. "Hold your hands out in front of you."

"You don't need to do that."

"Don't play games with me."

With a sinking feeling, he followed her order as she secured the cuffs around his wrists. No gun, no light, nothing he could use to pick the lock on the cuffs. How the hell was he going to get out of this? How had he managed to underestimate her? She'd seemed like a ditzy waitress, a redheaded bombshell who was mixed up in something she didn't understand. Nothing more than that.

"Did your boyfriend put you up to this?" he tried. "Because you deserve a lot better than Chris McAllister."

Jenna actually snorted. "I said don't play games," she said. "That includes puerile attempts to use reverse psychology on me. And not that it's any of your business, but Chris is not my boyfriend."

"You could've fooled me," he said, forcing himself to remain calm as they negotiated through the dimly lit tunnels. "And I guess you fooled him too. If my memory serves me right, he nearly shot up a bunch of innocent people this morning because he thought you were two-timing him with me."

They came to a fork where two tunnels met and Jenna hesitated, but only for a moment before using the gun to force him to the right. He made a note of it. If he were ever planning on getting back he'd need to remember every turn. Otherwise he'd be wandering in the tunnels until he died.

"Quit stalling," she said, shoving him forward with the butt of the gun. "Chris is an idiot. If he had half a brain in his head he would've figured out you weren't the one I was cheating on him with."

He was glad she couldn't see his face. The more she talked, the more distracted she'd be. Keep her talking. "So who were you cheating on him with?"

"This isn't twenty questions," she said abruptly. "Keep moving."

When he turned back he saw she was looking at her watch. "I'm not making you late, am I?"

"Shut up."

"What difference does it make if you tell me who you're dating? You're going to kill me, right?"

"You bet your sweet ass I'm going to kill you. You've caused enough problems as it is."

He got the impression she was about to say more but stopped herself just in time. It wasn't even a question of luring her into talking. She wanted to talk. And the conviction that she was going to kill him was making her careless.

"You know, it's not too late," he said. "If you go through with this you're going to end up in prison for a long time. Whoever your boyfriend is, I doubt he's going to wait around for twenty years or so."

"Really?" Jenna asked sarcastically. "That's the best you can do?"

"Unlock the cuffs and maybe I'll be able to think better."

"Cute."

Declan stopped walking and stood his ground, regardless of the gun pressed into his back. "You've had a good thing going for a while now. But the DEA and the Coast Guard are onto you."

"Okay, that's enough chit-chat," she said, raising the gun and hitting him in the back of the head with it. He winced at the pain radiating from the back of his skull. A trickle of wetness ran down his scalp. He was bleeding. "Even if you kill me, it's only a matter of time until you get caught."

"Please tell me you don't actually think that line's going to scare me. If you had the slightest idea I was involved you never would've shown up without a weapon. Move. Now."

Despite his efforts to track their course, there wasn't much chance he'd ever find his way back on his own. The web of tunnels was as intricate as a spider's web and whoever dug them had done that on purpose. More than once he thought he could hear the crash of waves against the shore, but then the sound would fade again as they descended ever deeper into the side of the cliff.

Rum-running tunnels. Declan wasn't all that surprised. As soon as he realized the smuggling operation was most likely operating out of the area surrounding the lighthouse that possibility presented itself to him. In part, that had been what prompted him to finagle Blake into giving him a job. Then he could explore the grounds without raising suspicions.

But apparently he'd done more than just raise suspicions. Somehow he'd blown his cover. As he reached his hand out to steady himself, he touched water and wondered just how secure the tunnels actually were. After all, it had been nearly a century since smugglers built them to transport liquor from the Canadian boats to hiding spots so deep in the sides of the cliffs that even the Coast Guard couldn't hope to penetrate them. How long would the web of tunnels last before it collapsed?

After they'd walked for a half hour or so they came to a crossroads where several tunnels intersected. Jenna stopped and shone her flashlight down each tunnel, as if she wasn't sure which way to turn. Would it be better or worse for them if they got lost? Declan wasn't sure, but either way things didn't look good.

She pulled a piece of paper out of her jacket and held it under the light. "Left," she said, shoving him forward into one of the corridors that led down at a steep angle.

The sound of the surf was much louder now.

"We're not going swimming, are we?" he asked lightly, remembering that Jenna was wearing rubber boots. "Because if we are I left my suit back in the car."

"I wouldn't worry about it," she said. "Swimming is optional."

"But drowning isn't?"

"Now you're catching on. Too bad you didn't work things out a little earlier. For you and your girlfriend. And Kelly's brat. But hey, shit happens."

"Why not just kill me now and get it over with?"

Jenna's lips curved in a feline smile. "If you turn up with a gunshot to the head, even that idiot Santos is going to get suspicious. Not to mention all your buddies at the DEA."

"You think drowning's going to convince them my death was an accident?" Declan didn't bother to hide his skepticism. "Seems a little naïve, if you ask me."

She shrugged. "Give me a little credit. Of course they'll be suspicious. But even if they are, they won't be able to prove it was murder. And it will be a hell of a lot harder for them to trace the crime back to me."

His jaw tensed at her words. He of all people should know the effect drugs had on people. He'd worked with drug dealers and addicts for most of his career. Friends were gunned down for the price of a hit, children pimped out to dealers in exchange for drugs. Even his own mother turned into a monster. He still remembered the things she'd said to his grandmother— the accusations and the lies she told—anything so she could scrape up enough money for her next hit. Yet somehow it always surprised him. Part of him still believed his mother would turn up at his doorstep and embrace him, telling him over and over again how sorry she was. He'd dreamed it so often he could call up the scene with almost no effort. She was always young, always beautiful. Always she stood before him with haunted eyes and told him how much she loved him.

The funny thing was it was never going to happen like that. His mother had been dead for more than twenty years, since his seventh birthday. He ran into her room to wake her one morning and found her staring at the ceiling, glassy eyed with a rubber tube wrapped around her forearm and a needle jutting out of a collapsed vein.

Declan nearly laughed aloud as he walked on, descending ever deeper into the tunnel as the water lapped at his shins. For his whole life, human depravity always surprised him, even though he'd seen far more of it than most people.

The tunnel widened considerably and he realized the floor lead down to a stone staircase. Cool air washed over his face and he knew they must be near the entrance.

If only he could figure out a way to get the damn handcuffs off.

"Watch your head," Jenna said, her voice echoing strangely as they emerged into a narrow cave with a curved ceiling. A low beam with a rope and pulley attached stood just ahead of them. At the center of the cave a set of stairs rose nearly to the ceiling. Despite the fact that he knew why they were there, there was something incongruous about a set of stairs in the middle of an empty cave.

Next to the stairs was a long, deep hole cut into the side of the rock, probably an old storage area for cases of liquor. And for drugs. Lots of drugs, judging by the size of the hole.

Jenna picked up a flashlight from one of the cubby holes that lined the cave and swung its beam around the perimeter of the room. "All right," she said, shining the light into his face and then aiming it at a flat stretch of hardened sand on the far side of the cave. "Over there. Up against the wall. And make sure you're against the wall. I don't want to see your face."

He walked over to the wall and waited. Icy water seeped into his sneakers, pooling around his feet. If the tide were coming in, which he was sure it was, it would likely rise almost to the level of the upper stairs and the storage area. Which was well over his head.

She followed behind him, the water squelching under her rubber boots. Kneeling down, she bound his feet with a length of rope and tied it off with an expert sailor's knot.

Should he attempt to tackle her and make a run for the entrance to the cave? *If I do, she'll shoot.* If he'd doubted her capacity for violence before, he had no such illusions now. Jenna pressed the gun against his gut as she tightened the knot with her free hand. And there was another reason he couldn't escape, not yet. He needed the deal to happen. If he did manage to overpower her and get hold of her gun, the smugglers would know something was up and head back over the border.

He wouldn't get another chance to capture them. He needed to wait.

"Guess you've had some practice," he remarked, watching her pull the line taut. "Do they teach you that at Cuppa Cafe?"

"Who do you think takes my boyfriend's boat out

at night." She snickered, not bothering to disguise her contempt—though whether it was for him or McAllister he couldn't say. "The harbor master thinks Chris has been out hauling lobsters after hours. Or maybe he suspects him of something worse, who knows."

"Doesn't it bother you at all, that you might be implicating him in something he has no involvement with?"

She tightened the knot so that it pressed hard against his jeans, chafing his skin. Giving him a withering look as she spun him toward the wall, she asked, "Are we talking about the guy who shot up my place of employment and nearly killed me? If it hadn't been for Tyler I'd be dead right now."

He nodded, but said nothing. Something in his memory clicked into place.

"Don't turn around. Don't try to play the hero. Just stay put or I'll shoot you before you know what hit you." He heard her boots squelching toward the other side of the cave and wondered how long it would take for the tide to rise to its full height. Should he fight her now? Every minute he spent in the cave was another minute away from Blake and Grace. Declan hoped Blake would stay put until the deal was done. If she did, the two of them might have a chance.

If not...he shook his head to rid himself of the thoughts pounding into his brain. Blake wasn't the sort of person to sit back and watch things happen. Damn the woman.

Jenna hadn't been kidding about drowning him either. Considering the icy water was already lapping at his ankles he guessed it wouldn't be too long before he was going to be wholly submerged. Glancing over his shoulder, he saw that Jenna climb to the top of the stairs and begin pacing back and forth across the narrow strip of concrete that led to the storage area. She held a walkie-talkie to her ear and an AK-47 hung across her chest. After a minute or so she walked over to the storage area and hoisted herself up into it. From what he could make out, she was crouched low over what looked like some type of safe.

Outside, he could hear the storm raging. From the muted sound of the wind, he guessed they were maybe a hundred yards beneath the interior of the cliffs. Far enough from shore for a drug-running motorboat to evade detection, but close enough to make a run for it if things went bad.

How much time did he have?

Chapter 16

Blake hugged the curve of the tower as she inched toward the door at its base. The rain pelted her windbreaker and the wind blew her hair into her eyes. Declan's Glock pressed against her belly as she made her way to her destination. Casting a quick glance back at the house, she prayed Grace was all right. Her heart hammered in her chest when she remembered setting the crying child down in her crib and walking out the bedroom door. "I'll be back," she'd whispered as Grace raised desperate eyes to her. "I promise."

Did Kelly tell her daughter the same thing?

Maybe. Because hard as it was to leave Grace alone, she couldn't sit by and wait for the killer to turn up at the house. At least this way she would have the advantage of surprise. Wrapping her fingers around the door handle, she tugged. It swung open easily. Whoever was up in the tower hadn't counted on any visitors. The place was isolated enough as it was, but nobody would be out in a storm of this magnitude.

Which was exactly what they were counting on. It was risky to smuggle drugs in the middle of a storm, but on the whole it was a lot less dangerous than transporting contraband at a time when someone might pick up on unusual activity. And the lighthouse minimized the risk more than a little. Even if somebody did notice the light, they would most likely dismiss it. If anything, they might think the light was intended to help boats maneuver through the inclement weather. Which it was—the only problem was that the boats in question were owned by drug smugglers.

As she felt her way toward the spiral staircase at its center, her thoughts returned again to Grace. If only there was a way to call out or even text someone. But with the storm raging, communication with anyone in town was impossible. The lights in the keeper's house would be visible to whoever was in the tower, but she doubted they would cause much concern. After all, how much damage could a defenseless woman and a one-year-old cause?

More than you know. As she had stood watching the light shining from the tower Blake remembered two things. The name of her father's sailboat and the first six digits of the second string of numbers. She hadn't thought about the boat for years, barely even remembered they owned a boat for a summer. But when she closed her eyes she saw *Dorothy* painted on its side as clearly as if she was ten years old again. Ruby E. wasn't a guest, or even a drug. It was the name of a boat—the boat that would be crossing the Canadian border loaded with its party guests—Heroin, Crystal Meth, Cocaine.

After that, figuring out the rest was easy. The first six numbers in the sequence were 582400. August fifth—today's date. The meaning of the next four numbers was less clear. Blake ran through anything she could think of that related to the number 24 before it hit her. 2400, twenty four hundred hours—twelve p.m. military time. A look at her watch told her it was a quarter to midnight, fifteen minutes before the smugglers were due with their shipment. Now that she deciphered the message it seemed perfectly clear. How had it taken her so long it took her to work it out?

Who was Monk? She guessed he must be the person behind the smuggling operation. The person who sent the bomb. But the question was a riddle within a riddle or a series of Chinese boxes, each one opening to reveal another box. If Monk was the person behind the smuggling, then who was he? Was he a local, or somebody who lived far away? Could it be a woman?

Blake had no idea. But she was going to find out.

She switched her flashlight on then off again, just long enough to get an idea how far she was from the spiral staircase. The trap door far above was closed but Blake didn't want to risk using a light. As stealthily as she could she crept over to the base of the staircase and pulled herself onto the first metal step. The stairs were slick with moisture, making every step an accident about to happen. She climbed slowly, glad the darkness made it impossible to see how high she needed to ascend.

She tried not to think about what she was going to do once she got to the top. *Wing it,* she told herself. *You've got a gun, you can use if you have to.*

Right.

Anyway, she wasn't planning on any heroics. Her goal wasn't to capture Monk. It was simply to keep the smuggler up in the tower until the authorities arrived.

A small voice deep inside her asked "What authorities?" but she forced it into silence. She'd tried texting both Angie and the police before she left the house but neither attempt was successful. As a last ditch-effort, she left a note propped up on the mantel in the living room but if something happened to her wouldn't it be too late? Once Monk realized she understood what was going on it would be easy for him to get rid of her then disappear for a while. As for the Canadian suppliers, they would probably disappear as well. At least long enough for the authorities to forget about them and focus their efforts elsewhere. As she climbed Blake got the distinct impression she wasn't rising but falling.

No, she told herself firmly, *Declan will be back soon.* The Sheriff would be there. The Coast Guard and the DEA would be there. All she needed to do was keep Monk from getting away. How hard could that be? She'd seen it a thousand times on television and nothing ever went wrong in the end.

The voice made another attempt at protest but she squelched it. The truth was she hadn't been able to contact the sheriff or Angie. As for the Coast Guard, could she rely on them to detect the light in the tower and investigate? Somehow she doubted it. In a storm like this they had better things to do than investigate spooky lights. And Declan?

She didn't want to think about Declan.

He'll be here, she told herself resolutely.

The floor of the lantern room was much closer now, maybe twenty feet above her. Her left hand gripped the staircase railing so tightly it throbbed. As she drew closer to the top her legs started shaking. By the time she was within reach of the trap door, the shaking was so violent she could hardly go on climbing. Just a few more steps and she would be close enough to touch the door.

She was inches away when her foot slipped. Crying out in pain, she reached out and wrapped her arms around the center pole. The metallic clang that rang out across the hollow space seemed deafening, though it all happened so quickly Blake knew the sound was barely noticeable over the roaring wind. For several minutes all she could do was lay unmoving on the stairs, clinging to the pole as if her life depended on it.

Which it did. For the first time since she began climbing, she was glad she couldn't see anything. She didn't want to know how much of a drop it was to the concrete floor below. Breathing in ragged gasps, she raised herself up into a sitting position without letting go of the pole.

She took a step, and another. *Just keep going,* she told herself. If she turned back now it would mean more threats from Monk, or maybe much worse. ACCIDENTS HAPPEN. The shaking started up again as she recalled the message written on the inside of paper the bomb was wrapped in. If she didn't deal with Monk now she would be forced to live in fear. Neither she nor Grace would be safe until he was captured and the smuggling operation was shut down.

Taking a final step, Blake lifted her hands and placed both palms against the trap door. She had to move fast. If she hesitated, even for a second, she would lose the advantage of surprise. Silently counting down, she braced herself for what was about to happen.

Three, two, one.

Using all her strength to push the trap door upward, she heard the joints click into a lock position and leapt through the opening onto the lantern room floor. She pulled the Glock out and held it in front of her in what seemed like a single, continuous motion. There was a dreamlike quality to her actions, as if she were an actress in a movie. For the first time in her life she felt graceful, powerful, and in control.

The feeling only lasted about a second.

Tyler Burke—computer whiz kid and unexpected hero—sat in a folding chair next to the portable lens. He wore a baseball cap that obscured his face and his legs were crossed at the ankles. On a small TV table by his side was what appeared to be a portable radio, a laptop computer and a Coke. If it weren't for the fact that an AK-47 hung from a strap across his chest, the scene would have been strikingly ordinary. He held the machine gun loosely, almost casually, in both hands. "You're about an hour later than I expected you," he said, glancing at his watch. "But better late than never."

She held the gun steady. "Shoot me and you're going to die right along with me."

Tyler regarded her almost kindly. "Forgive me for asking," he said, "but have you ever even held a weapon before?"

Oddly, the shaking stopped. Blake was more frightened than she'd ever been in her life but for some reason she was able to mask it. She knew all too well what the consequences would be if she couldn't hide her feelings. "Ever heard of beginner's luck," she said evenly.

"Very good!" Tyler beamed like a parent whose child had just mastered the multiplication tables. "Bravo! If I could set down this gun, I'd burst into applause. But for the time being, I'm going to refrain. Until we get things sorted out."

"There's nothing to sort out. This is my property

and I want you off it."

He raised an eyebrow. "I'm afraid I can't do that. Don't get me wrong, it wasn't my intention to kill you. Agent Hunter is a different story. Killing federal agents comes with the territory and I can't trouble my conscience about them. But I have nothing personal against you *per se*. Granted, I've got a substantial amount of residual resentment toward you. I'll admit that. Still, I'd rather not kill you if I didn't have to."

If she shot him at this close range there was a good chance she would hit him, even if she hadn't ever fired a gun. But he was right about one thing—he would most certainly be able to fire off several rounds before he died. And she would die too. As he reached for his Coke and took a long swig, she cast around for a way to catch him off guard. It wouldn't be easy. Despite his casual demeanor, Tyler was watching her closely.

Like a cat watches a mouse, she thought. *Well, the cat doesn't always win. Not if he's outsmarted.* Of course, she hadn't exactly outdone herself when it came to cleverness.

Outside, the storm was still at its peak. Rain pelted the lantern room windows, making it impossible to see anything beyond the catwalk. Even the oscillating beam of light that shone from the portable lens illuminated nothing but gray mist. Bolts of lightning snaked across the sky at regular intervals, followed by thunder so loud it rattled the enormous windows.

"Why don't you have a seat?" he asked, setting down his soda and glancing at his computer screen. "We've still got a bit of a wait."

Blake didn't move or lower the Glock, despite the fact that her hand ached. "Just answer me one thing."

"Oh, I very much doubt it will be just one. I mean, here you are with the mastermind—there must be so many things you want to clear up. But go ahead, shoot." He gave a tight little laugh. "Excuse the pun."

Despite the dripping irony in his tone, it was impossible not to notice the light that flared in Tyler's eyes when he mentioned the term mastermind. His ego, she realized with a start, was colossal. Could she use that somehow?

She let go of the gun and watched it skitter across the floor before sitting down cross-legged on the wooden floor. She wasn't sure what the hell she was doing, but an idea was beginning to form. "You're already filthy rich," she said, trying to imbue her words with as much awe as she could stomach, "and incredibly successful. You travel the world and eat expensive caviar and chat it up with a bunch of geniuses on a regular basis. You've got pretty much everything you could ever want without having to even try. So why risk it? Why get involved in this kind of thing when you don't really gain anything from it?"

"Good girl." Tyler watched the gun skid to a stop and nodded in a pleased sort of way. "Not only did you acknowledge your helplessness, but you stated the problem succinctly and convincingly. At least your legal background's coming in handy. Not much use for it up here, is there?"

"Looks like you read me pretty well." She could almost see his ego inflating with every compliment. His hold on the machine gun slackened. He'd let down his guard. Not by much, but it was a start.

He leaned to one side and lifted up a transmitter attached to the radio. Mumbling a series of phrases in

French into it, he listened as a mix of static and garbled words erupted into the room. She didn't speak the language, but from the tone of his voice she gathered that things were proceeding according to plan. When Tyler turned his attention back toward her, he seemed euphoric to the point of mania.

All the better.

She edged closer toward him but stopped when he raised the gun. "Are you going to answer my question or aren't you?" she asked. A little too belligerent, but she couldn't help herself.

Her tone apparently annoyed him. Pressing his lips together, he fidgeted with the lens before returning his eyes to her. "Have you ever walked into a room and wondered if maybe you weren't better than everybody else?" he asked. Not waiting for an answer, he went on, "I doubt it. Before I even researched you I knew you were from money. You look rich, you talk rich, you think rich. I, on the other hand, walk into a room and wonder if it's immediately obvious."

"That what's obvious?" she prompted when his voice trailed off.

His eyes settled on her. She hadn't noticed how green they were until that moment. They were eerily focused, as if he knew exactly what she was planning. "Do you know who had the highest I.Q. ever recorded at my high school?"

"Let me guess," she said. "You."

"I graduated at sixteen and got through Yale in three years. I owned my first company at twenty-one and by the time I was twenty-six I was a multi-millionaire. Right now I'm richer than a handful of third-world countries."

Despite herself, Blake couldn't stop listening to his story. Leaning forward with her arms resting on her knees, she studied his unlined face, his chiseled features. He wasn't lying, she was pretty sure of that. "So what's the point of all this?" she asked. "With every drug deal you set up, people are going to die."

He shrugged. "People always die. We're all going to eventually. And if drugs give people a little happiness—a high that takes them over the rainbow, who am I to stand in the way of that?"

"You're doing more than stepping out of the way," she said. "You're making it happen. You make drugs sound like candy bars. But people are dying from the stuff you ship into this country every day. Look at what happened to Kelly."

At the mention of people dying, Tyler's expression barely changed. He looked like he had the first day she met him in town—cold, gorgeous in a glittering sort of way, removed from everything happening around him. But the mention of Kelly's name shook him. A surge of adrenaline rushed through her and it was all she could do to avert her gaze so he wouldn't see the triumph in her eyes.

She could beat him.

"Kelly didn't die of a drug overdose," he said. The machine gun rested against his thighs now, the strap across his chest slack.

She turned her gaze back toward him. "No," she said slowly. "You killed her."

He licked his lips uncomfortably. "It had to be done. Kelly hacked into Jenna's email and showed up with Grace one night when Jenna was up here working the light. Predictably, Jenna panicked, but she at least managed to get rid of Kelly on her own that time. Mainly because she threatened to kill the kid and Kelly freaked."

Recalling Santos' condescending treatment at the sheriff's office, Blake couldn't help feeling a small surge of triumph. So she really had heard a baby crying that night. And Kelly probably dropped the pacifier in her rush to get Grace away from the lighthouse. *But why would Kelly have risked her child's life like that in the first place?* It still didn't make sense. Unless Kelly wanted back in. Unless she couldn't beat her drug habit. For some reason, that thought bothered her. Almost against her will, Blake forced herself to ask the next question. "Was Kelly trying to convince Jenna to let her back in on the smuggling ring?"

Tyler made the sound of a buzzer. "Negative," he said in a boisterous game-show-host voice.

"Then why would Kelly would show up out here?" Blake persisted, despite the fact that Tyler seemed to be deliberately baiting her. "Angie said she was clean."

"She *was* clean, for once in her life. That was the problem apparently. Seems she wanted to confront Jenna about Chris McAllister of all things. She'd gotten it into her head that Jenna convinced Grace's daddy to involve himself in our little scheme and she didn't want that. She'd introduced Jenna to me and got the bizarre idea that Jenna had done the same for Chris. God knows why, but the girl still loved the idiot. Didn't want him to get mixed up in anything unsavory. And maybe she thought if Jenna and Chris weren't working together they'd break up. Who knows what went through her tiny little brain. She showed up and kept threatening to go the police, you know the spiel. Didn't even want money, the little idiot. She could've used it to get that kid of hers into modeling like she always talked about. But apparently she decided she knew right from wrong. She was going to try and stop the big bad guy all by herself. Even brought the kid along to try to convince Jenna what was at stake." At this, he couldn't help breaking into a high-pitched giggle. Apparently the thought of anyone appealing to Jenna's sense of sympathy struck him as preposterous.

Blake had been stalling for time, but now she was almost wholly focused on the story. "But she wasn't killed that night," she said, working it through. "She came back the next night. Without Grace."

Tyler nodded, leaning back in his chair. "Stupid, stupid move. If only she'd stayed away after that first night. But she wasn't going to give up. Oh no, not our Kelly."

Despite his air of nonchalance, Burke was edgy. *It bothers him,* Blake realized, somewhat surprised that anything fazed him. "So you pushed her off the tower."

It wasn't a question.

Tyler sighed. "Jenna talks a good game but underneath the veneer she is one scared little girl. Couldn't take care of things herself so she locked Kelly out on the catwalk and waited for somebody else to do the dirty work."

He doesn't want to talk about Kelly's death. That much was obvious. "You never killed anybody before, did you?" she guessed. "You let the drugs do that. Or the people who worked for you. But you never actually killed anybody. Not before Kelly."

He made a dismissive gesture. "Nice theory."

"And Jenna wrote the suicide note," she continued,

fighting the urge to point out that he hadn't denied that she was right about Kelly being his first murder.

At that, he emitted another clipped laugh, devoid of amusement. "To be honest, I knew I should've killed her as soon as she wanted to stop working for me."

"Then why didn't you?"

Tyler shrugged but she pressed on, knowing she'd struck a vulnerable spot.

"Did you care for Kelly? You did, didn't you?"

His contempt was palpable. "Kelly?" he said, unable to keep the disdain out of his voice. "At least give me credit for having a modicum of taste. If I made any mistake at all, it was in underestimating how annoyingly persistent the girl could be. All in the name of some brat she probably didn't even know the father of. She was a very weak opponent overall. Almost not worth the effort. The only surprising thing was that she figured out how to get into Jenna's email. That, at least, was something I didn't predict."

For some reason Blake was oddly relieved to learn that Grace's mother died trying to do the right thing. Some day—if she ever made it out of the lighthouse tower alive—she would tell Grace how brave her mother was. Still, she couldn't quite believe McAllister hadn't done anything besides date the wrong woman. "So Chris wasn't involved at all," she said doubtfully.

"Oh, God, no," Tyler said. "If he weren't so stupid I wouldn't mind having his help—or at least his boat. But he can't control his temper. As I'm sure you're well aware, considering his little outburst this afternoon."

Her head swam. Even now, certain things didn't make sense. "But you saved him," she said, rubbing the bridge of her nose. "He was going to kill himself and you talked him out of it."

"I would've liked to have him out of the way," he admitted. "But I didn't want to risk him blowing Jenna away and ruining tonight's plans. Or myself, of course."

Of course. "He could've turned on you."

Tyler seemed to consider this. "I doubt it. Chris has three primary settings—anger, selfishness, and lust. Once I convinced him his life was going to hell if he pulled that trigger, he collapsed like a house of cards. Perfectly predictable. Ever play video games, Ms. Cartwright?"

Predictable. There was that word again. With dawning horror, Blake understood why Tyler risked everything when he didn't need to. She also understood how he could kill without compunction. To him, life had somehow morphed into one giant videogame. Playing online didn't give him enough of a jolt anymore, so he needed to take the game to a higher level. As she watched him caress the machine gun in his lap she wondered if it was real to him at all. Did he ever have any guilt? Any regrets? Or was it all just another rush, the same kind he experienced when he blew up an opponent on the screen?

The walkie-talkie next to the radio crackled to life before he could answer. Picking it up and holding it to his ear, he got up and walked to the front of the lantern room, being careful not to turn his back on Blake. In a low voice, he muttered a few sentences.

He spoke in English this time, she was sure of it, even though he was talking too softly for her to hear what he was saying. When he sat again he spent a few minutes on the computer before returning his attention to her. Had something gone wrong?

He didn't seem all that upset but some of the euphoria went out of his expression as he listened to whoever was on the other end. Mumbling something inaudible, he turned to gaze out at the horizon. She followed his gaze but could see nothing but darkness. No ship, no lights, nothing but rain and endless fog.

He hadn't turned his back on her. And the AK-47 was still slung across his chest. But his attention was on whatever was on the far side of the storm, not on her.

Now or never.

She reached for the gun, stretching her fingertips until they closed around its barrel, hardly daring to breathe, and pulled the trigger. Tyler spun around at the sound of the shot, lifting his weapon and spraying bullets across the tower as she dove for cover behind the chest where the lens had been.

Shattered glass rained down, catching in her hair and skittering across her back. Blake crouched in a ball behind the chest, praying she'd hit him but knowing she hadn't. The only sound was the screaming of the wind, flowing into the tower through gaping holes in the thick glass windows.

Blake crept to the edge of the chest and tried to raise the gun with both hands. She was shaking badly, so badly any attempt to get off another shot would be farcical.

She was going to die.

Well, she might as well make a grand exit.

She took a deep breath and managed to steady her hands enough to hold the gun out in front of her. As she rose from behind the chest and pulled the trigger, everything went black.

Chapter 17

"You know, I really wish you hadn't done that," Jenna said.

As Declan stood at the top of the stairs inside the cave, he realized he'd misjudged her yet again. She didn't look frightened or shocked or even angry. She simply looked annoyed.

Well, she wasn't the only one. It took him the better part of an hour to use a broken piece of glass to sever the rope that bound his feet. Not only had he cut his foot locating the shard, but he'd been forced to use his manacled hands to cut the rope underwater. By the time the rope finally split the water was up to his waist. He was half frozen, his hands were cuffed, and the gash in his foot bled profusely but he didn't plan on letting Jenna get the best of him a second time.

Jenna set down the briefcase in her left hand and reached for the gun stashed under her belt. She moved lightning fast and the cocked gun was level with his chest in less time that it took for him to kick the briefcase off the platform into the dark water below.

Her glance flicked to the case as it sank. "You think you're so smart," she said angrily, keeping the gun level. "Now you can go in and get it."

"I don't think so." He gave her a slow smile. "Though I sure hope that briefcase is waterproof." He stood unmoving with the barrel of the gun trained on him, trying to look puzzled. "I suppose you can tell them to just give you the drugs and let the money dry when they get back across the border."

For several seconds the only sound was the water sloshing against the base of the stairway. Declan watched impassively as Jenna's rage reached a boiling point. She didn't want to kill him, but she wasn't about to let the water ruin thousands of dollars either. "Just get the damn briefcase."

He pursed his lips and pretended to consider her command. "No," he said simply.

"You better move and you better do it right now," she shouted, brandishing the gun. "Or you will die. Blake's already dead and there's no reason you shouldn't join her."

Her words knocked the wind out of him. She was lying, she had to be. He could see the stealthy look of superiority in her face—the one that said, *I know exactly what I can use to win, and I'm going to do it.* Declan closed his eyes for long enough to convince himself that it wasn't true.

"I doubt it," he said launching himself at her, knocking her onto back as she released the trigger and the shot went wild. She got off another shot as they struggled but it ricocheted off the cave walls, echoing crazily.

Jenna screamed as the gun slipped from her grasp and tottered on the edge of the landing. He pinned her down against the concrete and she flailed at him, scratching his face with her nails then kneeing him in the crotch. Declan winced in pain, rolling off her and shielding himself from another blow with his manacled hands. She was on her feet again, moving toward the edge of the platform with startling speed.

Her hand closed around the gun just as he rose to his feet and threw himself at her ankles with all his strength. The gun sailed in an arc and splashed into the water as Jenna reeled back, her arms flailing wildly in an attempt to keep her balance on the edge of the platform.

Her eyes widened in fear. He read the recognition in her gaze. She knew she was going to fall. Reaching out with both hands, she grabbed onto his shirt and pulled him over the edge with her.

Even after spending an hour soaked to the waist, the shock of the cold was agonizing. An enormous splash sounded as they both hit the water at the same time and the sea closed over them. He could sense Jenna's body beside him and opened his eyes but saw nothing but blackness. Before he could surface her hands clamped over his head, forcing him down as he thrashed to loosen her grasp.

Twisting away from her, he came up for air, inhaling enormous mouthfuls as if he'd never breathed before. The water was at chest-level now for him but Jenna was submerged nearly to her neck. He took one last great gulp of air and raised his arms high over his head, launching at Jenna a final time. She guessed his intent immediately and turned toward the mostly submerged staircase in an attempt to scramble to safety.

Jenna had reached the top stair when he brought his arms over her head and pulled his handcuffs up against her neck. She clawed at his arms, frantically trying to loosen his iron grip, then slackened abruptly.

When he released his hold she was ready. Springing backward into the water she let her body fall onto his like a dead-weight, not even trying to save herself. *She's trying to kill both of us,* he thought in amazement as they sank below the surface.

The cave pool was jagged with rocks. A dozen sharp points pressed into his back and his thighs as the two of them hit bottom, the impact even more painful because of Jenna's weight on top of him. With a dawning sense of horror, Declan realized that what he thought were rocks weren't rocks at all. He was lying directly on top of a human skeleton. Forcing himself not to panic at the sensation of bones scraping against his back, he braced himself then pushed up as hard as he could.

There was no time to breathe when he reached the surface. Jenna was thrashing like a wild animal in his grip, her screams bouncing off the walls in an almost unbearable cacophony. Something clicked into place and he began strangling her methodically, efficiently as an assassin on automatic pilot. He shut out the sound of her screams then pulled the chain between the cuffs up against her neck and held it there until he felt her go slack in the water.

After that it was only a matter of seconds until he hauled her up the stairs and raised his arms over her head to free her from his grip. He watched her limp body collapse onto the landing and feared for a moment he really had killed the girl. A deep red mark cut across her neck where the handcuff chain had cut into it. He knelt over her and searched for a pulse, relaxing slightly when he found it.

There wasn't much time.

Unzipping her jacket pocket and clasping his fingers around the key to the cuffs, Declan freed himself and stood rubbing his raw wrists just long enough to see Jenna's eyelids flutter awake then close.

He didn't want her to die. But he sure as hell didn't want a repeat of their wrestling match. Pulling her arms behind her back, he clamped on the cuffs and dragged her toward the storage area. He spotted a coil of rope at the edge of the opening. After binding Jenna's feet, he took one deep breath and hoisted her up onto the rocky shelf. He tried not to think about the fact that her carelessness in fastening the handcuffs in front rather than in back of him saved his life. He'd made a rookie mistake by misreading her and was damn lucky to be alive. But he had other things to worry about.

How long until the smugglers arrived?

He guessed it would be soon. The level of the water was almost to the top of the stairwell now and the cave was half submerged. A flat-bottomed motorboat could easily dock inside and then retreat without touching the jagged rocks. It would be a matter of minutes to haul the cases of drugs up the staircase and stack them deep into the carved out area in the side of the cave. Jenna and whoever she was working with could ship the drugs out via the tunnel that night or they could leave the contraband there until later. Now that he'd seen the caves he understood exactly how the operation worked. They waited for heavy fog or, even better, a full-blown storm, then used the tower to radio to their cohorts on the other side of the Canadian border. Once the drugs were en route to the cave whoever was up in the tower could use the portable lens to communicate with the dealers and make-sure they wouldn't lose their bearings as they approached the rocky coastline.

It was a perfect setup.

No wonder the smugglers wanted Blake out of the picture. How long had they been running drugs out of Eagle Point? The DEA had been tracking a major operation in the vicinity for the past two to three years, which coincided with the death of the previous owner. With a vacant lighthouse and a clear stretch of coast, not to mention endless tunnels and caves just waiting to be used again, it was surprising nobody thought of it sooner. He didn't know how much money was involved, but he guessed it must run into the millions.

Millions. With a groan, he remembered the fallen briefcase and gingerly lowered himself back into the freezing water. How the hell was he going to find a black briefcase in black water? Wading to the spot where he thought it fell, he used his feet to search the bottom. The water was up to his neck now and the flashlight was essentially useless. He'd gone about three feet when his foot hit something hard.

With a whoop of triumph, he reached down and lifted the case out of the water. It was soaked and Declan knew the money inside would be too, but he didn't care.

All he needed was the case.

He set it down on a table at the corner of the landing when he heard the sound of a motor. The briefcase had a combination lock on it and he could only hope that he'd overpower the smugglers before they realized he didn't know how to open it. Of course it would have been a lot easier if Jenna hadn't thrown the gun into the water. There were other guns, he was certain, but he didn't have time to figure out where. A quick inspection of the storage area with a flashlight revealed nothing and he wasn't sure where else to look. So he would have to count on being able to use their own weapons against them. Which might be a problem, considering he wasn't exactly at his best.

There was another problem as well.

If Jenna woke up he was in trouble.

He stood with his back to the wall as the motorboat appeared inside the cave. The man at the wheel cut the engine and looked across at him, his expression wary. Clearly, he expected Jenna not Declan. Another was positioned at the back of the boat, sitting a few feet from about a dozen heavy crates. Both of them were armed.

Three outboard motors lined the back of the cigarette boat, which was narrow and made of fiberglass. The name *Ruby E.* curved across the back of the boat. He wondered who it really belonged to, or if it was in fact owned by the smugglers. Would the name be painted over once it returned to its destination across the border?

Though he knew its purpose, Declan couldn't help admiring the beauty of the boat's construction and smooth lines. The fiberglass and the speed made the boat almost impossible to detect by radar, which was exactly why smugglers used it. It was fast—able to reach fifty knots in a matter of seconds—and it was easy to maneuver. Ideally suited for transporting thousands of dollars of contraband and making a clean escape.

"Not this time," Declan said under his breath.

Lifting the case off the table, he approached the edge of the landing, just at the point where the top stairs met the platform. He smiled as warmly as he could manage and held out his hand. "Bon soir, mes amies," he said. "Welcome."

The first man smiled back and his eyes flicked hungrily to the briefcase, but his expression held deep skepticism. "Who are you," he said from the boat, his eyes coming to rest on Declan's soaked clothing and scratched face. "Where's the girl?"

With an inward sigh, he realized he wasn't going to fool them. Jumping down into the boat with his leg straight out in front of him, he kicked the gun out of the first man's hand and caught him in a strangle-hold before the second registered what was happening. With the efficiency of a trained fighter, Declan caught hold of the man's arm and pressed down on the elbow, snapping the bone and knocking the wind out of him. He leapt up onto the crates and grabbed the ankles of the second, bracing himself to take the impact of the man's fall. A surge of euphoria shot through him as he grabbed the submachine gun and cradled it in his arm. Taking aim on the smuggler at his feet, he got off two quick shots, one at each knee. The man screamed in pain as the other came to, just in time for Declan to shoot out both his knees as well. He scooped up the second weapon without thinking and set it out of reach.

Hauling the two men up onto the landing took longer than he planned and Declan cursed at the wasted time. With Blake out at the keeper's house while a killer radioed instructions from the tower, anything could happen.

He didn't want to lose her. The realization that he might was far worse than anything he'd encountered during the past hour. Had Jenna been telling the truth? He prayed she hadn't. He needed to get to the lighthouse and to do it fast.

Fortunately, the solution to his problem was only a few feet away.

Jumping down into the cigarette boat, he turned the key in the ignition and smiled grimly as all three motors roared to life.

****

Blake stood frozen in the darkened lighthouse tower. Wind tore through the gaping holes in the lantern room windows, whipping her hair into her eyes and making it impossible to see.

Not that she could have seen anyway. The tower was pitch black, an impenetrable darkness. Holding the gun out in front of her, she wondered again if she were going to die.

It didn't look good.

On the other hand, if she couldn't see a thing then neither could Tyler. As long as she didn't move or make any noise she was safe. As safe as she could be, considering she was a hundred feet above a roiling sea in a shot-up lighthouse tower with a *bona fide* evil genius.

She nearly laughed.

"Come out, come out, wherever you are," Tyler called softly. On the surface, his voice was smooth as ever but beneath the disdainful tone was something truly frightening. Rage. With a flash of insight, Blake realized that Tyler wasn't oblivious to the pain he caused. She was part of an elaborate game but he wasn't so deluded that he didn't know the deaths were real.

She held her breath, willing herself not to move. Her entire body rebelled at the effort—goosebumps covered her arms and her stomach churned. The wind felt as if it was raking its fingers across her skin and gusts of rain hit her back. Her teeth chattered but she gritted them together, clenching her jaw so tightly the pain radiated across her face and down her neck.

"I know you're there," he whispered seductively. "There's no point in drawing this out any longer than we have to. We both know you're going to lose."

Blake thought of all the times she'd heard that before heading into court. She'd lost cases, but she won her share of them, too. She won a hell of a lot.

But that didn't mean she was going to win this time. A flicker of hope flared then died like a burnt match. She needed to think. Take a chance and shoot in the direction of his voice? Or draw out the silence for as long as she could?

She tried to consider each choice rationally. It was impossible. She couldn't think rationally, not under those circumstances. She would have to trust her instincts. She drew in her breath and closed her eyes.

Stay where she was or take a chance?

"Too bad about the baby," Tyler said into the darkness, his voice low and caressing. "I'm not altogether fond of infanticide. But on the other hand, I'll be doing her a favor. Life sucks. And then you die."

Blake knew he was playing her. He was deliberately baiting her, secretly laughing at her emotionalism and her naive stupidity. Yet she couldn't stop herself, couldn't stand there listening to him talk about Grace for one more second.

She stepped out from behind the chest and spoke. Her voice was calm and startlingly clear.

"You're right about one thing," she told him,

immediately aware of the sound of him moving toward her. "Life does suck for you. And now you're going to die."

She raised the gun and fired several shots at the sounds. A flash of light pierced the black, illuminating Tyler's pale face. His eyes were fiercely triumphant yet the rest of his expression was oddly self-contained, as if he'd just forced an opponent into checkmate in a friendly game of chess. Or gunned down a particularly irritating avatar in World of Warcraft.

Bullets shot through the glass and she watched in amazement as cracks webbed across it. For a second she stared, awed at its intricacy. She watched in amazement as the entire window shattered.

Glass rained onto the room and she covered her head with her hands, shutting her eyes tightly and letting the gun drop. Wind tore into the tower, its force pushing her to the floor.

Where was Tyler?

At the moment the window shattered Blake thought she heard a cry, but all was quiet now. She grabbed the gun. "Tyler—" she called to him, forcing down her fear. "If you're going to kill me then you'd better hurry up. Because I'm getting just a little bit bored with you."

On the far side of the lantern room came the sound of a man scrambling to his feet. "Likewise," he hissed, moving toward her.

She raced to the sound, knocking into him and trying to hit the side of his head with the gun. He was stronger than he looked. Despite his wiry appearance, his arms were surprisingly powerful. Declan's gun flew out of her hand, but a sharp jab with her elbow caused him to drop his weapon as well.

Which was when she realized they were directly in front of the shattered window.

The intensity of the wind was beyond anything she'd ever experienced. Suddenly she wasn't fighting Tyler anymore. She was hanging onto to him trying to stop the two of them from hurtling through the opening onto the narrow catwalk.

"Now this," he said maniacally, diving onto the catwalk and dragging her along with him, "is one triple A game."

She fell backwards and slid across the catwalk, still staring up at him. His tangled hair hung down around him in wild disarray and his eyes were feverish with excitement. The wetness of the metal seeped through her jacket and the rain pelted down onto her face. Far below, the crash of the waves against the rocks was deafening.

Blake realized she was crying.

With the strange clarity that comes only once in a lifetime, she realized that she wasn't crying because she was going to die. She was crying because Grace was going to grow up an orphan, bounced from foster home to foster home as Declan had been. She was crying because she was never going to have the chance to tell Declan she loved him.

Just like Lucy, she thought as Tyler grabbed onto her jacket and lifted her head a few inches off the catwalk. She flailed and kicked at him, reaching for the railing above her. They skidded and slid across the catwalk as if it were coated with ice.

Suddenly there was nothing under her head and shoulders but air. The only thing stopping her from falling onto the rocks below was Tyler's own weight.

He sat with his legs on either side of her thighs, his hands clutching her jacket.

She wondered almost idly if they would both fall. Now that death was a certainty, not a possibility, she felt cut off from her emotions. It was as if she were watching someone else act out the scene of her death. Some actress in a movie maybe. Not her.

"I'm sorry, Grace," she whispered, closing her eyes.

What would it be like, plummeting through darkness?

She waited for everything to fall away, for the solidity of the metal to disappear from under her. Tyler's weight lifted off her and she knew he'd tired of the game.

Now it was time for him to annihilate the enemy.

But instead of hearing a euphoric cry of triumph, his battle cry turned into a scream of fear. When she opened her eyes Tyler lay a yard away, collapsed against one of the upright railings on the catwalk. Declan was rushing toward her when Tyler struggled to his feet and attacked him from behind.

Swinging around toward him, Declan shook him off his back in a single motion. Tyler went for the throat, wrapping his arms around his neck and pulling them back against the railing. Declan's arms went to Tyler's, clamping around them and slowly forcing them down. He loomed over the smaller man, breathing hard.

"You're going to jail," Declan said matter-of-factly, gripping Tyler's arm and shoving him down hard onto the catwalk. "Enjoy the view while you can."

Tyler nodded and flashed him an odd, crooked smile in return. Blake watched in terrified fascination as he swung his legs over the side of the catwalk. With a final turn of his head, his gaze came to rest on her. "Game over," he said, using both hands to propel himself into the empty air.

There was no scream. She waited for one, but it never came.

He was simply not there anymore.

Declan rushed back across the catwalk, standing above her and calling her name. Blake heard him as if he were calling to her from a great distance. His face, she noticed, was etched with anguish.

Belatedly, she understood why.

She was already sliding off the catwalk.

He was too late. What an odd way to say goodbye, she thought. "I love you," she tried to say as she slipped over the edge. But her voice wouldn't work.

Her hand hit one of the upright railings. Dazed, she realized she'd grabbed onto it. It was slick with rain. She wouldn't be able to hold on for long. Her other hand flailed uselessly at her side. Try as she might, she couldn't raise it high enough to catch hold of the edge of the catwalk. The pain was too intense. She must have hit her hand during her fight with Tyler but couldn't remember when.

Declan knelt before her, struggling to pull her to safety. "Give me your hand," he shouted as he reached out to her.

"I can't," she said in a whisper but her words were lost in the wind.

If she let go, she was going to fall. There wouldn't be enough time for her. But she couldn't hold on much longer. Declan was screaming, begging her to give him her hand, but she could barely hear him. It was as if she were watching TV with the volume muted.

She let go. Suddenly there was nothing beneath her, only a rush of air. She opened her mouth to scream but no sound came out.

Declan's hand caught hers and held it in an unbreakable grasp. He lifted her a few inches, just high enough to maneuver his arm around her. When he pulled her up onto the catwalk, she collapsed against him. Taking her into his arms, he held her so tightly she wasn't sure whose body was shaking.

"I thought I lost you," he said, nuzzling her hair. "Promise me you'll never leave me."

"I thought you didn't want to settle down," she said, gazing up into his dark eyes.

"I don't," he said, planting a messy kiss on the tip of her nose. "But it seems I can't live without you."

Epilogue

One year later

Blake walked out onto the front porch with Grace in her arms. The sleeping toddler snuggled against her, happily enmeshed in the snares of a dream. The rising sun cast its rays across the water, staining the ocean shades of deep crimson and orange. At the end of the jetty the lighthouse formed a dark silhouette against the streaked sky.

Declan stood with his back to her, holding a sketch pad. At the sound of her footsteps he turned and held his hand out to her. She took it and smiled, savoring its roughness and its warmth. A glance at the sketchpad told her that he was at it again—drawing yet another version of the renovations. Over the past month he must have drawn and redrawn the keeper's house a thousand times. After having lived with him for the past year, she was more certain than ever that renovation was his true passion.

So maybe he hadn't lied to her the day they met, when he'd described himself as a guy who renovated houses. He still hadn't given up his work for the DEA—and if she were honest with herself she'd have to concede he probably never would—but over the past few months he'd taken on on a different role at the agency. Maybe his boss sensed his growing reluctance to spend long periods of time away from Eagle Point, or maybe he realized what everybody else knew all along: that at this point in his career Declan's expertise would best be put to use training new agents. Nobody was better at his job than Declan, but with him overseeing training there were a lot more outstanding agents in the field.

"I thought I'd find you here," she said, setting Grace down in one of the Adirondack chairs that lined the porch. "Don't you ever sleep?"

He leaned forward to kiss her, then stooped to brush Grace's pale hair with his lips. "Guilty as charged," he said. "Just thought I'd try to get some ideas down on paper before the chaos begins."

Her smile blossomed into laughter. "That's not fair," she protested. "I've got everything perfectly under control."

She didn't, of course. Since The Lighthouse Inn opened a month before, her life had never been quite so busy. She advertised the inn as a place where guests could "get away from it all" and hoped to tap into city dwellers' desire to flee the stress of urban life. Aside from Henry—whose visit with his fiancée was far less awkward than she could ever have imagined—few of the guests genuinely wanted to "get away" from anything.

Henry had driven up from the city the previous week with his fiancée, a tax attorney with a penchant for Brahms and freshwater pearls. The fiancée seemed curious but hadn't asked Blake a thing. Henry hadn't spoken of the past either, other than to apologize for sending her an IPod Nano that nearly ended her life. "I knew I should have gone with the gift card," he remarked sheepishly after he'd seen the IPod on the kitchen counter. "I nearly got you killed."

Of course it hadn't been Henry who nearly got her killed. Tyler Burke had the monopoly on that one. According to Jenna's testimony, Tyler substituted his own version of a "welcoming present" for Henry's package on the porch in hopes that Blake's death—or her departure—would leave the place uninhabited once more. Much as she tried not to think about Tyler, he had a way of inserting himself into her thoughts.

Perhaps if she hadn't opened the inn he would have faded more quickly from memory. But Tyler, Blake soon learned, was what really interested her guests. She'd spent most of the past four weeks trying to dodge questions about her role in bringing down the East Coast's biggest drug smuggling ring. She also spent a considerable portion of time deflecting their inquiries about the ghost of Lucy Stone.

Much to their disappointment, her guests hadn't gotten much information out of her. Nor had anybody else. Despite a slew of offers, she decided to let the story of her near-death experience to remain a vague rumor rather than a made-for-TV movie. She also passed on the offers to publish Lucy Stone's diary and even thwarted the dogged efforts of *America's Haunted Places* to do a show about the lighthouse and the network of rum-running tunnels that crisscrossed the property. More than a few brave souls set out into the caves in search of Billy Stone's skeleton but at least none of them wanted any information out of her. Aside from her testimony against Jenna, Blake had said almost nothing at all about the case in public.

Jenna, on the other hand, was quite the celebrity. If

the rumors were correct, the former waitress was penning a tell-all account of her role in the former smuggling ring as well as an exposé on Tyler Burke. Whether the foxy redhead would profit from the sale of the books was open to debate. Kelly's stepfather—a recovering alcoholic who appeared out of the woodwork once the trial was underway—was suing for damages and hoped to gain the right to the profits from anything Jenna published about the drug smuggling operation. According to Angie, who was the town expert on the matter, he was also attempting to get ahold of a good chunk of Tyler Burke's multi-million-dollar empire. Shockingly, Burke died without leaving a will and no one came forward to claim kinship with him.

The more Blake thought about it the more Tyler puzzled her. On the surface, he'd appeared to have it all—wealth, intelligence, a beautiful home, the ability to travel anywhere in the world. But as the case went on and no one surfaced, not even a distant cousin, she fought the impulse to feel just a little bit sorry for the man. If there was someone, anyone at all, they would have come forward, if for no other reason than sheer greed. With every passing week she became more convinced that Tyler Burke had never been who he said he was. Like the gamer he had been, he'd taken on an identity that likely had little to do with the boy he grew up as. He'd mentioned a father who worked in a factory and Blake kept half-expecting the man to appear in town one day, beaten, grief stricken—and even a little envious of all the money his son amassed in such a short time.

As the weeks turned to months Blake came to

understand that no father would appear. She wondered if even the little Burke told her were true. Was even his working class father part of the fantasy world he spun for himself? Her instinct told her he probably was.

Had anyone ever been quite so alone? Had Tyler's isolation led him to become so enmeshed in the virtual world that he lost track of the real one? Or did his obsession with computers cause his isolation? Was he just another "mad scientist" whose gift for technology somehow eclipsed his sense of morality?

The questions were endless. And unanswered. She supposed she would never know the truth about him. Aside from the fact that his drug smuggling operation was merely an extension of operations he already oversaw in Asia and South America, his life was a mystery. Which, according to Declan, was why he'd always sensed something familiar about the smuggling ring. He'd been investigating Burke for a lot longer than the few months he spent in Eagle Point. He just hadn't known it.

As the criminal trial concluded and the civil trial got underway, Blake also wondered if more of Kelly's relatives might turn up but aside from the girl's stepfather nobody else came forward. She wasn't sure whether to be relieved or saddened by the fact that Grace would never know her birth mother's family.

Half of Eagle Point thought Blake was crazy to give up the money she could have made—either by suing for damages or selling her story—but then they thought she was mad to buy the lighthouse in the first place. Angie Corelli was especially despondent and told her so on a regular basis. Very regular, considering Angie had somehow conned Blake into cooking for her at the cafe a couple of times a week. Despite their differences, the two women were becoming good friends. Though Angie's cousin Mary still kept her distance—as if she were afraid Blake's propensity for ghosts and dangerous situations might somehow rub off on her.

She realized with a start that Declan was looking at her expectantly, awaiting a response. She had been so lost in her thoughts she hadn't heard a word he'd said to her. She leaned down to rearrange the blanket over Grace in an effort to stall for time.

Summoning her most endearing smile, Blake made a wild stab at answering him. "Um...I...like...it?" she said tentatively, guessing he'd asked her about his latest sketch. Which wasn't exactly a lie. She really didn't need to see his sketch up close to know it was good.

"You sure about that?" he asked, folding his arms across his chest. "It's not the kind of thing you should say yes to without giving it some serious thought."

"Um...then...no," she answered him. "Okay, I confess. I wasn't listening. I have no clue what you just said. Sorry."

Behind him, the sun had risen above the water and the crimson streaks were fading to pinks and blues. Sunlight glinted off the lighthouse tower's windows, making it seem almost welcoming. Which, she knew, it was. Just not for her. Not yet, anyways. Maybe with time she would be able to enter the tower without thinking of Kelly's death or her own experience there. But not yet.

Declan playfully wrapped a strand of her hair around his finger then grew serious. "I planned on waiting for the right moment," he said, "but it's been so busy around here I figured if I kept putting it off I'd never ask you.

"Ask me?"

"You didn't happen to catch the word 'wife' in what I just said by any chance, did you?"

"Oh God," she said, trying to quell the flutter in her belly. "Please tell me I didn't miss it."

He grinned, but his eyes remained serious. "I should've done it right the first time," he said, bending down on one knee. "But I haven't had much practice at this kind of thing."

Blake swallowed. For the past year she thought she had everything she could possibly want. She thought she didn't care whether or not she was Declan's wife. She'd been happy—more than happy—to have him as a lover and a best friend. When he hinted a few times that they should both adopt Grace she always put him off, not wanting him to feel obligated to take on a responsibility for something she initiated. But as she stood looking down at the vulnerability and hope in his face she realized marrying him did mean something. He was the man she wanted to spend the rest of her life with—and she wanted everybody this side of the Atlantic to know it. Most of all, she wanted him to know it.

"Blake Cartwright, will you marry me?"

At first all she could manage was a vigorous nod. "I will," she got out at last, hoping he wouldn't take the quaver in her voice as a sign of uneasiness. "I will marry you, Declan Hunter," she said, her voice stronger this time.

For a moment he seemed as unnerved as she had been a moment earlier. "You won't regret it," he said hoarsely, locking his dark eyes onto hers. "I haven't always been the ideal man, Blake. There are things, things in my past—"

She touched her finger to his lips, thinking of Lucy Stone. Lucy died without ever having the chance to really live, and Blake had no intention of suffering the same fate. "I think," she said slowly, feeling a little embarrassed by what she was about to say, "that the past isn't about regretting what we did, or even what we didn't do. I think the past is meant to guide us toward the future—to show us the way when we're lost." She smiled as he kissed her fingertip. "Pretty cheesy, huh."

Declan's only answer was to pull her down to him and kiss her again, on the lips this time. Her arms slid around his neck as she bent over him and settled in his lap. The warmth of his embrace enveloped her as their mouths touched, tenderly at first, then with growing ferocity. Blake reveled in the familiar scent of his aftershave and the fierce intensity of his lips pressing against hers. As their kiss deepened the evidence of his desire pressed against her cut-off jeans. Another minute and she would drag him upstairs and have her way with him, regardless of what needed to be done around the house.

"I'm probably going to have quit on Angie," she said nervously, breaking off the kiss almost against her will. Much as she wanted to lose herself in the moment, there was something else he needed to know.

He nodded. "Wedding's take a lot of planning. Some time off from the cafe would probably be a good idea," he said. "If she'll let you."

"I don't need her permission to quit," she said a little indignantly, then broke into laughter. When it came to Angie, Declan always seemed to think Blake was wrapped around the woman's little finger.

He raised an eyebrow. "Are you sure about that?"

She tried to look insulted and failed miserably. "I guess not," she said, giving him a sideways look. "Though I probably shouldn't be on my feet too much, considering."

If she hoped for a reaction, she got it. Declan paled beneath his tan then tried to speak and failed utterly. "Are you saying what I think you're saying?"

Blake gazed up at the lighthouse. The shadows had faded and the white tower shone brightly in the morning sun, its beacon blazing reflections so bright they were nearly blinding. Though she would never be able to explain it to Declan, she couldn't rid herself of the idea that the woman who lit its beacon nearly a century earlier had somehow played a role in her fate. "If she's a girl I thought we could name her Lucy."

A word about the author...

Gwenan Haines lives in New England with her daughter and a Siberian husky born on Halloween. She loves to travel and has visited Russia, Spain, France, Greece, and the Himalayas. Nowadays she's much more of a homebody, preferring to sit by the fire and spin twisted plots about strong heroines and sexy leading men.